PRAISE FOR THE DETECTIVE SHERIDAN HOLLER SERIES

'A brilliant debut!'

Steve Cavanagh

'T. M. Payne is one of the most exciting new voices in crime fiction… The comparisons to Val McDermid are well earned indeed'

Kia Abdullah

'A twisty, compelling, page-turning cracker of a debut. Full of great characters, T.M. Payne's Long Time Dead is so absorbing you'll miss your bus stop AND stay up past your bedtime. Perfect for fans of Val McDermid and Michael Connelly.'

Chris Merritt

'An excellent crime novel, full of humour and pathos as well as utterly realistic action. A stunning debut.'

Elly Griffiths

'Make way for the brilliant Detective Sheridan Holler! Urgent and artful storytelling for die-hard fans of crime fiction and new blood alike.'

A. J. West

'A thrilling debut . . . If you are a fan of police procedurals, this one set in the mean streets of Liverpool is for you.'

Mari Hannah

T0203587

'T. M. Payne has hit the ground running with *Long Time Dead*. Gritty, well-paced and packed with vividly drawn characters.'

M. W. Craven

'A gripping and gritty start to what promises to be an excellent new police procedural series.'

David Fennell

'An evocative, brilliantly plotted debut which I defy you to put down. I promise it will haunt you long after the end.'

Graham Bartlett

'Worth every interminable minute it takes to wind down.'

Kirkus Reviews

THIS
ENDS
NOW

ALSO BY T. M. PAYNE

Long Time Dead

THIS
ENDS
NOW

A DETECTIVE SHERIDAN HOLLER THRILLER

T. M. PAYNE

THOMAS & MERCER

This is a work of fiction. Names, characters, organizations, places, events, and incidents are either products of the author's imagination or are used fictitiously. Any resemblance to actual persons, living or dead, or actual events is purely coincidental.

Text copyright © 2024 by T. M. Payne
All rights reserved.

No part of this book may be reproduced, or stored in a retrieval system, or transmitted in any form or by any means, electronic, mechanical, photocopying, recording, or otherwise, without express written permission of the publisher.

Published by Thomas & Mercer, Seattle

www.apub.com

Amazon, the Amazon logo, and Thomas & Mercer are trademarks of Amazon.com, Inc., or its affiliates.

ISBN-13: 9781662511349
eISBN: 9781662511332

Cover design by Dan Mogford
Cover image: © Oliver Schwendener © Ryan Loughlin © Jakub Pabis / Unsplash; © railway fx / Shutterstock; © Rekha Garton / ArcAngel

Printed in the United States of America

For Susie
Dancing through this life with me

The water rises, dark and cold
I shall die here, I'll not grow old
I take a breath that seals my death
I'll be dead before the story's told

This ends now, I heard you say
And now I understand
As you turn away to go and play
With the watcher in the sand

PROLOGUE

Godfrey Stillman pulled the chair back to allow his wife, Martha, to sit down. She hadn't stopped moaning since they'd arrived at the restaurant, and it was sapping every ounce of his willpower not to put his hands around her scrawny neck and squeeze. Just a little bit.

'It's freezing up here, Godfrey. I can feel one of my turns coming on. Are you actually trying to kill me?'

'Perish the thought, darling.' Although *cherish the thought* had gone through his mind before he explained that as it was her birthday, he thought they would try something a little different. The 180 was a glitzy rooftop restaurant overlooking Liverpool. A novelty establishment standing at – as its name suggested – 180 feet tall, with 180-degree views across the city. Visitors could enjoy watching the sun going down in the summertime, and for the colder months the restaurant was transformed into a winter wonderland, sprinkled with the glittering lights of Liverpool.

'I'll have to leave my coat on,' Martha whined. 'Aren't there any seats inside?'

'It's a rooftop restaurant, Martha. There aren't seats inside, that's the whole point.' Godfrey sighed, peering at her over the rim of his glasses.

'It's very high up. I hope it doesn't set off my vertigo.' Martha nervously peered over the low glass barrier and shuddered all too dramatically.

'I thought perhaps the long lift ride might have given it away that we were going to be up high.' Godfrey removed his glasses and breathed on them.

'Why do you have to be so sarcastic?'

Just as a not unwelcome image of Martha plummeting to her death entered Godfrey's head, the waiter appeared.

'Good evening, folks. Have you been to The 180 before?' he asked cheerily, handing them a pair of menus.

'No. And I won't be coming again. Not if you don't have better heating,' Martha replied bluntly. 'I'll have a large gin and tonic and my husband will have a glass of water. He's driving.'

The waiter eyed Godfrey, who was cleaning his glasses with a napkin. 'Would you like ice and lemon?' the waiter asked, smiling sweetly at Martha.

'If I need ice, I'll just snap it off the edge of the table. You should warn people how cold it is up here.' Martha scowled at him. 'Are you a homosexual?' she asked, stretching out the word.

'Goodness, your powers of observation would give Miss Marple a run for her money,' he replied in the campest voice he could muster.

Godfrey suddenly had the urge to burst out laughing and give him a hug. Instead, he thought he should probably apologise for Martha's rudeness. 'I'm sorry about that. It's my wife's birthday and she had a wine gum before we came out. I think it may have gone to her head.'

The waiter threw his head back and laughed, before placing his hand on Martha's shoulder. 'Well, happy birthday. I'm sure you'll have a gay old time.' He flicked his hair to one side and waltzed off like a drag queen exiting the stage.

'He seems like fun,' Godfrey remarked.

'He's rude, and I've a good mind to complain. You didn't help with your ridiculous wine gum joke.' Martha picked the menu up and began reading each dish out loud, commenting on how exorbitant the prices were.

Godfrey ignored her as he glanced at the other tables. The young couple in the far corner, holding hands and sharing an enormous scarf. Clearly happy and oblivious to everyone around them. The family sitting near one of the large heaters, taking photographs on their mobiles of the stunning backdrop.

Then Godfrey noticed the woman sitting on her own. He noticed her because she was looking straight at him. Godfrey couldn't help smiling as she threw him a cheeky grin.

'Shall I order you the fish?' Martha asked, suddenly looking up for an answer. 'Who are you smiling at?' She spun round, just in time to catch the other woman turning her face away.

Martha slapped the menu down. 'Who's that? Do you know her?'

'Yes, she's a woman I had an illicit affair with while you were at one of your coffee mornings.' Godfrey shook his head. 'Of course I don't know her.' Slumping his elbows on the table, he resigned himself to yet another tedious evening.

As the waiter brought their drinks, Godfrey noticed the other woman was still eyeing him up. Just as he lifted his glass to his mouth, she raised hers to him and winked. And Godfrey Stillman did something he had never done in his life. He winked back.

While Martha inhaled her G'n'T, he piped up, 'I'll get you another, seeing as it's your birthday.' Pretending to look past

Martha for the waiter, he focused instead on the woman. She was elegant and attractive, probably in her late fifties. He studied her as she lit a cigarette and noted the wedding ring. *Widow maybe?*

'I can see you looking at her,' Martha hissed as she spun around to scowl at the woman, whose mobile had begun to ring.

'Oh, for heaven's sake, Martha, I'm looking for the waiter.' Godfrey watched as the woman blew cigarette smoke out just before she answered her phone.

He was still watching when she ended the call. Lifting her handbag from the chair next to her, she took out her make-up bag and using a small compact mirror, she applied a thick layer of lipstick. He couldn't take his eyes off her as she ran a hand through her hair before looking his way and holding his gaze. A moment later, she stood up, brushed her hands down her coat, picked up her glass and dragging her chair behind her, she made her way towards him.

Martha was about to point out something on the menu when she noticed the expression on Godfrey's face. She turned again to see the woman coming their way.

'Good God. Now she's coming to join us. Are you sure you don't know her, Godfrey?' Martha looked up just as the woman appeared beside them.

'Can I help you?' Martha snapped.

'Yes,' the woman replied, downing her drink and handing the empty glass to Martha. 'Could you hold this for me?'

Before Martha could answer, the woman took a deep breath, stood on the chair and threw herself over the balcony of The 180 Restaurant.

CHAPTER 1

Detective Inspector Sheridan Holler was half walking and half running as she headed down the corridor, just as Detective Sergeant Anna Markinson came up the stairs.

'What are you still doing here?' Anna asked, looking at her watch.

'I need you *right now*,' Sheridan whispered, grabbing Anna's arm and pulling her into her office before quickly closing the door. 'I'm meeting the new DCI in *one* minute.'

'Yeah, I know. And?' Anna crossed her arms.

'I've split my trousers.'

Sheridan turned around, bending over slightly, revealing a huge rip down the seam.

'Look.'

Anna burst out laughing as she put her hand to her mouth.

'It's not funny, Anna. I'm about to introduce myself to the new boss and my bloody arse is hanging out.' Sheridan shook her head. 'What am I going to do?'

'Just pull your shirt out. That'll cover it up.' Anna bit down on a grin. 'Or put your coat on.'

'My coat's too short. Lend me *your* trousers, we're about the same size.' Sheridan quickly undid her belt. 'You can stay in my office until I get back, I won't be long.'

Anna shook her head. 'Alright, but I'm not sitting here in my knickers. I'll put *your* trousers on until you get back.' She pulled her top out and unzipped her trousers.

Sheridan's phone rang and as she answered it, she swiped Anna's trousers with her free hand.

'DI Holler.' She nodded. 'Yes, ma'am, I'm literally on my way right now. I'll see you in *one* minute.' She looked at Anna, who was climbing into Sheridan's trousers. 'No, ma'am. Of course, ma'am, good idea. See you shortly.' Sheridan put the phone down.

She pulled Anna's trousers on and tucked her shirt in as Anna sat down.

'Don't be long. I mean it, Sheridan, I feel really uncomfortable like this.' Anna pulled a face as Sheridan grinned back at her. 'What?'

'The DCI thought it would be a good idea if you came, too.'

'Did you tell her I wasn't here? Please tell me you said I wasn't here.'

'No.'

'I can't go like this. Swap back.'

'No. Come on, she's waiting.'

Thirty seconds later Sheridan knocked on the DCI's door, while Anna squirmed behind her.

'Come in.' The booming voice behind the door beckoned them inside.

Sheridan entered, closely followed by Anna, who was fidgeting frantically, holding the bottom of her crumpled shirt down at the back to hide the gaping hole.

Detective Chief Inspector Hill Knowles looked up, smiling first at Sheridan but then frowning slightly at the state of Anna. 'Take a seat.'

'Thank you, ma'am,' they replied in unison, sitting to attention.

'Firstly, I'm not going to do a long-winded tedious introduction, you know who I am, and I know who you are. We'll be working together now, so we'll get to know each other in good time.' She leaned back in her chair. Before either of them could respond, she continued, 'And secondly, how are you doing now, Sheridan? I understand you were shot?' The bluntness of her statement left Sheridan very little room to respond.

'I was.' Sheridan shifted awkwardly in her seat. She had been working on a case, two years earlier, involving the murder of an off-duty police officer, when she was taken hostage and subsequently shot. Having recovered well from her injuries, she'd returned to work as soon as she was deemed fit for duty.

'I take it you had some counselling?'

'Yes, ma'am,' Sheridan replied. She had attended counselling sessions. Not because she felt she needed them but more because the force medical officer had thrown a fit when she'd told him it was a waste of time. He had also told her that if she didn't attend counselling, he wouldn't sign her off as being fit to return to work. And that wasn't an option for Sheridan.

'Good. Right, I wanted to talk to you about a job that fell flat in September.' Hill slid a bulging file across her desk towards Sheridan. 'Ronald Parks.' Sheridan turned the file round and opened it, making a mental note that Hill clearly didn't do empathy. Hill's predecessor, DCI Max Hall, had been one of the most understanding bosses she'd worked with. She had not only respected but had actually adored him.

'The guy who murdered his own son. The jury came back with a not guilty verdict.'

Sheridan nodded as she remembered the case. 'MIT dealt with it.'

'That's right. The case pretty much fell apart because there was doubt put to the jury that the evidence didn't hold up. Anyway, I want fresh eyes on this case. I want you and the team to go through it and find the golden nugget. The evidence is there. If Ronald Parks didn't kill his son, which I believe he did, then we need to establish who did kill him.'

DCI Hill Knowles stood up and retrieved her coat from the back of her chair.

'Sure.' Sheridan closed the file, remaining seated. 'How do MIT feel about this?'

'Well, technically they've still got a hand in it. Two of their DCs will be on attachment with us.' Hill Knowles buttoned up her coat. 'Right, well . . . Anna, it was good to meet you.' Then she said bluntly, 'I need a quick word with Sheridan.'

'Of course, ma'am.' Anna stood up and awkwardly backed out of the office, closing the door behind her.

Hill Knowles threw a thick woollen scarf around her neck. 'Sheridan, could you have a word with Anna? Ask her to smarten herself up a bit?'

'Yes, ma'am.' Sheridan nodded, biting her lip, trying not to laugh. 'No problem.'

'Thanks. Right, I'll see you on Monday.' And with that, Hill Knowles left.

Sheridan sat for a moment, rather bemused that Hill had left her sitting there, before she stood up and made her way back to her office. Slowly opening the door, she peered in to see Anna sitting at her desk with her arms crossed. 'Well, that was fun.'

Anna shook her head. 'You fucker, she must have thought I was mental, backing out of her office like that. What did she say after I left?'

'She said you need to smarten yourself up. Oh God, that was so funny.' Sheridan dissolved into a fit of uncontrollable laughter.

'Glad I amused you. Anyway, what did you think of her?'

'I liked her, I think we're going to get on brilliantly.'

'Really?'

'No.'

CHAPTER 2

Jennifer Parks looked up and smiled as a tall, blonde-haired woman ambled into the bookshop and smiled at her.

'I'm just browsing,' the woman said politely, if a little curtly.

Jennifer had owned the bookshop long enough to gauge almost every customer who walked through the door. She could usually tell what they were looking for before they even opened their mouths.

If Miss Blondie was going to buy something – which, apparently, she wasn't – it would probably be an autobiography by some washed-up celebrity, sharing their story with the world of how they fought drug and alcohol abuse before making millions on some reality show.

Jennifer loved to people watch. Loved to see what others didn't. Glancing out of the window, she spotted the homeless guy across the street, sat on his thick layer of cardboard with his knees pulled up tightly to his chest. A dark beard covered most of his face, and a heavy woollen hat was pulled down to his eyebrows. She passed him some mornings when she came to open the shop. Every now and then she would buy him a cup of coffee and place it at his feet.

Suddenly, Miss Blondie was standing in front of her, holding a copy of *My Story* – a washed-up celebrity's autobiography.

'Great choice,' said Jennifer with enthusiastic conviction, as she scanned the barcode.

'It's a present for my mother. She loves this sort of tacky crap.' Miss Blondie pushed her credit card into the machine, glancing at the poster on the wall just behind the till.

Jennifer had made the poster herself, asking for information about the murder of her brother, Daniel. It was one of a hundred posters she had placed all around Liverpool city centre and the surrounding areas. Most of them had by now blown away, whipped off lamp posts by the wind and rain. Some had been put up in shop windows, now replaced by 'Sale Now On' signs, ready for the Christmas rush.

No one looked at the remaining posters any more. Everyone knew that Daniel Parks was dead. Murdered apparently by their father, Ronald. His father, who had vehemently denied any involvement and was freed by the court after the jury had found him not guilty. The press had reported after the verdict that so many questions remained unanswered. If it wasn't his own father, then who *had* killed him? Why had they killed him? And what had they done with his body?

Jennifer felt her stomach tighten as she glanced at Daniel's picture on the poster. Daniel, the big brother who said he would always look after her. She had begged the police to never give up searching for his remains and had set up a local group of volunteers who went out with her most weekends, walking purposefully across fields and parks in the hope of spotting something the police might have missed, something out of place. But even the volunteers had stopped coming now. They all had their own lives, jobs and family commitments, they were all very sorry that they couldn't help Jennifer any more and she understood. But she told anyone who would listen that she would never give up looking.

Miss Blondie stared at Daniel's poster while she waited to punch in her pin number. 'Did they ever find out who killed him?'

'No. Not yet.' Jennifer slid Miss Blondie's book into a carrier bag.

'Terrible shame. He looks like a lovely lad.'

'He was,' Jennifer replied as the woman left the shop.

CHAPTER 3

Anna Markinson peered around the door of Sheridan Holler's office. 'Shouldn't you be getting home?'

'I will in a bit, I wanted to get a feel for this Ronald Parks job first.' She instinctively glanced up at the clock and then remembered it had stopped working weeks earlier.

'Well, avoid Queen's Road. Some woman's just jumped off the top of The 180 Restaurant.'

'That's one way to avoid paying the bill.' Sheridan raised an eyebrow.

Anna shook her head. 'You're terrible. Anyway, I'm going to shoot off, I'm on duty this weekend.'

'Ah, bad luck, mate. See you Monday.' Sheridan waved her off before picking up her mobile.

'Hello, you,' her girlfriend, Sam, answered.

'Hey, gorgeous person. Just a quick one . . . I'm going to be home a little bit late. What time is Joni coming over for dinner?'

'She's getting here for about eight.'

'Okay, I'll be home by then. I love you.'

'I love you too,' Sam replied, just as Maud, their cat, meowed loudly. 'And Maud loves you as well.'

Sheridan smiled and ended the call before turning to the case file summary on the Daniel Parks murder:

Ronald Parks (DOB 15/04/41) was arrested in January 2007 on suspicion of the murder of his son Daniel Parks (DOB 16/03/81)

Daniel had been reported missing on Friday 5th January by his sister Jennifer Parks (DOB 04/04/83)

Daniel Parks shared a cottage with his sister, Jennifer, in the grounds of their parents' land in Crosby, Liverpool. Their parents, Ronald and Rita (DOB 19/01/47) lived in the main house, which is set in five acres of land. Ronald is a builder by trade but was retired at the time of the murder.

Daniel and Jennifer jointly own a bookshop called Park and Read in Liverpool city centre and ran the business between them.

At the time Daniel went missing, Jennifer was at a book fair in Cardiff. The first night she was away, she sent several texts to Daniel, mostly describing the hotel she was staying at and the people she had met at the book fair. Initially, nothing in Daniel's responses indicated anything was wrong. However, the last messages that Daniel sent stated that their father was drunk and in a foul mood. Jennifer texted Daniel the next morning, but there was no reply. She called his mobile several times. Again, there was no answer. As it was extremely unusual for Daniel not to answer his phone, Jennifer cut short her trip and travelled home that morning.

When she arrived back at the cottage, Daniel was missing. His usually tidy bedroom was in disarray. His duvet was also missing, along with a white bath towel with the initial D embroidered on its corner. The towel was never recovered.

Daniel's wallet, keys and mobile phone were on the breakfast bar.

Jennifer stated that she walked across the yard to her parents' house to ask if they had seen Daniel, which they both initially denied. Jennifer noticed that her father had deep scratches to his face. When asked about these, he admitted having a fight with Daniel the night before.

Jennifer went back to the cottage and called the police to report Daniel missing.

The call-taker noted on the incident log that Jennifer sounded frantic, saying that something terrible may have happened to Daniel and the fact that his disappearance was totally out of character. The call-taker agreed to send a uniformed officer to the address.

On arrival at the location, the uniformed officer was met by Jennifer, who showed him the text messages from the previous night. The officer noted blood in Daniel's bedroom, and went to speak to the parents, Ronald and Rita.

The officer ascertained that Ronald and Daniel had argued the night before, although Ronald stated that he had been drinking and couldn't remember what the argument was about. He also stated that Daniel had attacked him, and he had only tried to defend himself and had not knowingly caused any injuries to Daniel. When asked to provide the clothes he had been wearing that evening, Ronald could not find them. His wife stated they may have been put in the washing machine, which the officer noted was on a wash cycle. The officer looked around the property and yard, and noticed an old spade in the back of Ronald's truck, which on closer examination appeared to have been scrubbed clean. When asked, Ronald denied any knowledge of how the spade had got there as it was usually kept in the shed, but did confirm that it was his spade but denied that he had cleaned it. Ronald Parks stated that after the argument with Daniel, he went back to the house, continued drinking with his wife and then went to bed at around 11 p.m. He stated he did not leave the house at any time after that.

The Parks' house is set in a relatively remote part of Crosby and there are few other properties in the area. The nearest property is situated further up the lane from the Parks' land and when the occupants were spoken to, they confirmed that they had CCTV that covered the lane. When this was checked by police, Ronald Parks' truck was seen to leave the address at 02.08 hours and return home at 04.05 hours that morning. Ronald Parks denied driving his vehicle.

A small blood sample was found on the keys to the truck.

During a search of the local area, Daniel's duvet was found in a field half a mile from the Parks' address. The duvet was examined, and traces of blood were found. These were a match for Daniel's blood.

The clothes that Ronald Parks had been wearing the night of the argument were examined and a blood sample matching Daniel's DNA was found.

A pair of work boots and a coat belonging to Ronald were missing. They were never located.

Ronald Parks' truck was examined, and hair and blood were found that also matched Daniel's, as did the blood on the keys.

The spade was forensically examined. It was determined that it had been cleaned with bleach.

Searches of the Parks' main house were carried out, but no further blood was found.

The cottage was examined, and Daniel's blood was discovered on his bedroom floor and wall, the living room floor and armchair and the kitchen floor and work surface.

A sperm sample was found on the living room carpet.

Jennifer stated that the sperm would be from a recent one-night stand with a male whose name and details she did not know.

DNA searches on the sperm sample were made and no match was found on the database.

Extensive searches within a five-mile radius of the Parks' property were carried out but Daniel's body was never found.

Ronald Parks was arrested on suspicion of murder.

Ronald Parks was interviewed in the presence of a solicitor. He answered 'no comment' to the majority of questions put to him.

He was charged with murder and remanded in custody awaiting trial.

The trial commenced in July 2007 and lasted 2 months. The defence based its case on the premise that, after Daniel and Ronald fought, Daniel may have received an injury that caused him to bleed.

This would account for the blood found in the cottage. The fact that his bedroom was in disarray was also a result of this altercation. Ronald had denied driving his truck away from the property and the CCTV image was poor and did not show who was driving. The defence stated that after the argument with his father, Daniel could have, in anger, gone for a drive in the truck to clear his head, which would account for his hair and blood being present. The truck was found to have an almost empty tank, and the heater wasn't working.

The defence suggested that Daniel may have planned to drive somewhere and sleep in the truck overnight, which is why he may have taken his duvet with him. It was January and, without heating, the temperature in the truck would have been freezing. Daniel didn't take his wallet with him, and therefore didn't have the means to refuel the vehicle.

Once he realised how little fuel was left in the truck, he headed home. This would account for the truck being seen returning to the property two hours later. The defence went on to suggest that Daniel's blood could have been on his duvet from the fight, and he simply threw it from the truck, hence it being found in the nearby field, the same for the white towel, which, although it was never located, could have been discarded somewhere. The defence also drew upon the fact that Ronald did not dispose of the clothes he was wearing during the fight with Daniel, his wife had simply put them in the wash.

The jury came back with a majority verdict of not guilty and Ronald Parks was released.

While he was on remand, Ronald Parks was visited by his wife, Rita, and his daughter, Jennifer.

Both Rita and Jennifer gave evidence at his trial. Rita Parks maintained her account that all she knew was that Ronald and Daniel had argued in the cottage, but she did not know what the argument was about. Ronald returned to the house a short while later, where they consumed some more alcohol and went to bed. She was not aware that Ronald left the house that night. She confirmed that she washed his clothes, but this was not out of the ordinary and was just a normal wash day.

Jennifer Parks maintained her account that she was very worried about Daniel as he would always respond to her calls or texts. She stated that Ronald was a wonderful father and had never been violent to her or Daniel and she did not believe that her father was capable of harming him.

Following the not guilty verdict, Ronald Parks returned to the house he shares with his wife.

Jennifer remained living in the cottage and still lives there alone. She continues to run the bookshop.

Daniel Parks was described as quiet, with very few friends. He spent most of his time either at home in the cottage or at work. He had a close relationship with his sister, Jennifer. The bookshop they jointly owned was doing reasonably well and they had no financial problems.

Daniel was single and had no known partner.

Jennifer was single at the time of Daniel's murder, but described having the occasional casual

*relationship in the recent past, although none that
would be relevant to these events.*

*During the police enquiry into Daniel's disappear-
ance, Jennifer had contacted the officer in the case over
thirty times to ask if police were still actively looking for
Daniel's body. She also set up a local volunteer group
that met up regularly to search the local area. As far as
the OIC was aware, this group no longer existed.*

*Ronald Parks had been married to his wife,
Rita, for twenty-seven years. She described their relationship as 'solid' with no matrimonial issues. She
confirmed that he had never been aggressive or violent towards her or their children and was a model
husband and father.*

*Daniel and Jennifer were their only children
together. Ronald Parks had a son, Jason, from a previous relationship with whom he had no contact.*

*Attempts were made to locate Jason and his
mother, Tanya Harris (Ronald's ex-partner).
Negative result.*

*Searches on the police crime system showed just
one call to police by Ronald Parks two years earlier,
in 2005, when he reported a theft of building equipment from his front yard. No arrests were made.*

*There were no other reports to police by any
of the Parks family and a search of the Police
National Computer system confirmed they were all
no trace.*

Sheridan stretched her back, yawned and closed the file. *Ronald
Parks got away with murder*, she thought. And she was going to put
that right.

CHAPTER 4

As she drove home, Sheridan's mind wandered to her own brother, Matthew, who had been murdered thirty years earlier. The case was still unsolved, and the pain of losing him in such a brutal manner still affected her and her parents.

She had lost a brother, just like Jennifer Parks. The difference being that Matthew's body *had* been found. His killer, on the other hand, had not. Yet.

She thought about Jennifer and how she had supported her father throughout his trial. Did she believe unreservedly that he was innocent? She had sat through the trial and heard the evidence against him. Maybe she had her own doubts about his account that night. And just maybe she had been swayed, like the jury, to believe he couldn't be guilty.

Ronald Parks had only been out of prison for two months, and was probably enjoying his freedom. Based on the evidence Sheridan had just been reading, she hoped it would be short-lived. To her mind, it seemed clear that the father was guilty. All she had to do was prove it.

Reaching into the glove compartment to grab a handful of change for the toll machine at the Kingsway Tunnel, she tried to clear her mind of work and smiled at the thought of getting home to Sam. They had met two years earlier when Sheridan had worked a case involving a resident at a nursing home. The same case that Hill Knowles had been referring to when she mentioned Sheridan having been shot. The morning Sheridan had arrived to interview the resident was the same morning that Sam had been visiting her best friend, Joni, who worked as a carer at the home.

The attraction between Sam and Sheridan had been instant and obvious. At the time, Sam and her beloved Maud had been living with Joni in Crosby, and they had met again when Sheridan needed to interview Joni at her flat. Sheridan had fallen in love very quickly. At first, with Sam's cat. But her love for Sam followed soon afterwards.

Turning right on to Bidston Hill, Sheridan could almost taste the large glass of wine that Sam would already have poured for her. As she parked on the drive, she saw Sam through the window, waving a tea towel around in the kitchen.

Maud, who was sitting on the back of the sofa by the window, stood up and stretched as Sheridan got out of the car. Sheridan stepped over to the window, tapping on the glass and smiling as Maud tapped back. Same thing every day.

As she walked through the front door, Sam called out from the kitchen, 'Hi, honey. Dinner's fucked.'

Sheridan grinned. As she hung up her coat, she called back, 'Is it salvageable or, like, really fucked?'

'It's quite bad,' Sam replied.

Walking into the kitchen, Sheridan coughed at the acridity of the smoke that hung in the air and tentatively stepped over to the cooker, bravely peering at what lurked inside.

'What do you think?' Sam handed Sheridan the – as expected – enormous glass of wine, before she opened the oven door and lifted out a cremated lump of meat. At least, Sheridan assumed it was some kind of meat. The state of the dinner made it a little difficult to be sure.

'What is it?' Sheridan took a sip of her drink and crouched down to pick up Maud, kissing the top of her head. Maud sniffed Sheridan's drink and tried to stick her paw in the glass.

'Beef Wellington.' Sam pulled a face. 'It's really hard to cook.'

'Clearly.' Sheridan smiled as the doorbell rang. 'That'll be Joni. I hope she's not hungry.' She gently put Maud down before opening the kitchen window slightly.

Sam greeted her best friend at the door. 'Hi, come on in. Slight change of plan, we're getting a takeaway.'

'You cocked the dinner up, didn't you?' Joni shook her head as she wiped her feet on the mat and closed the front door behind her. Following Sam into the kitchen, she hugged Sheridan and handed her a bottle of wine.

'And this is for you, Maud.' Joni knelt down, waving a catnip fish in front of Maud's face before dropping it on the floor. They all watched as Maud flicked the fish across the kitchen, ran after it, and then collapsed in a dramatic catnip-induced coma.

Later, as they all sat in the living room – their takeaway devoured – Sheridan rested her head back on a cushion and listened to Sam and Joni chatting. Every now and then, the Ronald Parks case crept into her thoughts, and she would close her eyes, trying to rid her mind of it, letting the rhythm of Sam and Joni's conversation envelop her.

Joni, who had met Sam at school when they were seven years old, was suggesting that Sam should take cookery classes as there was the distinct possibility that one day she might actually poison someone. Sam had initially been against the idea and fought her corner, reminding Joni that she had once made a rather exquisite pasta dish that looked worthy of being served up in a restaurant. Joni interjected with the reminder that in all the time they had lived together, that pasta dish was the *only* meal that had been remotely edible. And, she added, if Sam wasn't going to enrol in cooking classes, then she should consider a first-aid course.

'Why would I do that?' Sam retorted.

'Because if and when – and I emphasise the word *when* – someone actually starts choking to death on your hideous food, at least you'll know how to resuscitate them. Anyway, enough about your shit cooking, I've got a bit of news.' Joni shifted in her seat, prompting Maud – who was now clearly tired of her new catnip toy – to jump up and settle on her lap. 'I've got a new man in my life.'

Sheridan immediately opened her eyes and sat bolt upright. She'd known Joni for two years and had never once heard her speak about a boyfriend. Leaning forward to grab her glass of wine, she fired off questions. 'What's his name? What does he do? Where did you meet him?'

'I'm not telling you his name or anything about him.' Joni smiled as she cuddled up with Maud.

'When do we get to meet him?'

'When I think he's ready.'

Sam and Sheridan quickly glanced at each other before Sam piped up, 'Do you want to stay over tonight?' She knew that if they could get Joni drunk, she'd spill the beans about her mystery man.

'Yeah, okay.' Joni nodded and Sam flew into the kitchen to pour her a hefty bourbon and Coke.

Three large drinks later, and Joni had told them that her 'new man' was actually a cat she'd adopted called Newman and she had great hopes of the boy developing a blossoming relationship with Maud.

'I'm going to let him settle in properly before I bring him over. Do you think they'll get on?' Joni asked as she quickly sent a text to her mum asking her to stay with Newman overnight.

22

'It depends. Does he like playing poker?' Sam quipped, making herself chuckle before shrugging her shoulders when Joni raised her eyes to the ceiling.

Later, as they all headed up to bed, Maud tiptoed into the kitchen, deciding that the abandoned Beef Wellington required further investigation. She tapped the cremated lump several times, causing a piece to break off and get stuck in one of her claws. After several unsuccessful attempts to flick it off, she frantically raced through the living room and up the stairs until it dislodged itself. Once free of the meat monster, she ambled back downstairs and settled on the sofa, giving herself a thoroughly good wash.

CHAPTER 5

Mandy Tomkins strolled along the beach with her dog, Buddy. An early morning sun was rising in the sky, and she was taking advantage of the emptiness to simply drink in the beauty.

In the summertime, day trippers would fill the place with deckchairs, windbreakers and tents. Visitors would travel from miles around to witness the haunting Iron Men statues. Families would pitch up and tuck into their picnics, excited dogs would eagerly chase sand-covered tennis balls, and children with melted ice cream down their bare bellies would play for hours in the afternoon sun. At night, the Iron Men statues stood as silent witnesses to the sudden stillness, blindly watching as darkness fell upon them. Watching without seeing. Until the morning came.

Mandy loved this time of the day. There were few people around, which meant she could come armed with her camera to catch the perfect sunrise, or light bouncing off the water, or a ripple in the sand. Walking slowly, she headed for the far end of the beach, watching Buddy playing in the water as the tide receded further towards the horizon. As the morning wind blew across the sand, she stopped and stared, mesmerised by the Iron Men statues that pitted the shoreline.

Placed there two years earlier, the one hundred statues lined the estuary, facing out to sea. Many tourists visited Crosby Beach to soak up the atmosphere of these magnificent statues, touching them and admiring their simple beauty. Life-sized men made of iron. The Iron Men.

Mandy removed the lens cap from her camera as she crouched down, trying to capture a shot of one of the statues in the shimmering sand. Suddenly, she heard Buddy barking and looked up to see him circling another statue nearby, moving towards it, barking and then stepping back, before sitting down and staring up at it.

Mandy smiled and focused her camera on him, thinking that the scene would make a brilliant picture – if Buddy could sit still long enough for her to capture that perfect shot of him, his head tilted to one side, looking up at the statue. As she zoomed in, she noticed something odd about it. Something out of place. She took slow, deliberate steps across the sand towards the statue. On seeing her approach, Buddy jumped up and started barking again.

As Mandy got closer, her eyes widened, and her heart began to race.

Standing before her was an Iron Man statue. With a woman's dead body strapped to it.

CHAPTER 6

Sheridan poured a glass of orange juice and handed it to Sam, after taking a sip first. 'If Joni hasn't got any plans today, we could all go for a game of crazy golf at New Brighton?'

'Sounds good to me,' Sam said. 'If she ever gets out of bed.' She put the half-empty bottle of bourbon back in the cupboard just as the phone rang.

Sheridan swiped it from the kitchen worktop, answering it cheerily. 'Hellooooo?'

'Hi, mate. It's Anna, sorry to call you when you're meant to be off. Can you talk?'

'Yeah, go on, what's up?'

'A woman's body has been found at Crosby Beach, tied to one of the Iron Men statues.'

'Bloody hell. Any idea who she is?'

'No, not yet. MIT are all over it. But I've come down here in case we end up picking it up.'

'I'll be there within the hour,' Sheridan said, and ended the call.

'Everything okay?' Sam asked.

'Sorry, hun, I've got to go into work, they've found a body at Crosby Beach.'

'No worries.' Sam was used to the uncertain schedule of Sheridan's work, and the fact that any plans they made could be cancelled at a moment's notice. 'Someone drowned?'

'I don't know. Anna just said it's a woman.'

Half an hour later, as Sheridan drove through the Kingsway Tunnel, she thought about what had been found at Crosby and her head started to fill with questions.

She arrived at the beach to find the area swamped with police cars, CSI and coastguard vehicles. A helicopter flew overhead, scouring the beach, just as Sheridan reached the cordon. Flicking her warrant card at the young officer, she quickly ducked under the tape, just in time to see Anna heading her way.

'Hello, mate. Bloody weird one, this is.' Anna knew that Sheridan would want to see the body in situ, and escorted her quickly over to the woman strapped to the Iron Man.

The corpse was secured to the statue with two heavy straps and her hands were tied behind her back with cable ties. Her head was hanging down and wet auburn hair was stuck to her face, which was tinged with blue around her lips.

'Where's the witness who found the body?' Sheridan dug her hands into her pockets as a biting wind whipped around them.

Anna looked around to check. 'She's with MIT officers.'

'Hello, ladies.' A voice from behind made them both jump slightly. They turned to see DC Rob Wills standing there. 'This is an MIT job, isn't it? What are you two doing here?'

'Hello, Rob. What are *you* doing here, more like? I thought you were coming back to CID on Monday?' Sheridan frowned.

Rob had worked with Sheridan prior to his temporary attachment to the Major Investigation Team and she was pleased to see him again. Rob Wills was as solid as they came. Experienced and diligent, with a constant aura of calmness about him.

'I am indeed,' Rob said. 'It's my last day on attachment, but you know I can't resist a grisly murder. Talking of which, I understand you've picked up the Ronald Parks case?'

'Yeah, we have. I take it MIT are pissed off?'

'Not really. They're convinced he was guilty. They just couldn't prove it.'

Sheridan nodded towards the body on the Iron Man statue. 'Have you ever seen anything like this before?'

'No.' Rob shook his head. 'I got here the same time as the coastguard, and even with what those guys are used to seeing – bloated corpses in the water, all that sort of thing – they were pretty shaken up.'

'How long have we got until the tide comes in?' Sheridan checked her watch. 'It's almost ten now.'

'Coastguard says high tide is around half one, so we should be okay.'

'Have we checked all the other statues?' Sheridan watched a helicopter flying out towards the horizon.

'Yeah,' Rob said. 'The coastguard's been out to them all. Thankfully there's no more bodies.'

At that moment, several officers raced past them, heading away from the statues and towards the sand dunes. Sheridan, Rob and Anna instinctively hurried after them, throwing glances at each other, curious at the sudden burst of commotion. When they caught up with the officers, they stopped dead in their tracks in front of a small pile of driftwood logs.

'Christ,' Rob inhaled, as they stared in horror at the macabre scene before them.

CHAPTER 7

Jennifer Parks hurried along the street towards the bookshop. She hated opening late, especially on a Saturday, and even more especially in the early run-up to Christmas. She unlocked the shop doors, then flipped the sign to 'Open' before turning the lights on, just as her first customer of the day came in.

'Do you sell children's books?' The man wiped his feet on the mat and pulled his gloves off before tucking them into the pockets of his heavy coat.

'Yes, I'll show you.' Jennifer made her way towards the back of the shop, with the man in tow. She showed him the collection. Then, leaving him to it, she walked back to the counter, making a mental note of his book choice. She knew she hadn't seen him before. She prided herself on remembering her customers and the books they bought.

After Daniel's murder, the shop had seemed to attract more customers, business suddenly booming. She knew that most of the visitors were there to get a look at the woman whose brother had been murdered, and whose father had been charged with the crime.

Few of them mentioned it, although many stopped for a moment to look at the poster on the wall, pretending to have seen it for the first time, even though plenty more had been plastered all over Liverpool. Some pretended not to know who Daniel was, asking Jennifer questions about what had happened. Few people came into the shop and didn't purchase anything. It was as though they were buying a trophy from the shop where 'that guy whose dad killed him' had worked.

Except, as Jennifer had told the police and the court, her father wasn't capable of doing anything like that. And every day she had sat through the trial, she watched the jury also become more and more convinced that her father was innocent.

That day – two months ago – she had been sitting in the courtroom with her mother when the jury came back with their verdict. She remembered her father's face as the foreman said the words 'Not guilty'. She remembered hugging her mother and waiting outside the court for her father to be released. She remembered how he had half run towards them, ignoring the handful of journalists that shouted to him for a comment. All Ronald Parks had wanted to do was go home. All Rita Parks had wanted was for the gossip to die down so she could face her friends again. She knew that things would never be the same, she knew people would always believe the police had got the right man. Maybe they would have to sell up and move away. But Ronald Parks had made it very clear. He was innocent and nothing was going to make him run and hide. He hadn't done anything wrong.

All Jennifer Parks had said she wanted was to give her brother the funeral he deserved.

And all anybody else wanted was to know what really happened to Daniel Parks.

In the two months since her father's release, the three of them had barely talked about it. Ronald wanted to move on and try to exist under the shadow of prying, judging eyes. The police had failed to prove that he had murdered Daniel, and had therefore failed to find out who was actually responsible for his death. The one thing they all knew was that the life they had lived up until Daniel's death had changed forever.

Jennifer gazed out of the shop window, watching the street start to fill with people. Busy people rushing around like ants, scurrying in and out of shops, huddled inside cafés, chatting to their friends.

Her thoughts were broken as her first customer of the day approached the counter, after choosing his book. Or was it his memento?

CHAPTER 8

Sheridan stepped around the crime scene and crouched down, staring more closely at the man, who had been buried up to his neck in the sand and had a pair of binoculars crudely taped to his face.

'He's practically facing the dead woman on the Iron Man statue. Like he's watching her through the binoculars.'

Anna nodded. 'Do you think they were stuck to his face so that he could see her?'

Sheridan stepped back, making way for MIT and CSI officers to start examining the scene.

'No. The way they're taped to his face means he probably couldn't see clearly through them. It's purely symbolic. He was probably dead by the time he was posed this way. Plus, they've been here overnight, so there's no way he'd see her in the darkness.'

Sheridan looked over at the body on the Iron Man, then scanned the scene, slowly taking in every detail. Anna watched her, always ready to hear Sheridan's theory: she probably had one already. Anna loved working with Sheridan, they made a good team. Sheridan was an exceptional police officer with an exemplary record, and everyone on the team listened when she spoke. She was a detective in every sense of the word, and as she stood on the sand absorbing the scene before her, Anna could imagine the cogs turning in her mind.

'What are you thinking?'

Sheridan inhaled the sea air through her nose and puffed out her cheeks.

'I'm thinking that this wasn't *one* person.'

CHAPTER 9

Sam nudged Joni's bedroom door open with her knee, carrying in two cups of coffee. 'Jesus, you look rough.'

Joni opened one eye and tried to focus. Her mouth was as dry as old bones. She ran her tongue over her teeth. 'I can't believe you got me that drunk.'

She sat up gingerly before gratefully accepting the coffee, just as Maud made her entrance, jumping on the bed and rattling out a contented purr as she began kneading the duvet.

'It's like the good old days again,' Sam said. 'You and me getting smashed in your flat and you being all grumpy in the morning.' She set her mug down on the bedside table and climbed into the bed next to Joni. She screwed her nose up and frantically waved a hand around. 'Have you farted?'

'No, I bloody haven't,' Joni retorted, kicking Sam's leg.

'Sheridan had to go into work, they've found a body on Crosby Beach.'

'Really?' Joni sat up. 'Is it near to my flat?'

'I don't know.' Sam picked up her coffee cup and blew away the steam.

Joni's eyes were wide. 'Do they think it's murder?'

Sam shrugged. 'All I know is that it's a woman.'

Joni set her coffee cup down and sat up even straighter. 'I might know her, I might be a witness, how old is she?'

'I don't know.'

'How long has she been dead?'

'I don't know.'

'Was she strangled?'

'I don't know.'

'You're fucking rubbish.' Joni shook her head. 'What's the point in you having a detective for a girlfriend if you don't ask about any of this stuff?'

CHAPTER 10

Tony Harvey had spent the whole night pacing around his living room, thinking, trying to figure out how he was going to get out of this mess. His mind went over and over the situation until he suddenly felt sick and ran upstairs, throwing up in the toilet, breathing through his nose to stop himself from choking.

Reaching a hand across to the basin, he turned on the tap and splashed water on his face, closing his eyes to try and shut out the images. When he was able, he slowly eased himself up and realised the bathroom floor was covered in dark wet sand from his boots. His heart was beating so fast that he had to blink away white spots in his eyes.

His hands shook uncontrollably as he removed his boots and carried them downstairs.

Opening the kitchen drawer, he pulled out a bin liner and dropped the boots into it.

Now what? Bury them? Burn them? Put them in the car and throw them in the Mersey?

He swallowed as bile filled his mouth and quickly stepped over to the kitchen sink to spit it out, feeling the acid from his stomach burning his throat. His head was pounding and everything seemed blurred. He wanted to close his eyes and lie down. If he could just lie down for a moment, maybe he could figure out what to do.

He'd gone through every possible scenario and all he kept coming back to was that he had no choice. He had to run. The only problem was, he couldn't run without Helen.

Where the fuck is she?

He'd spotted her car was gone when he'd arrived home. He walked into the hallway, where he saw his own boot prints across the carpet. The sand that he'd carried back into the house was everywhere. He had to get rid of it. The evidence of what he'd done was all around him. He needed to clean the house up. He also needed to figure out how to get rid of any traces left in his car from where the bodies had been. He looked at the clock on the wall as he wiped a sleeve across his mouth.

He stood for a moment. Thinking.

And then the doorbell rang.

He looked through the blinds to see a police car outside and two uniformed officers standing at the front door. Just then, one of the officers spotted him.

'Fuck,' he said under his breath. 'Fuck.' He put the chain on the door before opening it.

'Hello, sir, are you Mr Harvey? Anthony Harvey?' the officer asked.

'What's this about?' Tony knew he could shut the door, make it to the back door and run into the woods behind his house. He could probably make it. But then what would he do? Where would he go? Where would he hide?

'Are you Anthony Harvey? We need to speak to you about your wife, Helen Harvey.'

'My wife isn't here. What's this about?'

'Can we come in, please?'

'It's not a good time. Has something happened?'

'We'd rather come in, Mr Harvey.'

Tony Harvey put his head down. Confused. *They're not here about the bodies at Crosby.*

He opened the door, and they followed him into the living room, before suggesting that he should sit down.

'Mr Harvey, we've been trying to contact you. I'm afraid we're here with some bad news.'

Tony Harvey swallowed. He felt his legs begin to shake and thought he was going to pass out. 'What bad news?'

'There's no easy way for me to say this, I'm afraid, but yesterday evening your wife took her own life.' The officer waited for Tony Harvey to absorb the words.

'What?' He felt his eyes fill with tears. 'Oh God. Where? No. Not Helen, you must have it wrong.' He stood up and put his hands on top of his head.

'What happened?' he sobbed.

'I'm so sorry to have to tell you that she jumped off the top of The 180 Restaurant in the city centre.'

CHAPTER 11

As Sheridan and Anna walked across the back yard of Hale Street Police Station, they spotted DCI Hill Knowles coming towards them.

'Have you been out to Crosby?' Hill called out, as she pulled her car keys from her pocket.

'Yes, ma'am,' Sheridan answered. 'We thought it would be a good idea to get a feel for the job in case it comes our way.'

'You didn't need to come in on your day off, Sheridan. MIT have got this one, I've just had a meeting with their DCI.' She stopped in front of them. 'I want you to concentrate on the Ronald Parks case.' Hill Knowles had a face that always looked like she was frowning – or was about to – and her greying short hair added an extra coldness to her thin, lined face.

'Of course, ma'am, I just thought—'

'I'm not bollocking you,' Hill said. 'I just know that the Parks job is going to be a bloody nightmare and I need you to give it your full attention.' She smiled. Sort of.

'I *will* give it my full attention, ma'am.' Sheridan tried not to sound riled.

'Good. Well, get yourself off home. I'll see you bright and early on Monday.' And with that, Hill got into her car and drove out of the back yard.

Sheridan and Anna made their way into the main building and up to the CID office. 'I'll have a quick coffee with you before I go home,' said Sheridan. As she walked up the stairs behind Anna, she noticed a line of dark bruises around her wrist.

In the office, Sheridan decided to broach the subject. 'What happened to your arm?' she asked.

Anna immediately pulled her sleeve back, revealing the marks. 'I was play-fighting with Steve, we were pretty pissed. I didn't even feel it until the next morning.' She pulled her sleeve back down. 'I look like a bloody DV victim, don't I?'

Sheridan raised an eyebrow. 'Don't even joke about it.'

Anna responded to the questioning look on Sheridan's face. 'Seriously? Come off it, Sheridan, Steve would never hit me. I'd fucking batter him.'

'Not if I got there first.' Sheridan smiled and finished her coffee. 'Right, I'm going home. I've got a game of crazy golf to play.'

CHAPTER 12

Jennifer Parks drove slowly down the country lane towards the cottage. It had been a long day and the bookshop busy. After closing up, she went to the gym and sweated her way through her regular two-hour workout. Having not eaten since breakfast, her stomach felt hollow.

As she turned down the track that led to the main house, she glanced at her parents' car, which was parked next to the row of conifers that ran alongside the house. She could see the light from the television flickering blue and white from the living room and she thought about going in, but changed her mind and carried on up to the cottage.

Once inside, she lit the fire and poured herself a glass of wine. When she was finished, she poured another, which she carried into the bathroom after turning the oven on, throwing in a meal for one.

After a long shower, she stepped out and wrapped herself in an enormous white towel. Wiping the condensation from the mirror, she stared at her reflection, leaning forward and noticing how old she looked for her twenty-four years. She could see the emptiness in her own eyes and quickly looked away, throwing on a pair of tracksuit bottoms and a jumper before resting back on the sofa, tucking her legs under her.

After devouring her dinner, she took the box file from the bookcase, laid it on the coffee table and stared at the large hand-written words on its spine: 'Daniel's File'. She'd read the contents a thousand times. The notes she had made during the police investigation into his murder, copies of the flyers she had put up, notes from her conversations with the officer in the case, notes of the evidence found in the cottage and in her father's truck. Questions she'd written herself, with blank spaces where the answers should be. So many questions left unanswered.

Jennifer opened the file and settled down to read its contents once again.

CHAPTER 13

Monday 5 November

Sheridan Holler glanced up as DCI Hill Knowles marched into her office. *Don't bother knocking*, she thought.

'Good morning, ma'am, how was your weekend?' Sheridan literally didn't give a shit but thought it would be polite to ask.

'Joyous. Are you ready to brief the team on the Ronald Parks case?' Hill Knowles's response was swimming in sarcasm, and she clearly didn't do small talk. Sheridan made a mental note not to bother asking in future.

'Aren't *you* doing the briefing, ma'am?' she asked.

'No, I'll leave it to you. I'll see you there in five minutes.' Hill Knowles gave Sheridan the thumbs up, then briskly tapped the corner of Sheridan's desk before leaving.

The annoying gesture prompted Sheridan to throw a pen at the door when Hill was gone, but it narrowly missed Anna Markinson as she walked into the office. She graciously bent down to retrieve it. 'Oh dear, is the boss getting on your tits already?' Anna handed Sheridan her pen back.

'She's just so bloody rude. And that thumbs up thing really fucks me off.'

'Word around the nick is that she lives on her own with thirteen cats.' Anna grinned as she perched herself on the edge of the desk.

Sheridan chuckled, scooped up the pile of papers in front of her and headed out the door, with Anna following closely behind. They walked into the briefing together and Sheridan made her way to the front of the room, spotting Hill Knowles sitting at the back by the window with her arms crossed and her chair tilted back on its hind legs.

'Good morning, everyone. Firstly, can I welcome back Rob Wills. He's seen the error of his ways on MIT and rejoined us from the dark side.'

Rob Wills winked at Sheridan.

'We've also got two DCs from MIT joining us later today. They're going to be on attachment for the duration of this enquiry.'

She paused, waiting for any reactions or questions. When none came, she continued.

'So, we are reopening the murder of Daniel Parks. His father – as you know – was found not guilty of Daniel's murder at trial earlier this year. Having read the file, I'm satisfied that the evidence was pretty much there, but the defence managed to put enough doubt in the jury's minds.' She took a sip of water before turning to the whiteboard behind her. 'I need everyone to know this case inside out. If Ronald Parks *did* kill Daniel, then we need to prove it, and if he didn't do it then the perpetrator is still out there. I also want us to really focus on locating Daniel's body – there is likely to be evidence on it that could nail this case once and for all.'

Sheridan went over the facts of the case for the benefit of her fellow officers, mentioning that Ronald's daughter had supported her father during the trial and had later set up a campaign to find Daniel's body, including flyering across the city.

As Sheridan briefed her team, she stole a glance in DCI Hill Knowles's direction, surprised to note the hint of a smile on her new boss's face. 'Right, any questions?' she asked.

DC Dipesh Mois put his hand up and Sheridan pointed to him. 'Yes, Dipesh?'

'What about Rita Parks? Is there any suspicion that she was involved?'

'No, MIT did a thorough job on her background checks and her account of what happened. There *was* suspicion regarding the fact that she washed Ronald's clothes, but in interview she admitted that while she knew Ronald and Daniel had argued, she didn't know what it was about. She claimed it occurred in the cottage while she was in the main house the whole time. Rita did see that Ronald had scratches on his face from where Daniel had apparently assaulted him and also noticed a small amount of blood on his clothes. She went on to say that she simply put them in the wash with some other items. There was literally nothing else to link Rita to the murder.' Sheridan allowed herself a smile. 'Unless, of course, you lot prove otherwise. Let's also concentrate on who else could have committed this murder if it wasn't Ronald.'

She looked around the room. 'Right then, I'll allocate jobs out to you all shortly. We need to go over all the evidence from the initial enquiry. If anyone has any questions, theories or moments of absolute genius, please don't keep them to yourselves.'

Hill Knowles followed Sheridan and Anna out of the room. 'Good briefing, Sheridan,' she said as she came up behind them.

'Thanks, ma'am. It's not my first disco.' Sheridan couldn't resist the sarcastic reply. She was aware of Anna putting her head down, not wanting the DCI to see her grinning.

Ignoring the comment, Hill Knowles continued walking past them towards her office, before stopping briefly to face them. 'I think you should go and see Jennifer Parks. She's a witness but she also needs to know that we're still looking into her brother's murder.'

'Absolutely. We'll go and see her at the bookshop rather than her home address. I don't want to bump into Ronald and Rita just yet. I'd rather Jennifer was on her own.' Sheridan forced a smile.

'Good. Keep me fully updated.' Hill Knowles put her thumb up, spun around and marched off down the corridor.

Sheridan looked at Anna. 'I'm actually getting to like her.'

'Really?'

'No.'

CHAPTER 14

Anna fed the parking meter before walking along the road with Sheridan, towards the bookshop. The area was busy with shoppers and the smell of fresh, warm doughnuts followed them down the street.

'This is it.' Sheridan stopped outside and peered in, before pushing the door open. They both immediately spotted the poster with Daniel Parks' face on it and snatched a look at each other. There were a couple of customers near the back of the shop and Jennifer, who was behind the counter, looked up as they walked in.

'Hi,' she greeted them cheerily. She was taller than Sheridan had imagined, slim but muscular, with defined features. Her short brown hair suited her softly chiselled face, and warm eyes gave her a certain beauty and presence.

'Jennifer Parks?' Sheridan kept her voice low, and her warrant card concealed in her hand.

'Yes.' Jennifer smiled again and then her face changed completely. Her eyes went from Sheridan to Anna, and back to Sheridan. 'Are you the police?'

Sheridan discreetly showed Jennifer her warrant card. 'Yes, but it's nothing to worry about, we just need to have a quick chat with you.'

Jennifer stepped around the counter and approached the two customers at the rear of the shop, politely advising them that she was shutting temporarily.

Once they had left, she flipped the 'Closed' sign over and locked the door.

'You've found Daniel's body, haven't you?' Her voice broke as she turned back to Sheridan and Anna, and her whole body began to tremble. She steadied herself, placing a hand on the counter as her eyes filled with heavy tears.

'No. I'm sorry, we haven't,' Sheridan said, worrying that the woman before her was about to collapse in a heap on the floor.

Anna pulled up a chair and eased Jennifer on to it. 'Give yourself a moment. Take some deep breaths.'

'I'm sorry.' Jennifer wiped her face and blew her cheeks out.

'It's okay. We didn't mean to upset you.'

'You didn't. I just really thought you were going to tell me that you'd found him.' She took deep breaths as she tried to blink away the tears. 'So, what can I do for you?'

'We just wanted to let you know that we've reopened Daniel's case.'

She waited for Jennifer to respond.

'Well, that's great news.' Jennifer stood up and reached over the counter for a tissue. 'So, what happens now?'

'We'd like to talk to you about the events leading up to Daniel's disappearance and just go over your original statement.'

'Okay. You mean *now*?'

'No, but could you come into Hale Street Police Station tomorrow morning? Say, ten o'clock?'

'Yes. Of course, that's fine.' Jennifer blew her nose. 'Have you spoken to my parents?'

'No, not yet,' Sheridan replied. 'We wanted to talk to you first. Is that okay? Will that cause a problem with them?'

'No, not at all, they'll be so relieved that you're reopening the case. We all just want to find out who killed Daniel.' She looked at the poster on the wall. 'Will you start searching for his body again?'

'Yes.'

'You probably know that I've been looking for him since he disappeared. I can give you maps of the areas I've already checked, if that helps.' She looked at Sheridan. 'Sorry, I know the police searched a huge area, but when they didn't find him, I set up a group myself. We used to go out checking fields and parks, any-where we thought he might be. It might save you a bit of time. Maybe you could start looking in other places?'

'That would be helpful, maybe if you bring the maps in tomorrow?' Sheridan smiled, not wanting to dampen Jennifer's enthusiasm.

As they left the shop, Anna turned to where they had parked their car but felt Sheridan's hand on her arm, pulling her in the opposite direction.

'We're going this way,' Sheridan said, taking her wallet out of her jacket pocket.

'Why?' Anna asked, trying to keep up with Sheridan, who was now striding down the road.

'Because those doughnuts smell fucking divine, and we're hav-ing one.'

CHAPTER 15

Tuesday 6 November

Early the next morning, Sheridan was back at her desk when Anna arrived carrying two mugs of coffee. 'I've just seen DCI Rowe from MIT coming out of Hill's office. He looked proper pissed off.'

'Oh great, so Hill's going to be in a bad mood all day,' said Sheridan.

A few moments later, Hill Knowles came into the office and closed the door behind her. 'MIT have just been to see me. They've identified the male body found at Crosby.'

'Okay.' Sheridan sat slightly forward.

'It's Ronald Parks.'

Sheridan stared at Hill Knowles in disbelief. 'Fuck.' She shook her head. 'What about the woman?'

'We think it's his wife, Rita.' Hill leaned back against the door. 'Ronald died of a heart attack. But his body also showed signs of crushing from being buried in the sand. He was dead before the water reached him.'

'What about Rita Parks?'

'She drowned. They both had their hands strapped with plastic cable ties. Their mouths were covered with duct tape. Rita was secured to the Iron Man by two ratchet straps – the type that are used to secure things down in transport. Ronald also had two of these strapped around *his* body.'

'Do we know how long they'd been dead?'

'Not very long. A few hours, apparently.'

Sheridan sat back and looked at Anna, just as her phone rang. She swiped at the receiver, answering quickly, 'DI Holler.'

'Hello, ma'am, it's Hazel from the front desk. There's a Jennifer Parks in reception to see you. She says you're expecting her.'

CHAPTER 16

Jennifer spent almost ten hours at the police station with Anna and Sheridan, going over her movements during the last few days. They put carefully formed questions to her, digging deep into her parents' lives. And they tentatively described their deaths, trying to gauge Jennifer's reaction to the details.

It was late in the evening by the time they were finished. Sheridan and Anna drove Jennifer back to the bookshop. During the short journey, she sat slumped in the back of the car. Silent. Broken.

Sheridan had delicately warned her that there would be police at the main house and cottage for a few days, searching for any clues that could lead them to whoever had killed her parents. Jennifer had been through this process when Daniel was murdered but this time it was different. She felt like nothing was real, like she was in someone else's body.

She had refused to stay in a hotel, and she didn't want to burden friends, insisting she would be fine at the bookshop. She and Daniel had often stayed there overnight if they were working late, cracking open a bottle of wine and chatting into the early hours. There were two rooms at the back of the shop. One had a sofa and camp bed, while the other had been converted into a small kitchen.

Jennifer declined Sheridan's offer to install a police alarm but had agreed that a marker should be placed on the shop, and Sheridan reassured her that marked police cars would drive past throughout the night.

Sheridan's concern was that whoever had killed her brother and parents might also target Jennifer. It appeared as though someone was trying to wipe out this whole family.

'Are you sure there's nowhere else you can stay?' Sheridan asked, turning in her seat to face the empty shell of Jennifer Parks.

'No. I'll be fine here.'

Sheridan got out of the car and opened the back door for her. 'I'll come in with you, just to make sure everything's okay.'

Ten minutes later, Sheridan emerged from the shop and got back into the car.

'I've just got that,' Anna said, pointing at the sign above the shop door. '"Park and Read". Like Park and Ride, but you park up and read a book rather than ride a bus into town. That's quite clever.'

'Well, aren't you the genius,' Sheridan replied sarcastically, shaking her head as she pulled her seatbelt on.

'Do you think she'll be okay?' Anna asked.

'I honestly don't know. She's lost everyone now. Losing her brother must have been hard enough but now her parents as well.'

'I forget sometimes,' Anna said.

'Forget what?'

'That you lost your brother. Is that terrible of me?'

Sheridan smiled as she started the engine. 'No, mate, of course not. I can relate a bit to how Jennifer feels about losing Daniel. But I can't even begin to imagine how losing her parents will affect her.' Sheridan looked back at the bookshop. 'The worst thing is, she believed that her father was innocent . . . but we could be about to prove that he wasn't.'

CHAPTER 17

Wednesday 7 November

'Nice area.' Sheridan undid her seatbelt. They were halfway along the lane that led to the Parks' property.

'Places around here are worth a bloody fortune.' Anna zipped her jacket up and got out of the car, showing her warrant card to the uniformed officer who had approached them.

'Morning.' He nodded at Anna.

'Good morning. We're just going to have a look around. Are CSI in the main house?' she asked, just as one of the CSI officers appeared in the front yard of the property and waved them over. 'Hi, Charlie, how's it going?' Anna smiled at the officer, whom she'd met at a number of previous crime scenes.

'Well, there's not much to tell you at the moment,' Charlie said. 'We can't get any tyre tracks, because the whole place is gravelled. And there's only one way in and out by car. Inside, the main house hasn't thrown up too much yet. There's no obvious sign of a struggle, and no blood that can be seen with the naked eye. Your lot have been through the place and taken what they need: computers, victims' mobiles, paperwork, all the usual stuff.'

'What about the property that Jennifer lives in?' Sheridan glanced at the little cottage at the end of the drive.

'Again, nothing to show that anything happened there but we're still working on it.'

'How long do you think until you're done?'

'Couple more days, I'd say.'

'Okay, cheers. We'll get kitted up and have a look around, if that's okay.'

'Sure.'

Sheridan left Anna talking to Charlie, and took a look around the scene. The main house was beautifully kept. The cottage that Jennifer lived in was bigger than she had realised from the photographs taken after Daniel's murder.

Walking past the building, Sheridan glanced inside the windows momentarily, before coming to a row of thick bramble bushes to the side of the cottage. She imagined Jennifer and Daniel playing here as children, perhaps playing hide and seek. As she came to the back of the cottage, she noticed a large tree that had fallen and stepped over to it, placing her hand on its dead bark, her imagination suddenly taking her to a stormy night where lightning had struck it and brought it down with a creaking and thunderous crash. She took a deep breath before sitting on the fallen tree, closing her eyes for a moment. It was such a beautiful place here, the perfect setting for two children to grow up in.

She opened her eyes. She wanted to be back here the night Daniel had disappeared. To stand silently and watch as the true events of that night unfolded. What would she see? All the questions she had would be answered.

What she did know was that she was going to find the truth.

What she didn't know was what lay buried deep in the ground, right under her feet.

CHAPTER 18

The briefing room was buzzing as Sheridan walked in. 'Good morning, everyone.' She set her coffee down on the desk in front of the whiteboard.

'Right, let's get started.' She inhaled. 'We have a development, as I'm sure you've all heard. The two bodies found at Crosby Beach have now been positively identified as Ronald and Rita Parks, the parents of our murder victim, Daniel Parks. Anna and myself have informed the daughter, Jennifer, and CSI are working at the Parks' property. So far there's nothing obvious there, but we'll see how they get on. I understand we've got Ronald and Rita's mobiles and computers, so they'll need to be examined along with the landline phone. Jennifer has confirmed that the binoculars taped to her father's face belonged to him. He'd had them since she was a child, and she remembers them very clearly as they are quite a distinctive design. She also confirms that her father kept some of his building gear at the property, including ratchet straps such as those that were found with his body. As we know, Ronald Parks was a retired builder and had often used these to strap materials down on his truck. The truck itself was seized when he was arrested for Daniel's murder back in January, but was eventually returned to him. He's since sold it on, however, and now just owns a car.'

She took a breath, and looked around the room to see that everyone was paying attention. 'Jennifer has decided to stay at the bookshop until she can return to the cottage, which will probably be in the next few days. My concern, obviously, is that someone might also be out to harm *her*. They've already killed her parents. It doesn't take a genius to work out that Jennifer could well be next. Although, let's not presume the same person or persons are responsible for these killings. Anna and I spent a long time with Jennifer yesterday, going through friends, family, associates of her parents – basically, anyone who would want them dead. She can't think of a single person who would do this. She's declined a family liaison officer, so myself and Anna will be keeping her updated as the investigation progresses. Jennifer states that the last time she saw her parents was about eight on Friday morning, before she left to go to the bookshop. She said they were both outside in the yard, and she waved at them. She was at work all day Friday, went to the gym at six p.m. and left there at eight p.m. She then drove home and arrived there at eight thirty p.m. She didn't go into her parents' house. Instead, she went straight to the cottage, where she stayed in all night, reading. The next morning, on the Saturday, she got up at around eight a.m., and arrived at the shop at around ten. When she finished work on Saturday at five p.m., she again went to the gym and got home at seven thirty p.m. Her parents' car was still parked outside the main house, and the television was on, but she didn't go in. On the Sunday, she went to the bookshop to do some paperwork and stocktaking, went to the gym and got home around nine p.m. Once there, she showered, had dinner and went to bed. Again, she didn't go to the main house. On the Monday, she was at work and that was when Anna and I visited her to tell her we were reopening Daniel's case, and of course then yesterday, we gave her the terrible news about her parents. She told us that it wasn't unusual to not see her parents for several days and even though they had a close relationship, they didn't live in each other's pockets. Let's keep Jennifer in our sights as a suspect for now. I want her story checked out. We also need to get into Ronald Parks' business affairs, phone and computer records. We need to find out everything we can about Rita Parks as well. The killer could be someone they owe money to, someone they've fallen out with, or even someone with a grudge against Ronald. Perhaps someone who believes he's responsible for Daniel's murder. He was found not guilty, but there has been a lot of doubt about the verdict even outside of the police force. I basically want to know everything about this family.'

CHAPTER 19

Jennifer Parks lay on the camp bed, staring up at the skylight. She hadn't slept all night. Every noise, every creak of the old building had kept her awake. She'd wandered around the shop into the early hours, aimlessly running her fingers along the rows of book spines, occasionally stopping at the window to sit and stare at the darkened empty street. The odd taxi and police car had driven past, and she'd watched a fox trotting along the pavement opposite. It had stopped to sniff a discarded takeaway carton before nervously scampering away.

Deciding there was no point trying to sleep any more, she got up and went into the small kitchen, flicking the kettle on and standing motionless until it had boiled.

Closing her eyes, she tried to imagine what her parents had gone through. How they would have suffered in their last moments. Out there in the icy water, cold and dark. She felt a sudden rush of panic wash over her body, her heart now beating so fast that she felt dizzy. Taking slow, deep breaths, she tried to focus on the simple task of making a cup of coffee, her hands shaking as she poured water into a mug.

Daniel's mug.

As she carried her coffee through to the shop, the street outside had suddenly come alive, pumping with people. Sitting behind the counter, she took a sheet of paper from the drawer and wrote a notice to put up in the window. *Due to unforeseen circumstances, this shop will be closed until further notice. Sorry for any inconvenience.* She read the words over and over, before screwing the paper up and throwing it in the bin, then staring out of the shop window at the world outside.

CHAPTER 20

Sheridan put the phone down as she sat back in her chair. A moment later and Anna walked in with a smirk on her face.

'Got an update for you,' Anna said as she sat on the chair opposite. 'As you know, in the original enquiry into Daniel Parks' murder, there was CCTV footage from a property just along the road. Rob has been out there today. The old couple that still live there – Mr and Mrs Atherton – still have the same CCTV system. Rob's had a look through the recordings, and we have a vehicle arriving at the Parks' house at 16.35 last Friday and leaving three hours later. The images aren't brilliant, but we've got an index number and a name. The vehicle is owned by an Anthony Harvey – a local guy in his late sixties. I'm just getting some checks done on him now.'

'Brilliant. Is he on his own in the car?'

'Appears so. But the CCTV also shows our victim, Ronald Parks, leaving the property in his own car at 14.30 that day and returning at 15.01, so he was alive until then at least. The only other images are of Jennifer leaving for work on the Friday and returning that evening. It's the same for Saturday, Sunday, Monday and Tuesday. Pretty much all the times she gave us. So, her account pans out so far. There's no image of Rita leaving the house at all on the day she was killed.'

'So,' Sheridan said, 'Anthony Harvey turns up at 16.35 on the Friday. CCTV shows that Ronald is back at the house by then and Rita's at home all day. We know that Ronald and Rita died at Crosby, so they were alive when they left the house. Let's have a closer look at the CCTV. Maybe they're in Anthony Harvey's car.'

They made their way to the CID office where swarms of officers were busy on phones, scrutinising their computer screens and talking across desks to each other.

Sheridan and Anna watched the CCTV footage closely. 'What do you think?' said Anna.

'It's way too dark to see anything clearly. But I don't think they're in the back seat.' She looked at Anna. 'They were both pretty small. Maybe they're in the boot.'

'We need to speak to Jennifer and find out if she knows Anthony Harvey.'

'I've just tried calling her, she's not picking up. Let's go out to the bookshop. You can drive and I'll keep trying her on the way.' Sheridan handed Anna the car keys as they made their way downstairs.

Twenty minutes later, Sheridan was peering through the bookshop window, holding her mobile to her ear, while Anna tried to listen for the sound of Jennifer's mobile ringing inside. Getting no response, they tried the landline as they walked down the alleyway at the side of the building.

The back door was locked.

'Let's give it a few minutes. Maybe she popped out to get some food or something.'

Suddenly, Anna's mobile rang. 'DS Markinson.' She put a finger in her ear to block out the traffic noise and Sheridan looked up and down the road for any sign of Jennifer.

Anna ended the call. 'This just gets more fucking weird. You remember the other day? When that woman jumped off the roof of The 180 Restaurant?'

'Yeah.'

'Well, *that* was Anthony Harvey's wife. Helen Harvey.'

'You're bloody joking.' Sheridan's eyes widened as her mind raced to fit this piece of the puzzle.

'Uniform were at his house on Saturday morning. They'd been trying to contact him since her identity was uncovered, and eventually found him at home. He said that Helen had a history of depression and had talked of suicide loads of times. He wanted to know where her car had been taken to, and if she'd left a suicide note. The officers explained that they weren't aware of any note, but that the car and contents have been seized. Post-mortem showed massive internal and external injuries. There was a slight trace of alcohol in her system, no drugs. She was in a bit of a mess, so they just got him to ID some of her belongings and then they took him home. Officers from Potters Road nick have been trying to contact him since then, but he's disappeared. He's not at home, his car's gone and he's not answering his mobile or landline. There's a marker on his car, and we're pinging his phone, but still nothing. The officers that were at the house are off duty, so Rob's going to text me their mobile numbers.'

Sheridan nodded and looked beyond Anna, to see Jennifer Parks walking towards them. 'Here's Jennifer.'

'Hi.' Jennifer tried a smile, but her face crumpled as she reached them. 'Sorry, I had to get out and go for a walk.' She unlocked the shop door. Sheridan and Anna followed her inside.

'How are you doing?' Sheridan asked, realising as soon as she asked that it was a ridiculous question.

Jennifer held her face in her hands and sobbed. Her strong shoulders dropped, and her chest heaved. 'I can't get my head around it all.' Her words were broken and almost inaudible, prompting Anna to step forward and place a comforting arm around her, before shepherding her to one of the back rooms as she spotted a customer peering through the locked door.

Sheridan arranged three chairs for them to sit on in the small kitchen and they all sat down. Both she and Anna waited patiently for Jennifer to try and compose herself before continuing.

'I'm so sorry,' Jennifer apologised, getting up to grab the kitchen roll from the worktop and tearing off a sheet to wipe her face and blow her nose.

'You don't need to apologise.' Sheridan's voice was low and calm, full of genuine empathy.

'I can't stop thinking about what my parents went through.' Jennifer lowered her head and tried to breathe slowly, swallowing as another sob rose in her throat.

As they waited, Anna's mobile pinged and she looked at the screen, which showed the names and mobile numbers of the two officers who had previously attended Anthony Harvey's house. She quickly stood up. 'Sorry, I need to make a couple of calls.'

Jennifer let her out of the shop and returned to the kitchen, where Sheridan was filling the kettle.

'Can I make you a hot drink?' Sheridan asked, noticing the name 'Daniel' on the mug in the sink. An unexpected sadness washed over her. Daniel was a victim of murder. He was someone she never had, and never would, meet. Seeing this simple, personal object, his mug, made her ache a little for Jennifer.

'No, thanks. But help yourself.' Jennifer sighed and sat down. 'Anyway, sorry, you probably came here to speak to me about the case.'

Sheridan switched the kettle off and sat opposite her. 'We wanted to make sure you're okay but yes, I have a question if you're up to it.'

'Yes, of course.'

'Does the name Anthony Harvey mean anything to you?'

Jennifer looked to the floor for a moment. She moved as though to shake her head, but suddenly her eyes widened, and she nodded. 'Sorry, you threw me for a second. Yes, I know him. But I'm not used to hearing him being called Anthony. We always called him Tony.' She looked at Sheridan. 'Why?'

'How do you know him?'

'He's a friend of my parents. Him and his wife, Helen, have known our family for years.'

'Tell me what you know about him.'

Jennifer explained how her parents had been friends with Tony and Helen Harvey since she could remember. Tony was a retired insurance consultant and his wife, Helen, had never worked as far as she knew. They had no children of their own but doted on her and Daniel. They would sometimes visit her parents for meals and drinks, often spending weekends there. 'Why do you want to know about Tony?' she asked.

'His car was at your parents' house last Friday. Did they mention that he was due to visit them?'

'No, they didn't.' Jennifer frowned. 'So, do you think Tony was the last person to see my parents alive?'

'Possibly. Do you know if Tony ever fell out with your parents?'

'Not that I know of.' She looked to the floor again. 'You don't think Tony had something to do with what happened, do you?'

'We don't know. Is there any connection between Crosby Beach, Tony Harvey and your parents?'

'We all went there a couple of times when Daniel and I were kids.'

'When was the last time you had any contact with Tony and Helen?'

'During my father's trial – they were really supportive. They called my mother all the time to check on her. They never believed that my father had anything to do with Daniel's murder.'

Sheridan shifted in her seat. 'Jennifer, I'm sorry, but I have to tell you that Helen took her own life last Friday.'

Jennifer's eyes widened and for a moment she didn't speak or move. Her eyes searched Sheridan's face and her mouth suddenly dried up. She stood up and poured herself a glass of water, taking a sip before she sat back down. 'I just can't believe it.' She looked up at the ceiling, slowly shaking her head. 'What the fuck is happening? It's like everyone I know is dying.'

At a loss to find the right words, Sheridan couldn't respond. She could see a physical change in Jennifer. She was breaking, slowly but surely, in front of Sheridan's eyes. For a split second, Sheridan's own parents' faces were in her head, and she was fourteen years old again, watching them gradually disappear beneath a cloud of grief after her brother's murder.

Her jaw tightened and she fought to shut the image out. She had never let what had happened to Matthew affect how she did her job. And she refused to let it now. What it did do was make her as determined as ever to find the killer in this case.

'How did she do it?' Jennifer asked.

'She jumped from the roof of a building,' Sheridan replied, realising there was really no easier way to describe it.

Jennifer absorbed the information. For a moment, they sat in silence. 'Did she leave a note or anything?'

'I don't know any details, I'm sorry. I've literally just found out myself.'

There was a knock on the shop window and Sheridan glanced around the kitchen door to see Anna standing there. Excusing herself, she made her way outside to hear what Anna had to say.

'I've spoken to the officers that went to Anthony Harvey's house on Saturday,' Anna told her. 'Apparently, he didn't want to let them in. But when he did, they noticed there was sand and dirt on the carpets.'

'You're shitting me.'

'Obviously, at that time they didn't know anything about the bodies at Crosby and, to be fair, no one would have made any connection between Anthony Harvey and the murders.'

Sheridan recounted the conversation she'd just had with Jennifer, before they went back inside. She and Anna tried to persuade Jennifer to stay with a friend so she wasn't on her own, but Jennifer insisted that she felt safe at the bookshop and would call the police immediately, should she need to.

CHAPTER 21

Sam smiled as Sheridan's car pulled on to the drive. She picked Maud up before opening the front door.

'Hello, you,' she said as Sheridan came into the house, kissing Sam first and then Maud, who inquisitively sniffed Sheridan's nose.

'Is there any chance there's a big glass of wine waiting for me?' Sheridan pulled off her coat and went into the kitchen, spotting the flickering candle that stood in the middle of the table, which was set for dinner.

'Sit down and relax. I've ordered a takeout.' Sam pulled out a chair with one hand and passed Sheridan a glass of wine with the other. 'Tell me all about your day.' She gently massaged Sheridan's head and neck and listened as Sheridan told her how the case was getting more complicated by the minute, and how Hill Knowles was the most annoying fucking woman she had ever worked with.

'Anyway, tell me about *your* day,' Sheridan said, finishing her wine and pouring them both another large one.

'One of my kids got a lump of plasticine stuck up her nose,' Sam said, accepting the wine and sitting back. 'And you think your job's stressful.' She grinned.

After dinner, they settled on the sofa, with Maud sprawled out across Sheridan's legs, her tail flicking every time Sheridan stroked her head.

'I think you should take your DCI out for a drink,' Sam suddenly piped up.

'Why the hell would I do that?'

'To clear the air. You've got to work with this woman and if you don't have it out with her then you'll always be butting heads. So, take her out for a drink and fix it.' Sam nodded her head once, as though this was the final word on the matter.

'That's a terrible idea.'

'It's a brilliant idea. Unless of course she's bloody stunning with a body to die for.'

'She looks like a skinny squirrel on speed.' Sheridan made herself chuckle with her analogy.

'Then, yes, you should definitely take her out for a drink.'

CHAPTER 22

Thursday 8 November

Hill Knowles walked into the briefing room, looked around, but clearly didn't see who she was looking for. She made to leave again, bumping into Sheridan as she turned.

'There you are,' she said. 'I've been looking for you, where were you?' Her abrupt tone made several heads turn, and immediately put Sheridan's nose out of joint.

'In the ladies, saying goodbye to the curry I had last night, ma'am.'

All heads went down as Hill Knowles inhaled through her nose. 'Can I see you in my office?'

Sheridan followed her down the corridor, feeling like a teenager about to be whacked across the backside by the headmistress. When they reached her office, Hill held the door open and then slammed it shut. Sheridan had barely stepped over the threshold.

'Let's get one thing straight, Sheridan. I don't give a flying fuck if you like me or not. I also don't give a flying fuck if the rest of the team don't like me. But I do demand respect and to be spoken to like I am actually the fucking detective chief inspector.'

'And I expect to be spoken to like I am actually the fucking detective inspector. Ma'am.'

They locked eyes, silently weighing each other up. It was a stand-off. The silence only broken by a tap on the door.

'Not now!' Hill shouted, her eyes fixed on Sheridan.

Sheridan took a deep breath and put her hands on her hips. 'What are you doing after work?'

'What?' Hill snapped.

'I think we should go out for a drink.'

Hill's astonished expression amused Sheridan, but she kept a straight face.

'Why the fuck would we do that?'

'Because my girlfriend thinks it would be a good idea. Personally, I think it's a very bad idea and I actually hope you'll say no.'

Hill's expression changed again; the frown ironed itself out and the corners of her mouth reluctantly began to turn skywards. Fighting the urge to smile, she looked to the floor.

'The Black Cat at six thirty,' Hill replied, before walking out of her office with Sheridan in tow.

The briefing room fell silent when they walked back in. Sheridan winked at Anna before making her way to the whiteboard, where Hill joined her, stiff-lipped and arms folded across her chest.

Sheridan began. 'Good morning, everyone. I'll quickly summarise where we are and what we need to do.' She unscrewed the top of her water bottle and took a sip.

She updated the team that Tony Harvey's wife, Helen, had been identified as the woman who had jumped from the roof of The 180 Restaurant. And the fact that when officers did eventually get hold of Tony Harvey at his home address the following morning, the carpets had been soiled with dirt and sand.

'As you know,' she said, 'Tony Harvey is the male whose car was seen to arrive and leave Ronald and Rita Parks' property on the Friday evening – before their bodies were found on Crosby beach.

Jennifer Parks tells us that Tony and Helen were friends of her parents and they had known each other for years. She's not aware of any arguments or issues between them. Since Tony was seen on Saturday by police, he's gone off radar. We've got a marker on his car, so hopefully ANPR will pick him up, and we've pinged his phone. It might be that Tony is so distraught by his wife's suicide that he's taken himself off somewhere, but with what we know so far, we need to find him urgently.'

DCI Hill Knowles looked around the room. 'I've been over to the magistrates' court. We now have a warrant to search Tony's address, which I want done this morning. We've got his wife's keys, so we don't need to be kicking any doors in.' She pointed to DC Dipesh Mois. 'What have you got on Tony's mobile so far?'

'On Friday, it pinged off a mast near his house. Then it shows him heading in the direction of the Parks' property. Later that evening, it pinged half a mile from Crosby Beach. Since then, we've got a hit in Liverpool city centre, but that's it.'

Rob Wills put his hand up. 'I've just finished checking through the CCTV at the gym that Jennifer goes to. She's clearly seen there on the dates and times she's previously given us. I've also got the CCTV near the bookshop and again, her timings are spot on.'

'Okay. Good work, Rob.' Hill gave a thumbs up. 'Let's crack on. I want Tony Harvey located as a matter of priority.'

CHAPTER 23

Sheridan walked into the pub and spotted Hill sitting in the corner by the window with her mobile pressed to her ear. She looked up and put her hand over the top of her glass; she didn't need another drink.

Sheridan got herself a tonic water and slid into the chair opposite.

'Thanks, Charlie, I'll let Sheridan know.' Hill ended the call and put her mobile on the table. 'CSI have finished up at the Parks' property, so Jennifer can go back there if she wants to.'

'Okay, I'll speak to her tomorrow. I want to get some safety measures in place first.' Sheridan sipped her tonic water.

'Sure.' Hill put her thumb up. 'Also let her know that we strongly advise against her staying at the cottage.'

'I will.'

There was an awkward silence before Hill spoke again, and when she did, her voice had softened. 'So, tell me . . . did you join the job because of your brother's murder?'

Sheridan didn't answer immediately. She had been unaware that Hill even knew about her brother's death. And she certainly hadn't expected it to be the first subject they discussed.

Taking another sip of her drink, she swallowed and put the glass down, staring at the bubbles rising to the top. 'Yeah,' she said. 'I always planned to become a detective. To solve his case.'

Hill nodded slowly. 'Tell me what happened.'

Sheridan described how, on a cold March day in 1977, twelve-year-old Matthew Holler went out to play football with two friends in Birkenhead Park and never came home.

One lad, Chris Hoe, had headed home early, leaving Matthew and his best friend, fourteen-year-old Andrew Longford, to carry on playing. According to Andrew, half an hour later they had spotted a man watching them from nearby. The man was white, medium build, with a beard, wearing blue jeans and a brown coat. Andrew said that he and Matthew decided to go home, walking to the pathway that crossed a small bridge before going their separate ways. Matthew was reported missing by Sheridan's parents later that evening and his body was found the next day, hidden near the bridge where Andrew Longford had last seen him.

The cause of death was a single blow to the forehead that fractured his skull. Although his clothes had been removed and were never found, there was no evidence that he had been sexually assaulted.

Andrew Longford and Chris Hoe both gave statements to the police at the time. Chris Hoe told police that he hadn't noticed anyone hanging around the park while he was there. Eleven years later, he was killed in an accident at work when he fell from scaffolding on a block of flats in Bootle.

Sheridan went on to tell Hill how the case had been reopened a few years earlier, but the police were no closer to solving the murder. Sheridan had herself made contact with Andrew Longford back in 2005. She described how, while sat in his cluttered living room, she had noticed a collage of photographs clipped into a frame on the wall. As she studied the pictures, she'd spotted a man in the background in one of the photographs and when she pointed him out, Andrew had remarked that he hadn't noticed him before. Then, after sifting through boxes of other old photographs taken by Andrew's father in Birkenhead Park, he'd spotted the same man, again standing in the background. In two of the pictures, the man was clean-shaven, but in the third he had a beard and was wearing a brown coat. Sheridan had handed the photos to the cold-case team, who were making enquiries to try and identify the male.

'So, Andrew Longford had never seen this male before?' Hill asked.

'No. And he couldn't be sure it was the man he'd seen on the day Matthew was killed. All he remembered was what the guy was wearing. He never really saw his face but just knew he had a beard.' Sheridan took another sip of her drink. 'Andrew's racked with guilt and has been his whole life. He's had a tough time of it, he's in remission from cancer and has some health issues. He's divorced and his dad died of cancer about thirteen years ago.'

'How have your parents coped with it all?'

Talking with Hill like this, away from work, Sheridan noticed that she felt a little more comfortable in her presence. Hill appeared to soften very slightly as she asked Sheridan about her brother.

'They live with it, like I do. They just want to know the truth. And I'll do whatever I can to find it.' Sheridan looked up and smiled. 'Anyway, enough about me.'

Hill stretched her back against the chair. 'Tell me about this girlfriend of yours who thought us having a drink together was such a good idea.' She cradled her glass.

Sheridan relaxed back in her seat and told Hill how she and Sam had met, a smile crossing her face as she spoke.

'So, what does Sam do for a living?'

'She's a schoolteacher.' Sheridan crossed her legs and folded her arms. Now she'd opened up to Hill, she wanted to hear *her* story. 'Well, that's me. Your turn.'

Hill pursed her lips. 'I'm not married, no kids, no tits, I love my job and I hate cats.'

Sheridan thought for a moment that she'd misheard. 'Sorry, did you just say "no tits"?'

'Yes. My family have a dodgy cancer gene, so I had a precautionary double mastectomy.' Hill lifted her glass and tilted her head to one side. 'Are we bonding?' she asked. Her comment drenched in sarcasm.

Sheridan couldn't help grinning. 'Possibly.'

'So, what did you say to Sam that prompted her to suggest this cosy little chat?'

Sheridan, deciding that the conversation was swaying towards brutal honesty, didn't hold back. 'I told her how annoying you are, how you rub people up the wrong way and when you do that thing with your thumb, I want to grab it and snap it off your hand.'

'Interesting.' Hill nodded. 'Well, I think *you're* the best DI that I've ever worked with. I think you're thorough and you completely motivate the team.'

'Thank you.' Sheridan half frowned and half smiled.

Hill's stoic expression didn't change.

Sheridan hesitated for a moment, before she asked, 'Why are you so pissed off all the time?'

'I'm not pissed off. I've just got a miserable face.' Hill suddenly stood up. 'Do you want another drink? Or are we done here?'

Sheridan raised her eyebrows at the abruptness of Hill's tone. 'I guess we're done,' she replied.

'Well, it's been magical. See you tomorrow.' Hill zipped her coat up, picked up her mobile and left. Sheridan watched as she walked past the pub window, stopped, backed up, looked at Sheridan and gave her a thumbs up.

CHAPTER 24

Friday 9 November

Sheridan and Jennifer pulled up at the cottage. Jennifer trembled as she got out of the car. She glanced back at her parents' house and wondered what she would face when she eventually walked through that door. Right now, she had no reason to go inside. Her parents were dead, and she hadn't lived there since she and Daniel had moved into the cottage seven years earlier.

Prior to that, the cottage had stood empty since the 1940s. It had originally been used for storage by Ronald after he bought the house and land in the seventies. It was a solid building with thick stone walls. Daniel had completed a lot of the renovation work himself, having learned the basics of the building trade from his father. Ronald had wanted Daniel to follow him into the business, often taking him on jobs at weekends, but although Daniel was a quick learner, it wasn't the life he wanted.

Daniel loved to read, as did Jennifer. They used to spend hours in the cottage together, noses pressed between the crisp white pages of any book they could get their hands on. Jennifer loved the cottage and all its quirkiness – the odd-sized rooms and tiny windows. Although it was surrounded by woodland and thick bramble bushes, she had always felt safe there. Even when darkness fell around the place and the moon was the only thing lighting up the back of the property, the eeriness never bothered her.

She stepped through the front door and let the smell of the cottage fill her nostrils. She was home.

Sheridan stood outside the main door for a moment, watching Jennifer as she slowly reacquainted herself with her surroundings. She had assured Sheridan that she would be fine here on her own and had accepted the offer of a police alarm. There was a police marker on the property and Sheridan had organised local patrols to drive past regularly and, if it wasn't too late at night, they would knock on the door to make sure Jennifer was okay. She had also arranged for a police car to be parked on the drive for a few days, just to give the illusion that police were there, should anyone be watching the place.

Sheridan's eyes moved around the room as she stepped inside. On one wall was a heavy oak bookcase lined with hardback novels, encyclopaedias, and a box file labelled 'Daniel's File'. She moved closer to the bookcase, tempted to take the box off the shelf and open it to see what was in there. Jennifer had told her that she'd kept notes during the investigation, a log of calls she'd made to the officer in the case, questions raised by the police, detailed maps of the area that the police had searched for Daniel's body, along with her own maps of the places she and her volunteer group had checked. She'd already given Sheridan a copy of these maps and Sheridan had politely taken them.

'That's the file I kept on Daniel when he disappeared,' Jennifer said, returning from the kitchen.

'May I?' Sheridan put a hand on the file.

'Yes, of course.' Jennifer lifted it off the bookcase and placed it down on the coffee table.

Sitting on the armchair, Sheridan gently opened the file. On top of the papers and notepads inside was a photograph of Daniel, his handsome, smiling face beaming back at her. He looked different to the photos that Sheridan had seen on the original case file. This version of Daniel seemed strangely real. Dark brown hair swept across his forehead, hazel eyes that glistened among long, rather feminine eyelashes. His high, strong cheekbones were made even more prominent by a close-cut beard, immaculately shaved into shape. He looked like a model.

'Daniel was very good-looking. How come he didn't have a girlfriend?' Sheridan asked, placing the photograph on the table before lifting out a large A4 notepad.

'He was quite shy. Girls used to fancy him, but he never had the confidence to really talk to any of them.' Jennifer sat perched on the edge of the coffee table as she stared pensively at the picture.

'Random question and I hope you don't mind me asking . . . but was there any chance that Daniel could have been gay?'

'No. Definitely not.' Jennifer reached into the file and took out one of the notepads, resting it on her lap. Suddenly bursting into tears, she put her hand to her mouth. 'I miss him so much.'

Sheridan sat quietly, waiting for Jennifer to regain her composure.

'I'm sorry,' Jennifer said eventually, 'I just want to know where he is. I want somewhere I can go to leave flowers, to sit and talk to him again.' Her tear-filled eyes looked straight at Sheridan. 'You will find out who killed my family, won't you?'

'I'll do everything I can, I promise,' Sheridan replied, before asking, 'Can I take this file?' Sheridan knew that even a nugget of information could be the key to solving the case. She often saw things that others missed. Even if Jennifer's files held nothing of note, asking about them was a way for Sheridan to perhaps learn more about Jennifer herself.

'Do you think it would help?' Jennifer asked.

'I don't know. I'm just thinking that you might have written something in it, a note or a thought and maybe you've forgotten it.'

'Sure, but will I be able to have it back?'

'Of course, I'll get it back to you as soon as I can.' Sheridan stood up. 'I should be going. I do have to say though, Jennifer, your staying here goes against our advice. I can't guarantee your safety if you stay. Is there no way I can convince you to stay somewhere else?'

'No, I'll be fine here. Thank you for everything.'

As Sheridan drove back to Hale Street, her mobile rang and she put it on loudspeaker. 'DI Holler.'

'It's Anna, are you free to speak?'

'Yeah, mate, I'm on my way back to the nick now.'

'Okay. I'll update you when you get here. You're going to love this.'

CHAPTER 25

Anna was in the CID office when Sheridan walked in, wrestling with the zip on her jacket.

'How did it go with Jennifer? Is she alright?' Anna asked.

'She's not too bad, but I've got a gut feeling that Daniel was gay and perhaps closeted . . . which may or may not be relevant. Anyway, what's this update you've got?'

'We've got the downloads from Helen Harvey's phone. It shows some contact between her and Rita Parks going back to when Ronald was on trial, nothing out of the ordinary as far as we can see. But just before she jumped off the restaurant roof, she got a call from Tony.'

'Okay.'

'Obviously, we don't know what was said during the call. But six hours later, he sends her a text message that reads, and I quote: "*I've sorted them both. We need to run, start packing, I'll be home soon.*" Now, obviously Helen didn't respond because she'd jumped by then, and we had possession of her phone.'

'And whatever he said to her, he didn't expect her to kill herself because if he did, he wouldn't have sent that text. It also sounds like he's not going after Jennifer. Any news on his car?' Sheridan asked.

'No, nothing yet.'

'I asked Jennifer if she knew of any connections Tony might have anywhere else in the country. But she can't think of anything.'

'What about Daniel? Why do you think he was gay?'

Sheridan showed Anna the photograph from Jennifer's file and told her the conversation they'd had about him never having had a girlfriend. Sheridan's latest theory was that maybe Ronald and Daniel's argument was about his sexuality. They were clearly very different. Ronald was a builder, whereas Daniel was an academic, a book lover, and had an almost androgenous look about him.

Hill Knowles walked into the office and made her way straight over to them. 'Tony Harvey's car has been found burnt out on wasteland on the Dock Road. CSI will examine it but apparently all that's left is the shell. His house has been searched and it looks like he's tried to clean up the carpets, but he hasn't done a very good job. There's no sign of anything that was used in the Parks' murders, but we've seized his computer. The neighbours haven't seen him.'

'Has he got access to another vehicle?' Anna asked.

'Not as far as we know, unless he's hired one. Or he could be travelling with someone else.'

Anna snapped a look at Sheridan, remembering her comment on the morning that Ronald and Rita's bodies had been found.

I'm thinking that this wasn't one *person.*

'You could be right,' she said. Anna nodded slowly as she spoke, before explaining to Hill what she was talking about.

Hill responded, 'If there is someone else involved, then we need to figure out who.'

◆ ◆ ◆

Later that afternoon, Anna stuck her head around the door to Sheridan's office. 'Fancy a quick one?'

'I hope you don't say that to all the girls.' Sheridan grinned and glanced up at the clock, which still wasn't working. 'I need to get some batteries for that.'

She stood up, quickly pushing her chair back, opening her desk drawer and lifting out the heavy file that Jennifer had kept on Daniel's murder.

'What's that?' Anna asked, craning her head to get a better look.

'Just taking a bit of light reading home with me,' Sheridan answered, raising an eyebrow: it would be anything but.

Anna turned to glance at the clock. 'I'll be back in a sec.'

Two minutes later she returned with two batteries, dragged a swivel chair over and went to stand on it. 'Can you hold the chair?'

Sheridan stood behind her and gripping the chair, put her other hand on Anna's back. 'Don't you dare fart.'

Anna tutted as she reached up for the clock, feeling the chair start to turn. 'Hold on tighter, it's going to spin round.'

Sheridan started laughing as Anna grabbed the clock from the wall and the chair turned 180 degrees, leaving her facing Sheridan. She stepped down. After changing the batteries, she reset the time and handed the clock to Sheridan. 'There, now you can put it back up.'

'I can't. I hate heights, you do it.' Sheridan pursed her lips. 'Please?'

Anna shook her head and put her knees on the chair, while she clung to the back of it. Sheridan started to spin it round, laughing as she did so. 'Stop it, Sheridan, I'll be sick.'

Sheridan spun the chair faster and faster, practically choking with laughter. After a few more spins, she stopped. 'Now get off and see if you can walk across the office without falling over.'

Anna climbed off just as Hill walked in to see her staggering across the office, arms outstretched, trying to focus on anything she could grab hold of.

'Good evening, ma'am.' Sheridan was almost sucking her own cheeks inside out, trying not to laugh.

'See you on Monday,' Hill curtly replied, giving Anna an incredulous look before she left.

CHAPTER 26

Jennifer Parks didn't know he was watching her through the kitchen window.

The thick bushes at the side of the cottage gave him the perfect vantage point. He'd been there earlier when the police had turned up, leaving a marked car on the drive outside the main house.

Since then, darkness had fallen, surrounding the cottage, and the stars were glistening in the crisp November sky. He watched as she wiped her hands on a tea towel, then picked up her glass of wine and nestled on to the sofa.

He quickly ducked down as headlights lit up the driveway, remaining motionless as another police car pulled up outside the door and two uniformed officers climbed out. Breathing as quietly as he could, he felt his own heartbeat thumping in his chest as he watched Jennifer opening the front door to step outside.

'Hello, Jennifer. I'm PC Morley, and this is my colleague PC Hunt. We're just checking everything's okay.'

'I'm fine, everything's fine, thank you.'

'We're on nights this week, so it'll probably be us that pop by in the evening. Some of our other colleagues will check on you during the day.'

'Thank you so much. Would you like to come in for a coffee or something?'

'I'm afraid we can't. Fridays are usually quite busy for us so we're just quickly checking in. Maybe next time.'

'Okay.'

'Well, you have a good evening. Call us if you need to.'

'I will, thank you again.' She forced a smile and watched as they turned the car around and drove slowly away, giving herself a moment to breathe in the fresh cold air. While she stood watching the police car weaving down the lane, he watched her.

She was right there – if he was quick enough, he could grab her before she went back inside. It would only take a second, he thought, as his hand tightened around the straps in his pocket.

CHAPTER 27

Sheridan walked into the pub with Anna, and immediately felt the heat from the open fire that blazed and crackled at the far end of the bar. She held her mobile to her ear as Anna went to get the drinks, and found them a quiet corner to sit in.

'Still no answer from Jennifer.' Sheridan ended the call and laid her mobile on the table as Anna put two tonic waters in front of them.

'Have you left a message?'

'Yeah.' Sheridan bit her bottom lip and checked her phone. Hesitating for a moment.

'I'm sure she's fine, Sheridan. Maybe she just wants some peace and quiet.'

'Yeah, but I did ask her to always answer *my* calls.' Sheridan tried Jennifer's number again. No reply. She looked at Anna. 'I'm ringing the nick.'

She spoke to the patrol sergeant, who confirmed that Jennifer had been visited at the cottage by uniformed officers less than half an hour before, and was alive and well.

'Now I can relax,' Sheridan said to Anna, sighing heavily as she slumped back in her seat. 'I meant to ask you . . . what's happening with your inspector's exam? Are you still thinking of going for it?'

'Not at the moment. I know I keep putting it off, but I need to be better prepared.'

'Well, don't put it off forever, you're not getting any younger.' Sheridan tilted her glass towards Anna.

'Cheeky bitch.'

'Anyway, what's your gut feeling about this job?'

Anna rested her arms on the table and spread her hands out before her as if she were about to play the piano. 'I think Ronald Parks *did* kill Daniel, and Tony Harvey killed Ronald and Rita. I also think Tony rang Helen to tell her he was going to do it. That's why she jumped. Apart from that, I'm not sure, until we get the phone checks and everything else back. It would have taken a lot of planning to get Ronald and Rita to Crosby alive, a lot of physical strength and time to even dig the hole in the sand. It wasn't a spur of the moment thing and the way the bodies were positioned was so symbolic, just as you said.'

Sheridan nodded slowly and took a sip of her drink. 'I know it's an old cliché, but I think we're missing something really obvious.'

CHAPTER 28

Saturday 10 November

Jennifer could feel the cold hard metal of the Iron Man statue against her back as the freezing water lapped around her feet. With her arms behind her, the muscles were beginning to ache, so she slowly turned her wrists until she could feel the rough metal against her palms.

Looking down at the incoming tide, she tried to turn her head to look back at the beach. She guessed it was around 2 a.m. by now. No one would be about at this time in the morning. No one would see her. If she screamed, would anybody even hear?

She felt like she was the only person left in the world. She tried to focus on something to take her mind off the bitterly cold wind that ripped through her clothing and right through to her bones.

She thought about the times she had come to Crosby as a child. Her parents would sit on the sand and watch her and Daniel playing together. She remembered when her father grabbed her mother's hand and tried to drag her to the water's edge. Her mother had started shaking and crying as the water touched her bare feet. Rita Parks had been terrified of the water.

It was the same day that Tony and Helen Harvey had come with them. She remembered Tony taking her by the hand to go and buy them all an ice cream. As they'd been walking back, she had dropped one of them and Tony had told her to stay where she was while he went back to the ice cream van.

That was the first time she was ever left alone. It was only for a few minutes. She remembered the man's face – the man who approached her and asked her if she was alright – asking if she was lost and was she with her parents? Did she need help finding them? She remembered staring at his face. He'd had kind features, like someone you would trust. But her parents had always drummed it into her and Daniel about talking to strangers. They said it almost every day: *Never ever trust a stranger*. She had always wondered if the same man would be there if she went back to the beach on another day. And if he had been there again, would things have been different if, the next time, she had screamed?

Her body shivered violently, bringing her back to the present as she realised the water was up to her knees. The freezing wind was now battering her face and she was struggling to breathe. She closed her eyes, with only one thought left in her head. What was the last thing that had gone through her mother's mind before the water consumed her?

CHAPTER 29

Sam sat on the toilet seat with Maud perched on her lap and watched Sheridan in the shower.

They'd spent the morning up in the loft, sorting through the Christmas decorations and debating whether this year they should put the fairy that had been in Sheridan's family for years on top of the tree, or choose Sam's favourite childhood hippopotamus, Hylda.

They had finally agreed to let Maud decide, placing both on the floor in front of her. Whichever one she patted, sniffed or attacked first would be the winner. After hissing at and tearing the shit out of the fairy, it was agreed that this year, Hylda the Hippo would take pride of place on top of the tree. And Sam would buy Sheridan a new fairy. And Maud was not allowed to be the decision-maker ever again.

As Sheridan stepped out of the shower, Sam handed her a towel from the radiator and laughed as she wrapped it around her head and proceeded to do a naked dance into the bedroom. After depositing Maud on the floor, Sam grabbed Sheridan's arm and pulled her on to the bed.

'Let's do rude stuff.' Sam grinned, but then Maud jumped up and strode across the duvet, purring loudly in Sheridan's face.

'Maybe not.' Sheridan laughed, but stopped suddenly as the sound of her phone ringing echoed from downstairs. 'Shit, that's my work mobile, can you grab it for me?'

Sam ran downstairs and grabbed the phone, before running back up and handing it to Sheridan, who had now wrapped the towel around herself. 'DI Holler.'

She listened as DC Rob Wills explained that uniformed officers had been to carry out a welfare check on Jennifer, but she wasn't answering the door. They had called her landline and mobile, both of which could be heard ringing from inside the property. Jennifer's car had been parked outside the cottage and the front door was locked. When officers gained entry to the property, nothing appeared out of place. They had then attended the bookshop, which was closed, with no sign of anyone inside. Entry was gained but once again, Jennifer wasn't there.

'I'm coming in.' Sheridan shook her head as she ended the call. 'Fuck.'

Twenty minutes later, Sheridan was throwing change into the toll at the Kingsway Tunnel when her mobile rang. She answered it and put her foot down. 'DI Holler.'

'It's Rob.' The voice started to crackle as Sheridan entered the tunnel.

'Say again,' Sheridan shouted.

'It's Rob, can you hear me?'

'Yes, but I'm just in the Kingsway Tunnel, you're breaking up.'

'We've just found Jennifer Parks.'

CHAPTER 30

Sheridan stared at the trainers Jennifer had been wearing when she was found, and the tracksuit bottoms, which were still soaking wet. Then she looked at Jennifer herself, lying there on the hospital trolley in one of the side rooms off the main A&E department. The department was busy: staff on telephones, nurses hurrying down corridors, doctors emerging from behind curtains and looking down at their notes. Phones rang constantly, and buzzers sounded every few minutes as paramedics wheeled in patient after patient.

Sheridan took a tentative step further into the room and closed the door behind her, to drown out the chaos outside. Noticing the blue tinge around Jennifer's lips, she instinctively pulled the blankets over her before turning to Rob, who was leaning against the wall with his arms crossed.

'What happened?' she whispered.

'She was found lying on the sand at Crosby, near to one of the Iron Men statues. They think she'd been there for a few hours.'

At that moment, the door opened, and a tall blonde doctor came in. 'I'm so sorry about this, we're very busy this morning.' She walked over to Jennifer and gently touched her face, waking her. 'How are you feeling?'

Jennifer put a fragile hand up to wipe her mouth. 'I'm alright,' she replied, suddenly noticing Sheridan standing behind the doctor. 'Sheridan, I'm so sorry.'

She burst into tears as the doctor put a comforting hand on her shoulder before checking her temperature. When she'd finished, she updated Jennifer's notes and quietly left the room.

'How did you end up at Crosby?' Sheridan pulled up a chair and sat by Jennifer's side.

There was a long silence before Jennifer answered. 'I needed to know,' she said. 'I'm so sorry if I worried anyone.'

'It's okay.'

'I can't stop thinking about my parents. My head is so full of questions. Who killed them? Why? But most of all, what did they feel before they died? I had to try and put myself there, where my mother had been, tied to that statue in the cold and dark. Maybe she tried to turn and see my father, maybe they tried to call out to each other.' She looked at Sheridan. 'I know you told me their mouths were taped up, but they might have tried. I wanted to know how my mother felt when the water started to come up around her.' She leaned back on the pillow, staring up at the ceiling. 'She must have been so frightened.'

Sheridan and Rob remained silent.

'I'm sorry,' Jennifer said. 'I'm really trying to be strong. I just feel so guilty that I'm here and they're all gone.' She tugged the blanket up to her chin.

'You *are* being strong, Jennifer,' Sheridan said. 'What you've been through would totally break most people. What you're experiencing now is probably something called survivor guilt and it's very common. You don't have to apologise to me or anyone else for how you're feeling.' Sheridan stopped short of using her own experience of loss to assure Jennifer that she understood completely.

'The strange thing is, when I was in the dark, standing in the water, a kind of peace came over me. It was like I was with my mother again. Like she was there. Is it weird that I feel like I've said goodbye to them?'

'No. It's not weird. Is that why you went there?'

'I didn't actually plan it, to be honest. After the police officers left the cottage last night, I wanted to get out and do something normal, like go for a run. I know that the police car you've parked on the drive is to help protect me, but if I'm being really honest, I hate looking at it, it reminds me that everything isn't normal and I just wanted to put my running gear on and go out, like I used to do. So, that's what I did and then I just kept running.' She allowed herself a smile. 'Like Forrest Gump.'

Sheridan grinned. She noticed that the colour was returning to Jennifer's cheeks.

'It made me feel alive to run and then it hit me that my parents aren't alive and how is it fair that I'm here and they're not? That was when I found myself on Crosby Beach.' She lifted her head and propped herself up on one elbow. 'And, however this sounds, I've made my peace with it a bit. I adored my parents, and I adored Daniel, and I'll miss them for as long as I live . . . but I have to get through this, or it's going to destroy me.'

'I know you're trying to be strong, but I'd like to leave the safety measures in for a bit longer.'

'I understand. I'm happy with the alarm and stuff, but do you have to leave the police car there?'

Sheridan sat forward, clasping her hands together. 'Jennifer, we haven't found Tony Harvey yet. We have evidence that might link him to your parents' deaths. I need to keep you safe.'

Jennifer said quickly, 'I can't believe Tony would hurt anyone, especially me. I've known him since I was a kid. Him and my parents were best friends for years. He was like family.'

'Why do you think he wouldn't hurt you?'

Jennifer hesitated, rubbing her face. 'Tony was like my father. It was like I had two dads. He adored me, and I adored him. He'd never hurt me.'

'Sometimes you think you know someone but then they turn out to be very different. I'd really like to leave the police car there a bit longer.'

'Okay,' Jennifer replied. 'But I honestly think you're wrong about Tony.'

◆ ◆ ◆

Pulling out of the hospital car park, Sheridan turned her mobile back on and listened to a voicemail from Anna. As she waited at the lights, she called her.

'Hi, Sheridan.'

'Hi, mate. You called me.'

'I did. How's Jennifer?'

'She'll be okay. I'll explain everything when I get back to the nick.'

'Okay. Anyway, I've got an update for you.'

'Go for it.'

'We've got CCTV of Tony Harvey going into a DIY shop, half an hour before he arrived at the Parks' house on the night they were taken.'

'Did he buy anything?'

'Yep. Cable ties. The exact same ones that were used on Ronald and Rita.'

CHAPTER 31

Sunday 11 November

Sam and Sheridan sat top to tail on the sofa. Sam was marking homework, while Sheridan was reading the file that Jennifer had kept on Daniel's murder. Deciding that she wasn't getting enough attention, Maud was busying herself trying to push piles of paperwork off the coffee table.

Studying the maps that Jennifer had marked up, Sheridan noted the dates when Jennifer and the volunteers had covered each area. She then took out the first of three thick notepads and began reading.

Jennifer had documented every conversation with the OIC and other officers, the time and date she had spoken to them and a summary of their conversation. There were pages of her own thoughts and memories of the day she had come home to find Daniel missing: the conversation with her parents and the call to the police. There were details of the trial, comments about the prosecution case and police evidence, even down to the reaction of jury members when certain evidence had been revealed. There was page upon page of notes, some of which read like a report and others like a diary. A very personal diary.

*I sit in the cottage alone. You've gone and my heart liter-
ally breaks. I can't think of one person who would ever
want to hurt you. You were so beautiful, so gentle and
kind. How could someone break our beautiful family?
How could anyone take you from us? Our perfect lives are
shattered. I miss you so much. It's hard to smile, it's hard
to think of my life without my big brother. Goodnight
Daniel. xxx*

As Sheridan turned the pages, she found she related to Jennifer's
pain with every word.

Lifting out the last notepad, she read some more recent entries.

*Monday 5th November – Two police officers, DI Holler
and DS Markinson, came to the bookshop to tell me
they're reopening Daniel's case. I'm going to the police
station tomorrow morning to go over my statement.*

*I pray they'll find out who really killed him. Maybe then
we'll finally get some peace and the three of us can try to
move on.*

Sheridan took her eyes off the page for a moment. Even as an experienced detective, she felt intrusive, like she wasn't supposed to be
reading Jennifer's innermost thoughts and feelings.

Thinking back on the numerous murders she'd investigated,
she couldn't recall a single one where the family had kept such
detailed notes about the enquiry. It reminded her of the diary and
notes she'd kept on Matthew's murder when she was fourteen.

She carried on reading until her head started to ache and letting the notepad rest on her legs for a moment, she closed her eyes.

'You okay?' Sam asked, looking up from her marking.

'Yeah. It's just heartbreaking to read Jennifer's comments about her brother.'

'It's reminding you of Matthew, isn't it?' Sam rubbed her hand gently up and down Sheridan's leg.

'In a way, yeah. I can relate to how Jennifer was consumed by it all. If we don't find out who killed her family, I'm not sure she'll ever move on from it.'

CHAPTER 32

Monday 12 November

Hill marched down the corridor, ignoring the 'Good morning, ma'am's from the officers left in her wake. She thundered into Sheridan's office, finding her on the phone. Sheridan abruptly looked up and put her hand in the air before finishing the call. 'That's brilliant, I'll be right there.'

Before Sheridan had even put the phone down, Hill said, 'Do you know a Sergeant Elfprick, or Allprick . . . whatever his fucking name is?'

'Sergeant Hallbick, yes, I know him.' Sheridan sat back, arms crossed, hiding a grin.

'Well, he wants his marked car back . . . the one that's parked outside Jennifer Parks' cottage.' She sat down as quickly as Sheridan stood up.

'Well, Jennifer will be pleased. She said it's a reminder that her life isn't normal at the moment. I take it you asked him *really* nicely if we could leave it there a bit longer?'

'Yes, I was very fucking polite. The upshot is, they've got two response cars off the road and need it back. I'll try and source one from somewhere else.'

'Thanks. I'm just off to CID – they've got the downloads from Ronald Parks' mobile phone.'

'I'm coming with you.'

'Bingo. Have a look at this.' Anna waved Sheridan and Hill over to her desk, where she handed Sheridan a printout. 'There's a few general texts over the last few months. Nothing of much interest. But then on the day the Parks were taken from the house to Crosby Beach, there are several texts and calls between Ronald Parks and Tony Harvey's mobile phones. Ronald rings Tony at 15.27 – the call lasts one minute. Then at 16.29 the text messages start between them.'

Sheridan and Hill studied the printout.

16.29 hours: Ronald Parks texts Tony Harvey: *You're not getting another penny until you tell me where Daniel's body is*

Tony to Ronald: *You said you didn't want to know what I did with him*

Ronald to Tony: *The police were supposed to have found him by now, this needs to be put to bed, it needs to end, where is he?*

Tony to Ronald: *Most of him is in one place and a bit in another place*

Ronald to Tony: *Did you cut him up?*

Tony to Ronald: *I tried, I'll tell you everything, but I want the other twenty, I'm just around the corner, get on to your bank.*

'So, Tony and Ronald were in it together.' Hill Knowles leaned against the back of the chair.

Sheridan reread the texts before asking Anna, 'Can you check the original file and see if there was a payment to Tony from Ronald before Daniel was murdered?'

'Yeah, no problem.'

101

'Now that we've identified a solid link to Tony Harvey for Daniel's murder, let's go and update the team.'

They made their way to the briefing room to let everyone know what they had found. Once they were gathered round, Sheridan launched right in.

'Okay. In relation to Ronald Parks' mobile phone . . . We've now retrieved some deleted texts between him and Tony Harvey on the day that Ronald and Rita were taken from the house.'

Sheridan read the text messages out loud as everyone listened intently. When she was finished, she headed back to her office to call Jennifer, leaving Hill to look around the room and decide who to shout at about Tony Harvey not having been located yet.

CHAPTER 33

Sheridan spoke to Jennifer, who had now been released from hospital and sounded a little bit brighter. Sheridan told her that the police car would be moved but they would be looking to replace it with another one as soon as they could. She didn't mention the text messages between Ronald and Tony.

Jennifer said she was planning to go to the bookshop as there were things she had to sort out.

Anna was waiting patiently in the doorway when Sheridan ended the call. She purposefully waved a sheet of paper in the air. 'Two weeks before Daniel went missing, Ronald paid thirty grand into Tony Harvey's bank account.'

'Was it questioned at the time?'

'Yep. Ronald Parks told police that he was repaying a debt from years ago, and Tony corroborated that statement.'

'So, it was all pre-planned? Ronald killed Daniel and paid Tony to get rid of the body. He gives him thirty grand up front, and was going to pay the other twenty later.' Sitting forward, Sheridan clasped her hands together and closed her eyes, as if to shut out everything except her thought processes. Anna didn't speak, but quietly sat down. Finally, Sheridan opened her eyes.

'But what doesn't make sense is the evidence in Ronald's truck. There's nothing to forensically link Tony to it.'

'We know they were working together. Ronald could have killed Daniel at the cottage, wrapped him in the white towel and then driven his body somewhere, met up with Tony, who then puts the body in *his* car, drives off and gets rid of him.'

'Possibly,' Sheridan agreed, 'but why chuck Daniel's duvet in one place and put the body in another? It doesn't add up.'

They sat for a moment, both going over in their heads the logistics of their theory, before Sheridan spoke.

'Maybe Ronald forgot to give the duvet to Tony, and so he decided to get rid of it himself on the way back from when they put Daniel's body in Tony's car?' She rubbed her face with her palm.

Anna spoke. 'But surely Ronald would have thrown the duvet further away from the house? He could have driven miles away to get rid of it . . .'

Sheridan snapped her fingers together. 'No. I think I know what he did do though.' She smiled. 'Ronald forgot to give the duvet to Tony and was almost home before he realised. His fuel tank was practically empty, so he couldn't drive too far, or he'd risk running out of diesel.'

'And he couldn't risk stopping to bury it, in case the fuel ran out and his truck wouldn't start. He had to get home as soon as he could.' Anna put her hand up and high-fived Sheridan.

'Thank fuck we've figured that out.' Sheridan puffed out her cheeks. 'But the question still remains, *why* did they want him dead?'

CHAPTER 34

The briefing was short. Sheridan tried to avoid looking to the back of the room where Hill sat, with her usual thunderous expression.

'It's been nine days since Ronald and Rita's bodies were found,' she said, 'and although we're making good progress, we really need to find Tony Harvey. With Jennifer declining a safer place to stay, we're leaving her so vulnerable. So, I want everyone to stay focused. You all know what tasks you have. This is a fast-moving enquiry and we're getting a lot of information coming through but we're sitting on a bloody time-bomb here.' She knew her team were giving everything to the enquiry and allowed her tone to soften a little. 'I know everyone's knackered. Look, you're doing a cracking job, but let's keep on top of it, eh? Let's find Tony Harvey and soon.' Sheridan smiled and wound up the briefing, telling those who had been on duty since early that morning to get themselves off home, before Hill got the chance to chip in with any negativity. Or start yelling again.

Driving out of Liverpool, Sheridan's mind chewed over the case. By the time she walked through the front door, she'd decided to try and switch off and give her head a rest. Hearing Christmas music coming from the living room made her smile, and she entered the kitchen to find Sam with her hands covered in a thick glue-like substance.

Sam pouted. 'I had a brilliant idea. I thought I'd make a practice Christmas dinner, so that when I have to cook the *actual* one, I won't fuck it up. So, I bought a chicken and some sprouts and a stuffing mix.'

'The oven's not on.' Sheridan frowned, amused by the look on Sam's face.

'Well, they didn't have any fresh chickens left, so I bought a frozen one and then Joni called, and we got chatting and she told me you can't cook a chicken from frozen . . . so it's still defrosting. Anyway, I thought I'd make the stuffing, as a starter.' Sam stopped for breath as she tried to pull the sticky substance off her fingers.

'What *is* that?'

'It's the stuffing. I think I put too much water in the mix and now it's just made a paste and I can't get it off.' Sam pursed her lips as Sheridan burst out laughing.

'Even Maud won't eat it. I tried to put a bit on her paw so she'd lick it off. But she just freaked out and ran upstairs like she was trying to get away from it.'

Sheridan laughed so hard that she had to put her hand on the back of the chair to steady herself. When she finally stopped crying with laughter, she kissed Sam on the nose and pulled a bottle of wine out of the fridge.

'That is hilarious. I bloody needed that.'

'Shit day?' Sam asked, scraping the stuffing mix from her fingers with a spatula.

'It's just this bloody Parks case, it's doing my head in.'

'Come and tell me all about it.'

◆　◆　◆

Later, as they sat on the sofa talking, Sheridan lay down to rest her head on Sam's lap. Maud stretched out across the coffee table, completely ignoring the lump of stuffing that had dried and cemented itself to the top of her paw. Sam listened as always while Sheridan recounted the basics of the enquiry.

'So, if you find and arrest this Tony fella, do you think he'll confess about where he's hidden Daniel's body?' Sam asked as she stroked Sheridan's forehead.

'Unlikely.'

'Can't you just beat the shit out of him and *make* him tell you?' Sam grinned.

'I wish it were that simple.'

'Have you got any clues at all about where Daniel's body is?'

'No. Tony's text just said most of it was in one place and some in another place.'

Sam stopped stroking Sheridan's forehead for a moment. 'Is that what he said?'

'Yeah.'

'Was that *exactly* what he said?'

'Yeah, pretty much, why?'

'Another place is where you found the bodies at Crosby.'

Sheridan craned her neck to look at Sam. 'What do you mean?'

'The Iron Men statues at Crosby were an idea by Antony Gormley, they're based on his actual body. He called it "Another Place".'

Sheridan's eyes widened as she quickly sat up. 'Are you sure?'

'Positive. We did a project on it a couple of years ago with the kids at school when the statues were first put there.' Sam got up off the sofa and walked into the kitchen, flicking on her laptop. Sheridan stood behind her as she googled the Iron Men statues. And there it was. On the screen was a selection of images of the statues with the words *Antony Gormley's Another Place, Crosby.*

Sheridan wrapped her arms around Sam and planted a kiss on her lips. 'You little beauty.'

CHAPTER 35

Jennifer locked the bookshop and wrapped her scarf around her neck as she made her way down the street. It had been a bitterly cold day. As evening shoppers filed past her, she contemplated going into the little café on the corner where she often sat and watched the world go by. But tonight, she just wanted to get home. Putting her head down against the freezing wind, she quickened her pace.

He crossed the road and began following her, staying far enough back not to be noticed, with his hands buried deep in his pockets.

At the corner, Jennifer turned left, making her way down the narrow, cobbled side street that she had walked a thousand times before, a handy short cut to the car park. Suddenly feeling the urge to look behind her, she stopped for a second and listened before quickly turning around. She spotted a woman weighed down with shopping bags coming towards her. Jennifer let her pass before continuing until she reached the end of the cobbles, and again looked behind before turning right.

Feeling her heart quicken, and seeing her own breath in the air, she stood for a moment, resting her back against the wall. Her eyes scanned left and right, spotting a few people heading over to the car park.

She didn't look back again. But he was there, walking slowly behind her.

CHAPTER 36

Pulling his cap down to cover his eyes, Tony Harvey climbed the steps into Liverpool Lime Street station and made his way to the destination boards.

A police officer stood in the middle of the concourse, watching a homeless man approaching people with his hand out. Commuters walked around the man as if he were invisible, and others just frowned as he approached, shaking their heads with a defiant 'no'. One woman, pulling an expensive suitcase, stopped as he limped towards her, his skinny legs drowning in filthy oversized jeans. She put her hand in her pocket and pulled out a few coins, which he gratefully accepted. The police officer pointed at him sternly and then indicated for him to move to the exit. The homeless man nodded and shuffled out of the station.

Tony watched the police officer slowly follow the homeless man outside, ensuring he left the station without bothering anyone else. He then looked back at the destination board as people milled around him, passed him, all busy, all going somewhere. He needed to get somewhere, too. Anywhere. He had to get away.

He'd had time, now, to think about what he'd done, how the police would find the evidence and come after him. Ronald and Rita Parks' faces were in his head all the time, everywhere he looked. He stared at the screens. All the destinations were right there for him to see.

All he had to do was choose one.

CHAPTER 37

Tuesday 13 November

Anna sat back with her hands behind her head as Sheridan walked in with a huge smile on her face.

'What?' Anna raised an eyebrow. 'Either you got some last night, or you're about to tell me you've solved the case and we can all go to the pub and get smashed.'

'No and no.' Sheridan leaned forward and whispered, 'I know where some of Daniel Parks' body is though.'

'Seriously? Where?'

Sheridan told her about the conversation she'd had with Sam the night before. As they made their way to the briefing room, they agreed that Sheridan would totally take the credit for working out the clue in Tony Harvey's text. And they were also clear that they wouldn't breathe a word to anyone about her discussing the case with Sam.

As the briefing room filled with officers, Hill walked in and made her way over to the front, nodding curtly at Sheridan, who reciprocated before addressing the team.

'Good morning, everyone. Quick update for you. I've been thinking about the text messages between Ronald and Tony, and last night I had a light-bulb moment.' Sheridan avoided making any eye contact with Anna, knowing that if she did, there was the distinct possibility that she'd start laughing.

'In the texts, Tony Harvey said that he'd put some of Daniel's body in one place and some in another place. Well, last night it suddenly dawned on me that "Another Place" is actually where Ronald and Rita's bodies were found. "Another Place" is the name for the Iron Men statues by Antony Gormley on Crosby Beach. So, I think the text that Tony sent is a hidden clue.'

'Wow. Well worked out, Sheridan.' Anna gave an exaggerated nod, purposefully trying to make Sheridan lose it. 'What made you think of that?'

'I don't know. It's been in the back of my mind, I guess, and it just came to me last night.' *You fucker*, she thought.

'Genius.' Anna grinned.

Hill jumped in. 'Right then, I'll speak to the super about getting a warrant to search the beach. Let's hope you're right, Sheridan.'

As Hill was about to wind up the briefing, Dipesh's phone rang and, after answering it, he immediately put his hand up to get Sheridan and Hill's attention.

'Yes, Dipesh? What is it?' Hill snapped at him as he ended the call.

'Tony Harvey's mobile just pinged off a mast in Birmingham.'

'So, he's either hired a car, is on a coach, has hitchhiked or he's got on a train. Whatever, I want him found and I want him found fucking *now*.' Hill swung round to walk out of the room. 'Keep me updated with his movements,' she barked at Dipesh as she left.

Silence hung in the room until everyone heard Hill's footsteps fading far enough away.

'You heard the boss,' Sheridan said. 'Let's check local car hire companies, coach companies and train stations, start with Lime Street, maybe we'll get lucky. Any questions?'

'Yeah, why is the DCI such a miserable fucker?' Rob Wills piped up.

The room rattled with chuckles and stifled laughs before Sheridan put her hand up. 'I don't want to hear shit like that, she's got enough on her plate without you lot backbiting.'

The room fell silent.

'I will, however, buy a pint for the first person who gets her face to crack a smile.'

CHAPTER 38

Sheridan headed back to her office and, after a long day, was about to pack up and head home when Anna called. 'Yes, mate?'

'Tony Harvey's in Southampton. Hampshire Police are on their way right now to a location near the port.'

'He's getting on a bloody boat. Meet me in CID.' Sheridan jumped up and made her way down the corridor.

'Sheridan.' Hill came up behind her. 'I take it you've heard.'

'Yeah, I guess he's hoping to skip the country.'

'We've got port alerts on him. He's not going anywhere.'

The room was eerily quiet as everyone waited for information from Hampshire Police. Some stared at computer screens, still working on the tasks they'd been given, while others quickly texted their partners to say they'd be home late. They took it in turns to ferry cups of coffee to tired colleagues and they flipped a coin to see who was doing the butty run.

Sheridan messaged Sam: *Hey gorgeous, I'm sorry but I'm going to be late home again, please eat and I'll text you when I'm leaving work. Miss you. Give Maud a scritch from me. xxx*

Sam texted back: *You just be careful out there. We'll be here when you get home. Maud's sitting in the bath staring at the taps. xxx*

Sheridan grinned as she pocketed her mobile.

'Boss,' Rob Wills called across the office, waving Sheridan and Hill over. 'I think we've got Tony Harvey on CCTV here.'

Sheridan and Hill quickly crossed the office to look over Rob's shoulder. He rewound the recording and played it again. 'This was yesterday evening at Liverpool Lime Street station.'

They watched as Tony Harvey walked through the main doors and made his way to the destination board. He then walked towards the toilets but the camera didn't cover that area and they watched, waiting for him to come back into view.

'That's him. I'm pretty sure that's him. So, he got on a train to Southampton.' Hill pushed her glasses on top of her head. 'Keep checking. See what train he got on and what changes he had to make. I want to know if he meets anyone.'

CHAPTER 39

Millside Police Station, Southampton
6.15 p.m.

Sergeant Phil Sturman briefed the firearms team before they headed out to Southampton Port. He had requested a dog unit to attend but none was available. Six units pulled out of the back of the police station, radios crackling with instructions. Sergeant Sturman was first to reach the lorry park where Tony Harvey's phone had last pinged, and other units arrived seconds later. There were four cars and two lorries parked up. Phil Sturman instructed his officers to take up tactical positions around the vehicles. The area was lit up from the police car headlights and officers' torches but with no sign of Tony Harvey, Phil Sturman requested the control room to ring the suspect's mobile phone.

All heads turned as they could just make out a faint ringing from one of the lorries. Phil Sturman pointed to it, giving the direction for his colleagues to surround it, as they all acknowledged that Tony was hiding underneath. Once everyone was in position, Phil Sturman gave the instruction.

'Armed police. Tony Harvey, we know you are under the lorry, and you are surrounded. Come out slowly with your hands in full view.'

Nothing. No sound. No movement.

He repeated the instruction. Still nothing.

He slowly crouched down and angled a mirror under the lorry, his weapon poised and ready as he peered underneath. The first thing he noticed was the strip of duct tape; one end had come away slightly and was gently flapping in the evening breeze. Then he angled the mirror to show what was directly above his head.

'Oh, shit.'

CHAPTER 40

Jennifer closed her book and got up from the sofa to stretch out the stiffness in her back. She hadn't been to the gym for a while. Her body was tense, not as supple and strong as usual. With her hands against the kitchen worktop, she did makeshift press-ups, counting to fifty before stretching out her legs, feeling the pull in her calf muscles. Suddenly, across the yard she saw the flash of headlights. She leaned towards the window to see a police car pulling up, followed by a second unmarked vehicle. She unlocked the front door and opened it.

Sheridan climbed out of the unmarked car, followed by Anna.

'What's wrong?' Jennifer asked, as she stepped on to the gravel drive.

'It's nothing to worry about. Can we come in?' Sheridan asked, nodding to the uniformed officers.

Jennifer stepped back into the house. 'Of course.'

They went into the living room and sat down.

'Has something happened?' Jennifer asked.

'We tracked Tony Harvey's phone to Southampton—'

'Has he been arrested?' she quickly jumped in.

'No.' Sheridan paused. 'We found his phone taped underneath a lorry. He obviously put it there to make us think that's where *he* was.'

'I see.'

'The uniformed officers are just going to have a look around outside, make sure he's not in the area.'

'You still think he might try to come after me?'

'We don't know, but we don't want to take any chances.'

'I really don't think he would, Sheridan. I just know Tony wouldn't hurt me.'

'You don't know what's going on in his head. Are you sure you don't want to stay somewhere else until we find him? I can't emphasise enough that we can't guarantee your safety here.'

'No. I'm fine. Honestly.'

Sheridan and Anna waited until the uniformed officers had finished checking the property, before heading back to the station.

Jennifer stood on the doorstep and watched them leave. She stayed there for a while, gazing up at the sky, Sheridan's words going round in her head. She rubbed her hands over her forearms as a chilly wind whipped across the yard.

CHAPTER 41

Friday 23 November

Sitting at the back of the church, Sheridan and Anna closely watched the handful of people who had turned up for Ronald and Rita Parks' funeral. At the front, Jennifer cast a lonely figure, sitting with her head down throughout the short service.

The vicar spoke about Ronald and Rita and how they had enjoyed twenty-seven years of marriage, before their lives were so tragically cut short. Ronald had left school at fifteen to work on building sites in all weathers, learning the trade before setting up his own successful business. A model father who provided for his family and doted on his two children.

Jennifer's eulogy described her mother, Rita, as a quiet woman, always happy and ready with a smile. She was a wonderful mother who cherished having her small, close-knit family around her. Loving and protective until the end.

Ronald and Rita were unassuming people, happy just to be in their own company. Their deaths had shocked the community, and everyone's thoughts and prayers were with their daughter, Jennifer.

Two parents now in God's heaven, reunited with their beautiful son.

Afterwards, as the small congregation quietly filed out of the church, Jennifer remained at the door to personally thank each person for coming. Some took her hand softly, saying how wonderful her parents were. Others hugged her gently and commented on the beautiful service. As they all headed back to their cars, Jennifer made her way over to Sheridan and Anna.

'Thank you so much for coming,' she said as she took Sheridan's hand. 'I don't know how I would have got through the last few weeks without you.'

They strolled through the cemetery, listening intently as Jennifer recited many stories from when she was a little girl and her life growing up with Daniel. She described how her parents were so protective of them both and how they had encouraged them to move into the cottage when they were in their late teens. She talked of how their mother dreaded the thought of them growing up, flying the nest, always wanting to keep them close and safe. Her voice broke as she described the happy days they had all spent together; how life had seemed so perfect back then.

As they walked her to her car, she turned, leaning back against the driver's door.

'I'm sorry there wasn't a wake, I just couldn't face it. Is that bad of me?'

'Not at all. Are you going to be okay?'

'I have to be. Because if I'm not, then what's the alternative?'

'Well, you call us if you need anything. We'll keep you posted on any progress.'

'Thanks,' Jennifer said, and forced a smile as she watched them walking back to their car.

◆ ◆ ◆

Anna, in the passenger seat, turned the heater on as they drove away and warmed her hands over the air vent. 'Do you think Jennifer will stay in the cottage?'

'I don't know. Maybe,' Sheridan replied.

'How much do you reckon the property's worth? The house, the cottage and five acres of land has got to be worth over a million, don't you think?'

'Probably. Plus, the bookshop business.'

Sheridan let this thought linger for a moment. It had crossed her mind more than once that Jennifer would end up very wealthy now that her family were gone. She had even toyed with the idea that Jennifer could be working with someone. Maybe she was pulling the strings, keeping herself away from suspicion by ensuring she had an alibi. But could she really be capable of such a crime? Her love for Daniel and her parents was evident, even palpable in the way she talked about them.

Anna spoke, breaking Sheridan's thoughts. 'Yeah, but like they say, money can't buy happiness. I'm sure Jennifer would have her family back in a heartbeat rather than all that money.'

'Unless she's somehow involved. People do strange things for money.'

'Do you suspect her?'

'I suspect everyone. I know there's no evidence pointing to her, but we can't rule her out.'

'There's no way she's working alone if she is involved though, eh?'

'Exactly. The question then would be, who is she working with? I mean, she doesn't appear to have anyone else in her life, so whoever it is, we're not aware of them.'

◆ ◆ ◆

Back at Hale Street, Hill met them on the stairs as they were returning to the office.

'How did the funeral go?'

'It was okay, not many people there.'

'Right, well, the good news is that the magistrates have issued a warrant for us to search Crosby Beach for Daniel's body. Only around the area that Ronald and Rita's bodies were found, no further. It's a logistical nightmare, with the tide times, but I'll set it up and see how we get on.'

'Thanks, Hill. I'll let Jennifer know.'

CHAPTER 42

After putting a pound coin in the vending machine, Sheridan put both hands on the glass and gave it another shove, finally loosening the chocolate bar that had hung temptingly close to dropping for the last two minutes.

Tearing the wrapper open with her teeth, she headed back to her office, quickening her pace as she heard her phone ringing, and promptly dropped the chocolate on the floor. 'Fuck's sake,' she mumbled, bending down to pick it up and throwing it into the bin under her desk, not trusting the three-second rule with a well-trodden police station floor, as she picked the phone up. 'DI Holler.'

'Sheridan, it's Ruth Manning from the cold-case team.'

'Hi, Ruth.' She felt a flutter in her chest. The familiar feeling that came over her whenever the team looking into her brother's murder called.

'You about this afternoon? I've got to pop to the nick anyway and thought I'd come and see you. Looks like we might have a bit of a lead in your brother's case.'

An hour later, Sheridan was at her desk with her hands clasped together in front of her when Ruth Manning knocked on her open office door.

'Come on in,' Sheridan said. 'So, what have you got?'

Ruth took a seat. 'Does the name Stubby mean anything to you?'

Sheridan sat back, thinking. 'No, I don't think so. Why?'

'We tracked down a woman in one of the photographs you gave us, and she remembered a guy who used to come and watch the football matches that her son and your brother Matthew played in.' Ruth looked down at her notes. 'She only saw him a couple of times but seems to think he was called Stubby, probably a nickname. Anyway, we've run the name "Stubby" through PNC but haven't come up with much. We've still got a few more people to trace and ask though.'

'Did she say if he was always alone? Could he have been just another dad watching his son, maybe?'

'She couldn't remember. She wasn't a hundred per cent about the name either. But hopefully we'll track down others in the photo and maybe they'll know him.'

'Have you spoken to Andrew Longford?'

'Yes, I called him this morning. He can't place the name but said he'll have a think and get back to me.'

'I'll ask my parents if the name rings any bells.' Sheridan made a mental note to speak to Andrew Longford herself. 'Have you looked at surnames like Stubb or Stubbs?'

Ruth smiled. 'We have. Nothing yet but like I say, we'll keep at it.'

'Thanks, Ruth.'

Sheridan walked Ruth to the door. As she watched her make her way down the corridor, Sheridan felt anxious, her hands tingled, and she grasped them together. Each piece of new evidence could mean a step towards finding Matthew's killer, or another dead end. Each time there was a development, Sheridan knew she had to tell her parents, the risk and worry for her being that it would lead nowhere, and they would be back to where they'd started. But Sheridan had to stay positive. And maybe 'Stubby' really was the man they'd been looking for all these years.

CHAPTER 43

Sunday 25 November

Rosie and Brian Holler were waiting at the front door when Sheridan and Sam arrived. As they got out of the car, the familiar smell of home baking wafted from the house. They all hugged before gathering around the kitchen table, chatting and tucking into home-made shortbread, which they then washed down with the copious amounts of tea that Rosie put in front of them.

'I had a visit from the cold-case team on Friday.' Sheridan had waited for the right moment to broach the subject. She didn't want to get her parents' hopes up that just because someone had put forward a name, it would lead to anything.

Rosie pulled her chair closer to the table and put her hand on Brian's.

Sheridan took a deep breath before continuing. 'They've tracked down a woman who was in one of the photos that Andrew Longford gave me and she thinks the man in the picture was called Stubby.' Sheridan searched her parents' faces for any sign that the name rang a bell. Neither of them had recognised the man in the photograph who stood alone, watching, as Matthew and his friends played in a football match.

'Stubby?' Rosie Holler frowned and looked at Brian, who shook his head.

'What about the surname Stubb or Stubbs?' Sheridan asked.

'I don't remember anyone with that name.' Brian rubbed his chin before taking a sip of his tea.

'Well, have a think about it and let me know if anything comes to mind.'

'Have your colleagues asked Andrew Longford if he knows the name?' Rosie asked, standing up to make yet another cup of tea.

'Yes. He said he can't think of anyone with a name like that. But I'm going to pop and see him now and have a chat with him.' She looked at Sam. 'Can I leave you here for a little while? I won't be long.'

'There's shortbread to be eaten, be as long as you like.' A moment later Sam was standing at the door, blowing a kiss to Sheridan as she drove away, heading to Andrew Longford's house.

When Sam went back inside, Rosie was still at the kitchen table.

'Where's Brian gone?' Sam asked, sitting down and reaching for the plate of shortbread.

'He's taken himself off into the garden.'

'Is he okay?'

Rosie ran her finger around the rim of her teacup. 'He gets frightened.'

'Frightened of what?'

'That we won't live long enough to see the day that Matthew's killer is found.'

Sam reached across the table and put her hand on Rosie's, squeezing it gently. 'Sheridan *will* find him.'

'I'm sure she would if she was actually dealing with his case. But there's only so much she can do from the sidelines.' She pulled a tissue out of her cardigan pocket and wiped her eyes. 'After Matthew was found, Sheridan used to sit in Birkenhead Park and watch the people there. She had a notebook that she used to write down the date, time and description of everyone that walked near to the scene where his body was left. She was only fourteen but even then, she acted like an adult. Like a police officer.'

'She joined the police because of Matthew, didn't she?'

'Yes. She told us a few weeks after Matthew died, when the police didn't have any leads, that she was going to become a detective and find his killer.'

Sam smiled. 'She was feisty even then, by the sounds of it.'

'She was the one that kept us going. Even though her heart was broken, she was so strong. If it wasn't for her then I don't think I'd be here now. Losing a child to murder rips your world apart, it takes everything away from you. Leaves you broken. If we didn't have Sheridan, I don't think Brian and I would have been able to carry on. It would have been easier to just give up. I know when he goes out into the garden that he's crying, but he doesn't want me to see.'

Sam noted the sadness in Rosie's eyes. She moved her chair around the table to sit beside her. 'Men don't like to show their feelings, do they?'

Rosie turned to Sam. 'He'll come in when he's ready and pretend that he's fine. He'll stand at the sink, wash his hands and come out with some joke or silly comment. He does the same thing every time.'

At that moment, Sam realised that Sheridan did exactly the same thing. Deciding not to mention this to Rosie, she just tapped the older woman's hand and said, 'He's a wonderful man. You've got yourself a good one there.'

Rosie smiled and touched Sam's face. 'You're a lovely girl, Sam. I'm so happy that Sheridan met you. I can see how good you are together.'

'I'll always look after her, Rosie.'

'I know you will. And she'll always look after you.'

At that moment, Brian came in from the garden and started washing his hands at the sink. 'A squirrel has buried his nuts in your plant pot, Rosie.'

'Have you left them there?' Rosie put her tissue back in her pocket and winked at Sam, who smiled and winked back.

'Of course I have. You never touch another man's nuts.'

'Brian.' Rosie shook her head.

'Sorry, I couldn't resist.' He smiled and kissed the top of her head. 'Right, unless Sam's eaten all that shortbread, I think I'll have some now. Do you two ladies want another cuppa?' he said cheerily, drying his hands before putting the kettle on.

◆ ◆ ◆

Sheridan was sitting in Andrew Longford's freezing-cold living room, her hands cupped tightly around a mug of coffee.

'Sorry about the temperature in here. Boiler's packed up. I'm waiting for the council to come and fix it. Hopefully they'll be here this afternoon.'

Sheridan noticed how dreadful he looked. His pale skin appeared almost translucent and tiny sores covered most of his face. He'd been in remission for some time, but it was clear that his cancer and subsequent health conditions had completely ravaged his body.

'I know I look like shit.' He grinned. 'I actually feel okay though.'

They chatted for a while, and eventually the conversation swung round to Matthew and the man in the photograph. Andrew had tried to associate the name Stubby with someone he remembered, but told her that he honestly couldn't link it to anyone.

He asked how her parents were doing and they talked about Christmas. Andrew would be alone but was happy to be. It was just another day, after all.

Sheridan got up to leave just as the boiler repair van appeared. She promised to keep Andrew updated with any developments and he gently took her hand as she reached the front door.

'Please tell your parents that I think about them.' His soft blue eyes looked straight into hers.

'I will.'

As she got into her car, she immediately put the blowers on and tried to thaw out her hands.

CHAPTER 44

Monday 26 November

Jennifer felt her jaw clench as she opened the front door to her parents' house. She hadn't stepped foot inside the place since before they were murdered and the thought of it filled her with dread. As she stepped into the hallway, she noticed how different the place smelt. Stopping to look at the pictures on the wall, she put out a hand to steady herself. Images flew through her mind of what had happened here. The fear they must have felt. The pain.

As she walked from room to room, the silence engulfed her. It all seemed so strange now; everything was the same and yet everything was different.

She pushed the door open to what was once her bedroom, just as empty as it had been since the day she and Daniel had moved into the cottage. The pink carpet had faded now. She stepped over to the window, staring out across the yard. She could see herself as a child, being chased by Daniel into the woods that stretched out across the five acres of land. She remembered the times she had hidden in the undergrowth, holding her breath so he couldn't hear her and then watching as he swished a stick in front of him, laughing and calling out her name. At that moment, it hit her, the reality of it all, and she put her hand to her chest, feeling her heartbeat pounding through her ribcage.

She took her mobile out of her pocket and sent a text to Sheridan: *Hi, I'm going to get away for a bit, stay with a friend, Izzy, in Cornwall. I'm going to get a train tonight. I'll keep my mobile with me in case you need to call me, and I'll text you when I get back.*

A moment later her phone rang as Sheridan's name popped up on the screen. 'Hi, Sheridan.'

'Hi. Just got your text and wanted to make sure you're okay.'

'I'm fine, I just need to take some time out.'

'I understand. How long will you be gone for?' Sheridan asked. Before Jennifer could answer, a piercing sound echoed down the line.

'I'm not sure. A few days probably.'

'Sorry, Jennifer. The fire alarm's going off. What's the address you'll be staying at?' Sheridan made her way downstairs, scribbling the address down on a piece of paper while struggling to hear Jennifer over the wailing of the fire alarm.

'Okay, I've got it. I'll speak to the local police down there, just to let them know you might be at risk.'

'I'll be fine. Tony doesn't know the address.'

'Okay. Let me know when you're due to come back and meanwhile I'll keep you updated if anything happens.'

'I will. Thanks, Sheridan.'

Ten minutes later, Jennifer closed the front door of her parents' house and headed back to the cottage. Feeling snowflakes landing on her, she put out her hand and watched as one drifted down and rested in her palm, only to melt away almost immediately. There one moment and gone the next, without anything to show that it had ever existed.

Feeling the heat from the open fire as she stepped through the front door, she turned into the kitchen.

And there he was. Standing right in front of her.

She stopped dead, feeling a rush of adrenaline course through her body. She opened her mouth to speak but couldn't form the words.

Then he broke the silence. 'Hello, Jen.'

CHAPTER 45

Once the fire drill was over, Sheridan made her way to Anna's office and, finding it empty, she headed further up the corridor into CID.

'Sheridan.' Anna waved her over. 'We've got the results for Tony Harvey's computer, there's nothing suspect on there at all. Same with Ronald and Rita's.'

'Okay.' Sheridan looked around the room.

Hill Knowles walked in and made a beeline for Sheridan and Anna, literally hurling a piece of paper on to the desk in front of them. 'Helen Harvey had no known mental health issues and had never indicated to her GP that she was suicidal or had ever had any thoughts of self-harm.'

'So, either Tony was lying, or Helen never told her doctor about any issues. I'd love to know what Tony said to her before she made the decision to jump,' Anna said.

'Me too. Must have been pretty fucking bad, whatever it was. Let's brief the team.' Hill scooped up the doctor's report and checked her watch.

The briefing was short. Hill summarised where they were in the investigation. When she was done, she said, 'The chief is kicking my arse over this job, we need to find Tony fucking Harvey. Right, get yourselves off home.' She put her thumb up before leaving the room.

Sheridan puffed out her cheeks and watched the room of tired faces as they turned off their computers, grabbed their bags and coats and wearily headed home.

As she headed back to her office, her mobile pinged with a message from Jennifer: *Tony here gun.*

CHAPTER 46

'Sit down, Jen.' Tony Harvey's legs were shaking. Beads of sweat glistened across his forehead.

'Have you come to kill me?' Jennifer sat on the arm of the chair, feeling pins and needles all over her body, like tiny slivers of glass cutting into her.

'Is this being recorded?' His breathing was laboured as he frantically looked around the room.

'Of course not. Why would it be?' Jennifer's mouth was dry. She licked her lips, trying to swallow.

Tony reached into his pocket, pulled out a note and as he held it in front of her to read, she could see his hands were trembling. She had to lean forward slightly to see the words scrawled on the paper and when she finished, he screwed it up and threw it into the fire.

'I don't know what you're talking about.' She held both hands out in front of her, palms skyward.

Tony looked up at the ceiling, fists clenched tightly by his sides. 'I could have killed you so many times. I've been watching you, Jen. I was here when they left that police car outside. Very clever. I sat up in the bushes one night, the night the two police officers came to check on you, and I was so close I could smell you. I was ready to grab you, strap you up like your parents, and throw you in a fucking ditch.'

'So, why didn't you?'

'Because I needed the disc. I thought that if I killed you then I'd never know where it was.' Tears poured down his face. 'I just want the disc.' He spat the words out through clenched teeth. 'Please just give it to me.'

'What disc? What are you talking about?'

'Don't fucking lie to me, Jen. You know what disc. The one that proves what happened here.'

'I swear I have no fucking idea what you're talking about.' Jennifer shook her head, watching him and waiting for the moment he took his eyes off her so she could press the alarm.

She had to press the alarm. What if Sheridan hadn't got her text?

'I really don't want to spell it out, but someone set up recording equipment and what happened here is on that disc.' He breathed in heavily. 'I'm sure you understand that I don't want the police to get their hands on anything that links me to it.' He put his hand on top of his head and began to sob. 'I know what I did was horrific, and I can't take it back.'

There was a silence before he spoke again. 'I know you hate me. I never thought I was capable of doing any of the things I've done.' His voice trailed off. 'Helen's dead.'

'I know.'

'She killed herself because of what we did.'

CHAPTER 47

Sheridan and Anna raced down the stairs, jumping into their car in the back yard and waiting for the armed response units to leave before pulling out behind them.

'I fucking knew he'd try to get to her.' Sheridan pulled on her seatbelt. 'She kept saying he'd never hurt her, but I *knew* he'd come for her.'

Anna adjusted the volume on her radio and spoke into it. 'Charlie Delta one-four, I'm with Charlie Delta six-six, en route to CAD 878. We'll hold back behind the firearms units.'

The control room operator acknowledged Anna and confirmed it would be a silent approach once units were nearer the scene.

'How the fuck do these people get hold of guns so easily? He's a retired insurance consultant, for God's sake.' Sheridan slowed down as the units ahead of them manoeuvred their way carefully through a red light.

Ten minutes later they pulled in just along the lane from the Parks' property and watched the armed units take up position.

'You okay?' Anna asked.

'Yeah, I'm fine, mate.' Sheridan nervously tapped the steering wheel. 'But I'll be even better if he doesn't fucking kill her.'

CHAPTER 48

Jennifer's eyes followed him around the room as he paced up and down.

'If the police turned up now, what would you say to them? Would you tell them everything? About Daniel? About my parents?'

'I don't know. I just thought if I had the disc then I might find a way out of this fucking mess.'

'There's no way out, Tony. The police know everything.' She turned her head towards the window. 'And they're outside.'

Tony looked up to see the police cars pulling on to the drive and armed officers getting out. He closed his eyes tightly, pushing out tears, and as he wiped his hand over his face he took slow, deliberate steps towards her. She felt every muscle in her body tense as he carried on past her and stopped briefly at the door. As he wrapped his fingers around the handle, he whispered, 'I'm so sorry, Jen.'

Watching as he turned the handle, she whispered back, 'The police think you've got a gun.'

He stopped, put his head down and then opened the front door, before lifting his hands above his head.

Jennifer watched as two armed officers slowly walked towards him, giving him clear instructions. She could feel her head pounding as she screamed out, 'Tony, I beg you, please don't!'

He craned his head round to look at her and, for a moment, their eyes locked. Then he nodded, reached into his jacket pocket and turned back to the officers, shouting, 'I'll fucking shoot the lot of you!'

Jennifer jolted sharply as she heard the crack of the gun and saw Tony Harvey's body hit the ground.

CHAPTER 49

Tony Harvey was still alive when the ambulance pulled out of the Parks' property. Anna was outside, listening to updates on the radio.

Sheridan was inside the cottage with Jennifer, waiting while a paramedic checked her over. As the paramedic was finishing up, Jennifer grabbed her hand. 'Is he going to die?'

'I honestly don't know, my love,' the paramedic replied.

'He can't die. He's the only one who knows where my brother's body is.'

'My colleagues will do everything they can.'

When the paramedics were gone, Jennifer told Sheridan that after walking around her parents' house, she had returned to the cottage to find Tony standing in the kitchen. She'd asked him if he was going to kill her and he had patted his jacket pocket, so she assumed he had a gun. When he told her to sit down, he'd stepped over to the window to look outside, and that was when she had sent Sheridan the text message. She'd wanted to press her alarm, but he had been standing so near to the remote-control device that she never got the chance to activate it. She said that Tony had asked about some recording. He seemed to think that what happened to Daniel in the cottage had been taped, and he wanted the disc because it incriminated him somehow. Tony had appeared paranoid that the cottage still had recording equipment in it and had shown her a handwritten note that read *I'll tell you where I buried Daniel if you give me the disc* before he threw it on the fire.

'What would make him think there was recording equipment in the cottage?' Sheridan knew the place had been thoroughly searched and no such equipment was ever found.

'I have no idea and I kept telling him that. He was crying at one point and said he was so sorry about what he'd done.' She looked to the floor. 'I asked him if he would tell the police everything, if he'd tell the truth, and he just said, "I don't know" and went on about the disc.' She looked at Sheridan. 'That's when the officers turned up and he walked out.'

'Do you know anything about this disc?'

'No. I have no idea what he was talking about.'

'Did he say anything about killing Daniel or your parents?'

'Not really. I wanted him to talk about it but to be honest, I probably wasn't thinking straight, I was just so bloody terrified.'

'I'm sure you were. It's okay, I just want to know his motives.'

Jennifer didn't respond.

'The armed officers said that you shouted, "Please don't, I beg you" to Tony. What did you mean by that?'

'Just as he got to the door, he said he was sorry. I thought he was going out to shoot the officers. I didn't want anyone to get hurt. I can't believe he had a gun.'

'He didn't have a gun.'

'So why did he threaten to shoot everyone?'

'We don't know. Maybe it was his way out, perhaps he knew they'd shoot him if he made the threat first.'

'Is he going to die?'

'I don't know. I'm going to need to get a full statement from you, though. Do you feel up to it?'

'Yes, of course.'

'Are you still thinking of going to Cornwall?'

'No. Not now.'

In that moment, Sheridan silently prayed that Tony Harvey would survive. After all, he was the one who held the answers. He was the one who could put this to rest, allowing Jennifer to know the truth behind the murders of her family. She also felt a sense of relief, as even if Tony Harvey did survive, he wouldn't be a danger to Jennifer for a very long time.

Unless, Sheridan thought, their conclusion was right . . . and he hadn't been working alone.

CHAPTER 50

Thursday 29 November

Sheridan was at her desk when Anna walked in.

'Want the bad news?' Anna sat down.

'Go on.' Sheridan's shoulders dropped.

'Tony Harvey died half an hour ago.'

'Bollocks.' Sheridan sighed heavily. 'Fucking bollocks. That's a real pain in the arse.'

She crossed her arms and slumped back in her chair. 'What has Hill said?'

'Right now, she's on the phone to the chief. And I doubt her thumb's in the air.'

'She'd better not wind down this investigation. There's still way too many unanswered questions. Why did Tony Harvey kill Ronald and Rita Parks? Why did Ronald pay Tony to dispose of Daniel's body? Why did Helen Harvey kill herself? Where exactly did Tony bury Daniel? Why did Tony leave Ronald and Rita the way he did, why not just dispose of them, rather than draw attention to them? What's this disc that Tony was banging on about? I don't feel comfortable just binning it because everyone's fucking dead.'

'Neither do I.' Hill had suddenly appeared, leaning against the door frame. 'But the chief wants to see me this afternoon, so

I'm going to ask for more time. We need to be sure that we haven't missed anything.'

'What do you think he'll say?'

'I know exactly what he'll say. He'll tell me to start winding it down. Our main suspect is dead, and we've got a shit-load of evidence to prove he was our man.' She looked at Anna and Sheridan in turn. 'So, if you've got anything I can take to him to prove otherwise, now would be a really good bloody time to tell me.' She held out her hands expectantly.

'Can't you postpone the meeting? It's Friday tomorrow, so if we could have tomorrow and the weekend, we might come up with something.'

Hill bit her bottom lip and looked at the floor. 'What are we still waiting on?'

'The results of Tony Harvey's mobile interrogation and the CCTV from when he was at Lime Street. We need to know if he met anyone. Plus, the search at Crosby Beach, and we need to be looking for this disc. From what Tony Harvey was saying, there could even be a recording of Daniel's murder.'

'That might not be enough to keep the case fully open.'

'I want the house and cottage searched again, maybe the disc is there somewhere,' Sheridan added.

'Alright, go and see Jennifer. She needs to know that Tony Harvey's dead anyway.'

Sheridan nodded. 'Do you think you can stall the chief?'

Hill tapped the door frame. 'I don't know. We need something to convince him, and we need it *now*, Sheridan.'

CHAPTER 51

Sheridan drove slowly down the lane that led to the Parks' property. She pulled over, looking out of her window at the nearby neighbours' house with the CCTV.

'What's wrong?' Anna asked, leaning forward to see what Sheridan was looking at.

'Nothing. I was just wondering if Tony Harvey knew about the CCTV on that house.'

'What do you mean?'

'Well, he could have easily found out from Daniel's murder trial that Ronald's truck was captured on CCTV. So, if he knew that, and if Ronald and Rita's murders were so premeditated and planned, then why did he drive here in his own car and let himself be clearly seen on camera?' She rested her head back.

'By the wording of the texts between Tony and Ronald, it's clear they'd probably had an argument beforehand. Maybe he was so angry that he forgot about the cameras. Plus, there's no other way to get to the Parks' place. You have to go past that camera if you're in a car.'

'Yeah, I guess. But it's like he thought some of it through to the last detail, and the rest of it he totally fucked up. Like stopping on the way to buy cable ties.'

'True.'

'Ronald knew about the cameras.' Sheridan inhaled, suddenly remembering a small detail from the original case files. 'There was a record on the crime system from 2005. Ronald had reported a theft of building equipment from the yard at their house. The uniform who dealt with it back then did some house to house and got the CCTV from there.' She pointed a thumb towards the property. 'The images weren't good enough to ID anyone, but Ronald then knew they had a camera that would pick up anyone going to *his* place.'

'So, he knew his own truck would be seen the night he killed Daniel?'

'Exactly.'

'Unless he'd forgotten about the CCTV.'

'Maybe. But highly unlikely.' Sheridan got out of the car. 'I'm going to speak to them quickly. It's Mr and Mrs Atherton, isn't it?'

Anna followed her up the pathway that led to the house. 'Yeah. What are you going to say?'

Sheridan pressed the doorbell and glanced up at the CCTV camera. 'I'll wing it.'

The door was answered by a tiny little man in his eighties with his trousers pulled halfway up his belly and the collar of his shirt badly worn away.

Sheridan smiled at the huge ginger cat that ambled up the hallway to inspect who was at the door, and showed her warrant card to the old man.

'We're sorry to bother you, Mr Atherton. Just wondered if we could have a really quick word?'

'Of course. Come on in, we're getting used to police officers turning up now. I take it you need to look at the CCTV again?'

He held the door open, and they stepped inside.

'No, actually, we don't,' Sheridan said. 'I know someone from my office was here the other day, and I'm sorry for the intrusion.'

'Oh yes. I understand the police were at Jennifer's house with guns. It's all very worrying. Is Jennifer alright? We haven't been to see her. It all feels a bit awkward.'

'She's doing okay. Did you know the family well?' Sheridan looked up to see Mrs Atherton tottering in, carrying two cups of tea.

'When the children were young, they used to play along the lane and often stop and natter to us. We never had much to do with the parents, they kept themselves to themselves most of the time. When they got a bit older, Daniel and Jennifer sometimes popped in for a cuppa. Would you like a cup of tea?' Mr Atherton asked.

Sheridan turned to Anna, who put her hand up. 'No, we're fine, thank you.'

Mrs Atherton adjusted her hearing aid as she sat down next to her husband.

'My wife has hearing problems,' he explained. 'So you'll have to speak up.'

'I can hear you. I'm not deaf,' Mrs Atherton said, and winked at Sheridan.

'Selective hearing.' Mr Atherton grinned and squeezed his wife's knee.

Mrs Atherton took a handkerchief out of her cardigan pocket and blew her nose. 'Terrible business, isn't it? That poor boy, he was so handsome. I remember a few years ago, he was sat right there where you are, chatting away to me. He loved to come over to see Dave.'

'Dave?'

'Yes. Dave. Our cat. Daniel adored him, so did Jennifer.' Her voice trailed off as she took a sip of her tea.

'Would you like a cup of tea?' Mr Atherton asked again. 'Have I already offered you one?'

'You have, but we're fine, thank you.' Sheridan smiled.

'So, have you come for more CCTV?' Mrs Atherton put her cup down and got up, shuffling awkwardly in her oversized slippers towards the cupboard in the hallway.

'No. We don't need to see it,' Sheridan said and, realising that Mrs Atherton hadn't heard her, she walked into the hallway where Mrs Atherton was opening a small cupboard under the stairs.

'It's in there, help yourself.'

Sheridan peered in and spotted the CCTV box flashing in the corner. It was an old system, and Sheridan noticed that the digital time display lights weren't all working.

'Who installed it?'

'Our son. He used to live around the corner but he married a German girl and moved over there about ten years ago. He thought it would make us feel safer. To be honest, we've always felt safe here anyway, never had any problems, but he insisted. He also put an alarm in, but Dave used to set it off when we were out, so we turned it off.'

Sheridan glanced at her watch just as she felt Dave push himself against her leg. Unable to resist, she reached down and stroked his head. Looking back at the time display, she noticed something odd and checked her watch again.

'I'm just popping outside,' she said, going out of the front door, walking down the path, and then turning around to walk back. When she came back into the hallway, Mrs Atherton had returned to the living room.

Sheridan opened the cupboard door and rewound the recording, just as Anna joined her.

'What's up?' Anna watched the replay of Sheridan outside.

Sheridan turned to her. 'We need to get back to the nick right now. I think we might have just found what Hill needs to keep this case going.'

CHAPTER 52

As the afternoon traffic began to build, Hill turned down a side street, only to be faced with a truck parked in the middle of the road, its hazard lights blinking.

'Bollocks,' she said, and put the car into reverse just as a lorry pulled up behind her. She was definitely trapped here. She checked the time on her watch, then sat tapping the steering wheel. She couldn't be late. She'd already pissed the chief off by asking for their meeting to be moved to Monday, the request met by a curt 'Not a fucking chance, Hill.'

Five minutes later, she gave up hitting her horn and got out of the car. Striding over to the truck and spotting the cab was empty, she looked up and down the road. As the driver came out of the building next to her, she proceeded to inform him that he was a prick and if he didn't move immediately, she would have his truck towed away. As he got back into his cab, he stuck his middle finger up at her and revved the engine several times, drowning out the sound of her mobile ringing in the car.

Sheridan and Anna ran up the stairs towards CID.

'Hill's not answering her mobile.' Sheridan made her way over to a desk by the window, opening the file and flicking through the pages. She pointed to the printout.

'Here it is.'

Sheridan read the texts again.

16.29 hours: Ronald Parks texts Tony Harvey: *You're not getting another penny until you tell me where Daniel's body is*

Tony to Ronald: *You said you didn't want to know what I did with him*

Ronald to Tony: *The police were supposed to have found him by now, this needs to be put to bed, it needs to end, where is he?*

Tony to Ronald: *Most of him is in one place and a bit in another place*

Ronald to Tony: *Did you cut him up?*

Tony to Ronald: *I tried, I'll tell you everything, but I want the other twenty, I'm just around the corner, get on to your bank.*

She then found the entry that showed the time when Tony Harvey's car was seen on CCTV as he arrived at the Parks' property.

Tony Harvey's car was seen to arrive at 16.35 hours.

'That's it.' Sheridan picked up the phone and dialled Hill's mobile again.

Hill quickly walked across the car park and made the mistake of looking up at the chief's window. He was staring down at her, impatiently tapping his watch.

'Oh, fuck off,' she said under her breath as she reached the main doors and yanked them open. Making her way up the stairs, her mobile rang, and she answered just as she reached the chief's door.

He opened it and stepped back.

'You're late.'

'Sorry, Mike,' Hill said, still holding her mobile against her ear as she put her briefcase down and unbuttoned her coat.

'Thank you, Sheridan,' she said, ending the call and sitting down, crossing one leg over the other.

'So, tell me you've got something that's going to convince me to keep the Parks case open.' The chief slid behind his desk and sat back, his hands behind his head.

'I've got something that's going to convince you to keep the Parks case open,' Hill said, and smiled.

CHAPTER 53

Sheridan and Anna had so far knocked on Jennifer's front door three times but there was still no answer.

'Her car's here, so I'm guessing she's around. Maybe she's at the main house.'

They were just making their way across the yard when Jennifer came around the corner. Her face was flushed, and it took a moment for her to catch her breath. 'Sorry, I've been out for a run.'

'I wish I had your energy,' Sheridan remarked as they followed her into the cottage.

They sat in the living room. As Sheridan told Jennifer that Tony Harvey was dead, she burst into tears and buried her face in her hands. 'Did he say anything before he died?' Her voice broke. She didn't even try to wipe away her tears.

'No,' Sheridan said. 'He never regained consciousness.'

'So now we'll never find Daniel.' Jennifer bent forward, staring at the carpet. 'Fucking bastard, fucking bastard!' she screamed, stood up and started to pace. Her anger was so tangible, it filled the room. 'Did they search him? Did he have any notes on him? He had a note that he showed me when he turned up here, the one I told you about. The one he threw in the fire. Did he have any other notes? Maybe he wrote other notes, have you searched his house?'

'Yes, we've searched everything and there are no other notes, I'm sorry.'

'So, that's it?' she sobbed. 'You're not going to try and find Daniel's body now, are you?'

'We still have officers searching at Crosby Beach . . .'

'So, you're keeping the case open?'

'We're waiting for the authority to carry on with the investigation.' Sheridan shifted in her seat. 'However, I was wondering if you would allow us to carry out a thorough search of the cottage and main house?'

'What for?'

'Well, you said that Tony was talking about some recording of what happened here in relation to Daniel, and that he mentioned a disc. I know you said there was no recording equipment, but we need to be absolutely certain of that.'

'You mean a hidden device or something?'

'Yes. But who would have set it up, and why?'

'I have no idea.' Jennifer looked around. 'Surely I'd know if there was something in here.' She shook her head. 'When's all this going to be over?'

'I know how hard this is, Jennifer. Honestly, I do. But we need to make sure nothing has been missed. I could get a search authority but I'd rather you consented without one.'

Jennifer agreed to the search, and went to make arrangements to stay with her friend Izzy in Cornwall for a few days. The investigation had taken its toll, and she needed to get away from the place where her brother and parents had lived and died to try and clear her head.

She stopped in at the bookshop before catching the train down south. As the train flew past rolling hills and beautifully rich countryside, Jennifer felt a moment of peace wash over her. Closing her eyes, she silently prayed that the investigation would soon be over.

CHAPTER 54

Hill was already at Hale Street by the time Sheridan and Anna got back from Jennifer's. They walked into CID just as she was about to brief the team. 'Ah, Sheridan, good timing.'

Sheridan joined her at the front of the room. 'What did the chief say?' she asked.

Hill ignored Sheridan's question and filled a cup from the water machine before turning to the room and announcing, 'Sheridan made a rather interesting discovery earlier today, which she's about to tell you all.'

Clearing her throat, Sheridan addressed the team. 'Earlier today we visited Mr and Mrs Atherton and discovered that the time on their CCTV system is fifteen minutes fast. So, we originally thought Tony Harvey arrived at the Parks' place at 16.35 but we now know he actually arrived at 16.20. Now, we already know that he sent the texts to Ronald Parks at 16.29. So, the question is, why would he send a text message nine minutes *after* he arrived at the house?'

Hill was sitting at the back of the room. 'And that's one of the reasons why the chief is happy for us to continue, but with half of the team. He agrees that there are too many unanswered questions. The investigation will now lie solely with CID, but I want to thank all of you for your efforts so far. Everyone has worked relentlessly and doggedly to get to the bottom of this case and I'm confident we *will* solve it once and for all.' She turned to Sheridan. 'We'll have a full briefing with the team shortly and decide where we go from here. I've got a meeting at six, so I need to get going. Good work.' She almost smiled, before getting up and leaving the room.

Sheridan stood to face the team, grinning. 'I've also got a meeting at six. In The Black Cat. The drinks are on me.'

CHAPTER 55

Anna stepped out of the shower, wrapping a towel around herself as she walked into the dressing room. She stood looking at her own reflection in the full-length mirror as she ran her index finger across her bottom lip. For a moment she imagined being at work, sharing a joke with Sheridan, and she beamed. She turned sideways and stared at her profile, still smiling. The smile that everyone saw. The smile that fooled them all.

Snapping her back to reality, Steve called from the bottom of the stairs, 'Do you want a cup of tea?'

'Yes please,' she answered before turning back to look at herself in the mirror.

And then she dropped the towel.

Her eyes fell on the dark purple bruises across her ribs and stomach. She twisted her hips to reveal the blackness across her back. Lifting her arms above her head, she stared at herself and realised what she had become. A master of pretence. The smiles she displayed to everyone around her were well practised; a perfect charade. No one would ever suspect what was really happening behind closed doors.

She put her dressing gown on and, with one hand on the banister, she slowly made her way back downstairs.

CHAPTER 56

Monday 3 December

Sheridan was sitting in Hill's office and as she waited for her to finish a phone call, she looked around the bare walls. A dead plant stood miserably on the windowsill. She made a mental note to steal it and try to revive it somehow. Perhaps wrap it up and give it back to Hill for Christmas. Dead or alive.

Sheridan still hadn't really figured Hill out, but in a strange way the new boss was growing on her. She was still as annoying as fuck, but her heart was in the right place, and she was passionate about her job. More than that, she didn't care who she pissed off in order to get a result.

The latest gossip in the office was that she was gay, living with a partner twenty years her junior and at least six cats, all named after characters from _Star Trek_. Her partner didn't work, and Hill's real first name wasn't Hill. Several officers had laid down a tenner and a guess as to what it really was. There were various entries, including Hillary, Hillman and Hill Billy.

As soon as Sheridan had got wind of the bet, she abruptly told those involved that office gossip was cruel and childish, and they all needed to grow up and concentrate on the fucking job. But, yes, she'd stick a tenner on Hilda.

Hill ended the call and turned her attention to Sheridan. 'So, what are your thoughts about the text messages?'

'All we know is that they were sent nine minutes *after* Tony arrived at the house. The only explanation I can think of is that he's driven past the CCTV and parked up for some reason. But why would he park up right by the drive and send a text message? Plus, the first text was sent by Ronald, so it's not like Tony parked up to *send* a text. And like I say, why put in a text what you can say to someone's face? I mean, he was there, he was right there by the house.'

'And we're sure on the timings?'

'Positive.' Sheridan crossed her arms. 'Unless Ronald sent the text to Tony because he was planning to come to us and tell us that Tony killed Daniel and the texts between them could be evidential. The texts that Tony sent back are pretty damning.'

'But they also incriminate Ronald himself.'

'True.'

'Plus, we don't know what was said during the phone call between them an hour or so earlier. Maybe Ronald tried to get Tony to say something about killing Daniel, and that's what riled Tony to do what he did. Maybe Ronald threatened to go to the police. Don't forget the money that Tony mentioned in the texts. Ronald might have been thinking he could tell the police that Tony was blackmailing him.'

'Possibly. I would question, though . . . If Tony had Ronald and Rita tied up at the house, why didn't he take Ronald's phone? There's also the fact that he kept hold of his own phone right up until he taped it to the lorry. He had the foresight to delete the texts between them, probably thinking that once they were deleted, we couldn't retrieve them.'

'Maybe he forgot that he'd left Ronald's mobile at the house,' Hill said. 'Remind me, where was it found?'

'Down the side of the sofa.'

There was a knock on the door, and Anna peered in from the corridor. 'Boss, the search team have finished at the cottage. Nothing found, there's definitely no recording devices in there, or in the main house.'

'What about this disc?'

'Again, nothing.'

'Thanks, Anna. Grab a seat. We're just discussing our theories.'

Anna pulled a chair over next to Sheridan.

'What's Jennifer Parks like?' Hill asked. 'Have either of you got any concerns that she's involved?'

Sheridan spoke first. 'I don't think so. And Anna will tell you that I suspect *everyone*.'

'True,' Anna agreed, nodding.

'I'd never completely rule her out though.' Sheridan sighed. 'But she definitely wasn't there the night Daniel was killed, there's literally no evidence of her being involved in anything and she's been honest and upfront throughout.'

'How's she holding up generally?'

Anna replied, 'She's doing pretty well, considering. She's a strong person, mentally *and* physically.'

Hill responded, 'She's got a lot to gain financially now that Daniel and her parents are dead.'

Sheridan agreed. 'True. But if she's involved in any of this, then she hasn't been acting alone. And if that's the case, then we've missed something. Or someone.'

CHAPTER 57

Wednesday 5 December

Sheridan's eyes searched the CID office until they fell on DC Rob Wills. She casually meandered over to him. For the last few days, more and more questions had started to rumble around her head as she found herself doubting everything. The fact that the case was complex didn't bother her, she relished a challenge, but the more she thought about it, she realised that she had more questions than answers.

Rob looked up as she approached. 'You okay, boss?' he asked, smiling. He knew that look – the one she gave him when she needed him to check something out, but didn't want to share it with the whole team.

Sheridan sat in the chair next to him, pretending to read what was on his computer screen, but her eyes were slowly scanning the room. Once she was satisfied that everyone had their heads buried in their work, she turned to him and grinned. 'You know how much you love me?'

Rob sat back and raised an eyebrow. 'Yes, Sheridan?'

'Can I ask you to do me a teeny favour?'

'Probably.'

'Thank you.' She slid a piece of paper across the desk and tapped it with her finger.

He leaned forward and read what was written on the paper. Twice. His puzzled expression didn't surprise her.

Folding the note up and putting it in his pocket, he nodded. 'I'll see what I can do.'

Sheridan placed her hand on his and squeezed it. 'Thank you.'

As she walked back to her office, she spotted Hill making her way downstairs and quickly took the opportunity to grab the dying plant from her windowsill. As she emerged, mission accomplished, she bumped into Anna in the corridor.

'What are you up to?' Anna tried to peek at whatever Sheridan was hiding behind her back.

'Stealing stuff. Do you fancy getting out of the office, grab a quick coffee?'

'Sure.'

After hiding the deceased plant in her filing cabinet, Sheridan and Anna walked into town. They stopped every now and then to glance in shop windows at the displays that were becoming increasingly festive. Liverpool was buzzing with Christmas shoppers, so they escaped the crowds by ducking into a café and pitching up in a cosy seat by the window.

'What are you and Steve doing for Christmas?' Sheridan asked, scooping the chocolate powder off the top of her cappuccino with a teaspoon.

'Not much, we're just having a quiet one together,' Anna replied, unwrapping the tiny complimentary biscuit that came with her latte.

'But you normally go to your parents'?'

'Yeah, I know. But I'm working on Boxing Day and Steve wanted it to be just the two of us this year. What about you and Sam?'

'My mum and dad are coming over. You and Steve should come to ours for dinner one night. We haven't done that in ages. I promise I won't let Sam cook.'

Anna laughed. 'I really need that in writing.'

Sheridan's mobile rang. 'DI Holler.' She suddenly stood up, lifting her coat from the back of the chair.

'We're on our way.' Sheridan ended the call and, glancing around to make sure no one was in earshot, she leaned over the table and whispered to Anna, 'We're going to Crosby Beach.'

'What for?'

'The search team looking for Daniel's body have found something.'

CHAPTER 58

The light was already beginning to fade by the time Sheridan and Anna arrived at Crosby Beach. They walked carefully across the sand towards the CSI team.

'Hi, Charlie,' Sheridan said. 'So where was it found?' She had to raise her voice over the wind that had suddenly picked up.

'Over there.' Charlie pointed. 'Actually, pretty close to where Ronald Parks' body was found. It was buried about twelve inches down.'

They followed him across the sand and stood near to where the finger had been located. After discussing the possibility that more body parts would be found, Sheridan asked, 'And it's just one finger?'

'So far, yes. We'll get it examined and I'll let you know the results as soon as I can.'

'Can you tell which finger it was?'

'If I had to hazard a guess? I'd say the little finger.'

'Okay.' Sheridan cupped her hands and blew into them, having left her gloves in the car. 'Well, we'll leave you to it. Really great work, Charlie.'

'Anything for my two favourite detectives.' He smiled broadly, before turning and heading back to the CSI van.

Sheridan stood where she was for a moment, thinking out loud. 'So, if that *is* Daniel Parks' finger, and let's say it *was* Ronald who killed him and Tony who disposed of his body, then Tony put the finger here nine months before he killed Ronald and Rita. So, he knew where he was going to put them, even back then.'

'Unless he kept the finger and put it here *after* he buried Ronald.'

Sheridan pulled a face. 'That's fucked up.'

'Possible, though.'

'How does someone go from being an insurance consultant to a calculated, murdering finger hoarder?' She heard how it sounded the moment the words left her lips and allowed herself a grin, which was mirrored by Anna, who repeated 'finger hoarder' before snort-laughing.

They walked back to the car and Sheridan started the engine to warm them up.

'Do you think Tony *did* cut Daniel into pieces?' Anna asked.

'No. From the wording in the text messages, I think he was going to but couldn't go through with it.'

They sat for a while, looking out over Crosby Beach. The Iron Men statues were now fading into haunting silhouettes along the misted shoreline.

'I've asked Rob Wills to check out the CCTV at the train station.'

'Which CCTV?' Anna asked.

'Lime Street to Newquay.'

Anna turned to look at her. 'You're checking that Jennifer actually went to Cornwall?'

'Yeah.'

'Are you starting to not trust her story?'

'I just don't want anything to be missed.'

CHAPTER 59

As she came through the front door, Sheridan handed Sam the dead plant that she'd taken from Hill's office.

'For me? You really shouldn't have.' Sam peered closer at the plant and screwed her nose up.

'We're on a mission.' Sheridan kissed Sam as she took off her coat.

'To collect dead things?'

'No, to revive dead things.'

'Oh God, please tell me you're not going to start bringing dead bodies home, are you?'

Sheridan pulled off her boots, took the plant from Sam and walked into the kitchen. 'It's my boss's. I took it out of her office. I'm going to try and bring it back to life and give it to her for Christmas.'

'Why is your boss growing onions in her office?'

'I don't think it's an onion.'

After dinner, they sat hunched over Sam's laptop, googling houseplants, and every now and then removing Maud's sticky paw from the keyboard. They scrolled through pages of pictures until they finally discovered that the onion was more likely to be an amaryllis.

'We'll see if it grows and then I'll take it back in to her.'

'Has she not noticed it's gone?' Sam shut the laptop and Maud promptly spread herself across it, feeling its warmth on her belly.

'Well, she hasn't mentioned anything yet.'

'What if Hill finds out you've taken it, and we accidentally kill it? What if Maud eats it?'

'Then I'll be back in uniform by Christmas.'

CHAPTER 60

Friday 7 December

Hill stood gazing out of Sheridan's window as they discussed where the investigation was going, when there was a knock on the door.

'Come in,' Sheridan answered, as the door opened and Rob stepped in.

'Oh sorry, I didn't realise you were here, ma'am,' he said to Hill, and turned to leave.

'What is it, Rob?' Hill snapped, crossing her arms.

Rob hesitated. He knew that when Sheridan had asked him to check the CCTV on Jennifer Parks, she hadn't told anyone else about her suspicions, and he didn't want to drop her in it.

Sheridan, on the other hand, now saw a perfect opportunity to wind him up.

'Yes Rob, what *is* it?' Sheridan asked, crossing her arms to mimic Hill.

Rob instantly spotted that mischievous glint in her eye. 'It's okay. I'll come back a bit later.' He nodded as he went to make his escape.

'Is it that thing I asked you to do for me?' *Get out of that one,* Sheridan thought, turning her head slightly to hide her grin.

'What thing?' Hill asked impatiently.

'Sheridan asked me to pick something up from the chemist for her and I just came to let her know.' He turned to face Sheridan, totally straight-faced. 'To let *you* know that the pharmacist said you'll need a prescription for that type of cream.'

'Thanks, Rob.' Sheridan narrowed her eyes.

Five minutes later, after Hill had left, Sheridan sent Rob a text: *You fucker*

He texted back: *You started it*

She replied: *Well played, by the way*

He responded: *Thanks. I've got what you asked for. Meet me where the black raven flies at midnight. Wear a flower in your lapel*

Sheridan burst out laughing and replied: *That's too funny. CID 2 mins*

◆ ◆ ◆

Sheridan winked at Rob as she slid into the chair next to him. 'Tell me something that's going to make the hairs on the back of my neck stand up.' She put her hands together in prayer.

'Jennifer met a guy at Lime Street. They had a coffee together before she got on the train alone.' Rob pointed at his computer screen as Sheridan leaned in closer to see the image of the male. He stood around six feet tall, with dark hair and a beaming white smile. Sheridan watched as he approached Jennifer while she was reading the destination board.

He smiled, she smiled back, and they walked into the station's coffee shop. Half an hour later, she emerged alone and made her way to the platform to board her train. The man came out of the coffee shop five minutes later and left.

'So, this guy didn't get on a train?'

'Nope. I've gone back and I can't even find him arriving, so God knows where he came from.'

'And I take it there's no CCTV inside the coffee shop?'

'Sadly not. Anyway, I've got the CCTV of Jennifer arriving at Newquay station, she got into a taxi. I've also done a voter's check on the address that she said she was staying at. There's four people listed there. All with the surname Duncan, but they might not live there any more. The electoral register can be out of date, as you know. What's Izzy's surname?'

'Come to think of it, I don't actually know. I didn't ask.'

'That's not like you.' Rob frowned.

'Is there an Izzy or Isabelle Duncan registered?'

'No. There's a Thomas, Michelle, Hayley and Jack. But no one called Izzy or Isabelle.'

'Wasn't Isabelle Duncan the name of a famous actress?' Sheridan asked.

'No, that was Isadora Duncan, and she was a dancer.'

'That's right. Didn't she die in a plane crash?'

'No, she died when her scarf got caught in the spokes of her car.'

Sheridan frowned and stared at him for a moment. 'How do you know all this stuff?'

'I'm interested in dead people. Especially those who died in strange and tragic circumstances.'

'Do you bore your wife with all this weird trivia?' Sheridan grinned.

'You know she doesn't listen to a word I say.' He smiled. Jo, his wife, was profoundly deaf.

Sheridan raised her eyes to the ceiling at his joke, slapped his arm and leaned back in her chair.

Rob rubbed his arm in mock pain. 'I've also been going through the CCTV at Lime Street from when Tony Harvey was seen there. When we looked at it originally, we saw him walk in, check the destination board, look around a bit and then go into the toilets. When he comes out, he goes back to the destination board and then leaves. I've only managed to track him down for a few minutes after that because he goes off CCTV, but from what I've got so far, he doesn't meet with anyone else.'

'Okay, that's fine.' Sheridan put her hands behind her head. 'Can you do me one more favour?'

'Sure.'

'There was DNA found at the cottage when Daniel was murdered. A sperm sample that Jennifer said was from a one-night stand, but she couldn't remember any details of the mystery man. Can you run it for me again?'

'Sure. But what makes you think we'll get a hit this time?'

'DNA samples get added to the database every day. Maybe whoever's sperm it was, they're now on the system.'

CHAPTER 61

Saturday 8 December

Hill closed her front door. She was about to get into her car when she noticed her neighbour's curtains were still closed. Checking her watch, she tutted, locked the car again, crossed the road and knocked on the door. She could hear Barney, her neighbour's dog, barking. She knocked again and waited for a few moments before deciding to go in. Putting her key in the lock, she could hear Barney sniffing at the door, and as she opened it he wagged his tail furiously and jumped up at her.

'Hey, Barney.' Hill stroked his head before stepping inside and pushing the living room door open.

'Gloria?' she called out and Barney immediately turned and ran upstairs.

Hill followed him, calling out Gloria's name as she reached the landing. Gloria's bedroom door was ajar. Hill could see one of her feet sticking out from under the duvet.

'Oh shit,' she said under her breath, taking a tentative step forward and slowly pushing the door open.

'Gloria?' she whispered, pausing momentarily before making her way around the side of the bed.

As she leaned over her, Hill noticed that her eyes were shut, and she was deathly still. Then she saw the wires.

'What the hell are you doing?' Gloria screamed, as she opened her eyes to see Hill's face just inches from her own.

Hill jumped back. 'Your bloody curtains are closed.'

'What?' Gloria pulled the headphones out of her ears.

'Your curtains are closed. It's gone ten, your curtains are never closed at this time of the morning.'

Gloria grinned. 'You thought I was dead, didn't you?'

'Of course I thought you were bloody dead. You're eighty-one with a dodgy ticker. Why are you still in bed?'

'Not that it's any of your business but I'm listening to an audio-book. Is there a law against that?' Gloria shook her head and leaned forward, fluffed up her pillow and flopped her head back into it.

'I'll leave you to it then.' Hill took her keys out of her pocket. 'Do you fancy a cup of tea?'

Hill checked her watch again. 'No, I'm fine, I've got things to do. Can I get you anything before I go?'

'I thought the offer of a cup of tea might be a hint.'

'You want *me* to make *you* a cup of tea?'

'That would be lovely. Two sugars. I'd get up and do it myself, but I'm at a really good bit in this book. Do you want me to tell you the plot? Maybe you can work out who the murderer is, seeing as you're a big hotshot detective?'

'No. I really don't.' Hill turned and went down to the kitchen. After making Gloria a cup of tea, she gave Barney a quick kiss on his head and made her way back downstairs.

'Hill?' Gloria called out from her bedroom as Hill was about to open the front door.

'What?' Hill called back.

'Thanks for checking in on me.'

Hill replied, 'You're welcome.'

'Nosey old cow.'

Hill smiled broadly and, without responding, she made her way across the road and back to her car.

◆ ◆ ◆

Half an hour later, she unwrapped the flowers and bent down, carefully placing them in the vase. She stood up and stepped back with her head bowed and eyes closed. The sun was trying to shine through the clouds, every now and then breaking through and shimmering off the rain-soaked grass.

The cemetery was always busy at this time of year. Families tending their loved ones' graves, laying wreaths over crosses, lighting candles that flickered precariously under glass domes, protecting the delicate and vulnerable flame from the wind if only for a moment, before it was snuffed out.

The dark clouds moved slowly and heavily above her, covering the last rays of sunshine and turning the sky black. And then the rain came, hard and unforgiving.

She kissed the tips of her fingers and ran them over the words engraved on the headstone.

'I miss you,' she whispered, and her words carried gently on the breeze. 'I miss you so much.'

CHAPTER 62

Anna walked into the kitchen, following the smell of bacon that wafted through the house.

Steve turned and smiled at her. 'Good morning. Thought I'd cook us a proper breakfast.'

'Smells divine.' She flicked the kettle on. 'Sheridan asked me if we wanted to go over to her and Sam's for dinner one night, do you fancy it?'

'Maybe.' He flipped the bacon. 'I just always got the impression that Sheridan didn't like me very much.'

'What makes you think that?'

'I don't know, just a feeling I get. If I'm honest, I've always felt a bit uncomfortable around her.' He leaned forward and kissed her cheek. 'Maybe it's just me.'

Anna didn't answer, instead walking into the living room, where she sat on the arm of the sofa, feeling tears stinging her eyes as she unconsciously touched her side. The bruises had faded now, and he had sworn on his life that he would never hit her again. He had sobbed like a child when she told him that if he did, she'd leave him. This was his last chance.

CHAPTER 63

Jennifer rested her head back as the train rumbled out of the station, bound for Liverpool. The carriages were busy and almost every seat was taken. Opening her book, she tried to concentrate on the words, but the noise from two lads in the seats behind distracted her. And everyone else.

She heard the hiss of a beer can being opened and something tap her on the head. She looked up just in time to catch a glimpse of the lads ducking back down and laughing. As the train picked up speed, she felt another tap and looked up again. Nothing.

Glancing around the carriage, she noticed that everyone was trying desperately to ignore the two lads. Their absent faces bowed, pretending to read their mobile phones, newspapers or books. Some just stared out at the scenery.

Then came another tap. This time she stood up and eased herself past the woman sitting next to her and, holding on to the top of the seat, she stood in the aisle.

The two lads looked at her, grinning. 'Alright, love?'

'If you touch me again, I'll break your fucking hand,' she said calmly, the hint of a smile on her face.

One of the lads stood up and faced her. 'It was just a joke.' He looked her up and down and leaned forward, his lips puckered. 'Kiss and make up?'

His mate burst out laughing and took a sip from his beer can, just as Jennifer pushed him so hard in the chest that he fell backwards on to his mate. 'Shut up, you silly little prick,' she said, before returning to her seat.

The carriage became deafeningly quiet as the other commuters silently high-fived her in their heads.

CHAPTER 64

Monday 10 December

Hill was already in a foul mood before she even arrived at work. And it only got worse when she walked into her office and saw the empty windowsill. She turned on her heels and made her way down the corridor to CID. No one was in yet, so she took the opportunity to rifle through the cabinets under their desks.

As she opened Rob's drawer, she spotted the envelope marked *Guess Boss's Real Name.* She opened it, reading the list of officers who had bet what 'Hill' was short for. She absorbed the information and put the envelope back. After a final cursory check around, she returned to her office to watch as the back yard began to fill with cars. When she was sure everyone was in, she marched down the corridor and burst through the door to CID.

Sheridan was updating the whiteboard. She jumped as Hill's voice boomed behind her. 'Someone please tell me we're making progress on this job.' Hill looked around. 'Someone? Anyone?'

Sheridan put the black marker pen down. 'Hill, it's a complex case and we're—'

'I know it's fucking complex, Sheridan, but I need to go back to the chief with something soon. Otherwise, *this* time, he will shut it down.'

'We're waiting on the results of the finger found at Crosby—'

'And you're all sitting here waiting for that?' She shook her head. 'Well, I'll just go and sit in my office and wait as well, shall I?' she shouted. 'I'll tell you something, if that's *not* Daniel Parks' finger, then when I meet the chief next week, he *will* have this case closed.'

No one spoke. No one moved. No one dared suggest that if it wasn't Daniel Parks' finger then there was the distinct possibility that they would need to investigate whose it actually was.

Hill stormed out, slamming the door behind her.

Rob's phone rang, and he picked it up. He stared at his keyboard as everyone focused on him.

'Okay, thanks,' he said, and put the phone down. He took a deep breath before saying, 'The DNA's not a match. It's not Daniel's finger.'

'You're fucking joking.' Sheridan slapped the desk. All heads went down in stunned silence.

'Yeah, I'm joking. It's a definite match.'

The room erupted as a sigh of relief went round like a Mexican wave.

'What else do we know about it?' Sheridan asked excitedly, putting her hands on top of her head. She was ready to forgive the joke given how good this news was.

'It's the little finger of his left hand. Clean cut through the bone.'

Sheridan practically skipped down the corridor towards Hill's office and tapped on the open door three times. Hill was standing with her hands behind her back, staring out of the window.

Sheridan hovered in the doorway. 'I've got some good news.'

Hill didn't turn round. 'What is it?'

'Just got the results back. The finger found at Crosby *is* Daniel's.'

'Good—' Hill cleared her throat. 'Good work.'

'You alright?' Sheridan stepped into the office as Hill turned round.

'No, I'm not alright. Some bastard has nicked my plant.'

Sheridan's eyes widened. 'Plant?'

'I had an amaryllis on my window ledge and now it's gone.'

'Oh yeah, I remember seeing it. It looked a bit dead to me,' Sheridan replied as casually as she could.

'It wasn't dead.' Hill looked back at the spot where the plant had been and shook her head.

Sheridan was about to confess when Hill suddenly pushed past her and left the room. Sheridan watched as she went into the toilets. She was about to follow her in when Anna came out. Her eyes were red; Sheridan could see she'd been crying. Without a word, Sheridan shepherded her into her office and closed the door.

'What's wrong?' She sat Anna down on the chair. Crouching in front of her, Sheridan peeled her hands away from her face. 'Anna, whatever it is, you can tell me.'

'I've wanted to tell you before.' Anna raised her head and wiped tears away with the back of her hand. 'I just didn't want to believe it myself.'

'Believe what?' Sheridan gently squeezed her hands.

'I need to tell you something. I need your support, nothing else.' She inhaled deeply. 'I'll sort it, that's all you need to know.'

A thought flashed through Sheridan's head. The bruises she'd seen on Anna's wrists, which Anna had passed off as being the result of a play-fight with Steve. The joke Anna had made about looking like a DV victim. Had Sheridan believed her too quickly? Had Anna been suffering in silence, too scared to tell her best friend? Because once Anna told her, Sheridan couldn't unknow it. Sheridan hesitated before answering, 'Okay. Just tell me.'

'I'm pregnant.'

At that moment, Sheridan's door flew open and Hill appeared. She looked down at Anna and Sheridan. 'What's going on?'

Anna stood up. 'Nothing, I just felt a bit faint for a second.'

'Do you need to go home?' Hill asked.

'No. I'm fine now, it's passed.'

'I can get someone to take you home . . .'

'I'm fine. Honestly.'

'Okay. Well, get yourselves over to Jennifer's. She needs to know that we've found Daniel's body part.'

And with that, she left as abruptly as she'd arrived.

'We'll talk in the car,' Sheridan whispered.

CHAPTER 65

Jennifer didn't speak. She sat staring at the floor, breathing in through her nose and blowing the air out of her mouth, like someone who was about to pass out.

Anna placed a cup of water next to her, and briefly touched her shoulder before joining Sheridan on the sofa. There was never an easy way to tell someone that their loved one had died, but in this case Jennifer already knew that Daniel was dead. What she didn't know was that someone had cut his finger off and buried it on the beach.

When she was able to speak, Jennifer asked the one question that Sheridan had dreaded. Did they think he'd been tortured? Sheridan was honest with her. It was possible.

Silence hung in the room as Jennifer tried to comprehend the fact. Slowly shaking her head as if to rid her mind of the images that filled it.

She finally looked up. 'So what happens now? Is the case closed?'

'Well, it depends. If we don't find anything else at Crosby, and if there's no other evidence to suggest someone else was involved, then . . . yes, there's a possibility the case could be closed.' Sheridan hesitated. 'But we've still got a couple of things to check.'

Sheridan explained that given everything they had found so far, it was highly likely that Ronald and Tony had colluded to kill Daniel and Tony had killed her parents. What was still unknown was why.

'I don't think I can stay here.' Jennifer blew her nose before running her hand through her hair. 'I need to move away and start again.'

'I completely understand. Where would you go?'

'I don't know. I need to try and sell the house. If anyone would buy it.' She glanced around the room. 'Who would want to buy a place where so much tragedy has happened?' Her eyes fell on Anna and Sheridan but neither of them had an answer.

'If nothing else is found at Crosby, will you keep looking for Daniel's body?'

'Probably not. But that's not to say that one day it won't be found,' Anna replied.

Jennifer looked at Sheridan. 'Have you finished with my file?'

'Oh, yes. I'll get it back to you.'

As they left, Jennifer hugged them both. 'I can't thank you enough for everything you've done. I really wouldn't have got through all of this without you both.'

She watched as they got back into the car and put her hand up as they drove off. Heading back inside, she instantly curled up into a ball on the sofa.

'Did anything strike you as a little bit odd?' Sheridan asked as they headed back to Hale Street.

'Yeah. When you said we've got a few things left to check, she didn't ask you what they were.' Anna turned to look at Sheridan. 'You said that just to see what her reaction would be, didn't you?'

'Yep.'

CHAPTER 66

Sam was trying to unravel Maud from a ball of string when Sheridan came through the front door. The living room was cluttered with boxes of baubles and tangled strings of Christmas lights covered the coffee table.

'Hello, you two.' Sheridan leaned down to kiss Sam, noticing a piece of tinsel sticking out of Maud's mouth.

'Have a look at this,' Sam said, taking Sheridan by the hand and marching her into the kitchen, where she pointed at the amaryllis plant on the window ledge. 'It's literally growing by the hour.' Sam beamed. 'We are bloody horticultural geniuses.'

'Thank God. Because my boss has noticed it's gone, and she got proper upset today. I need to take it back tomorrow.'

'Does she know it was you that took it?'

'Not yet.'

'Maybe you could sneak it back and not say anything.'

'I need a drink. And then we'll decorate the tree.' Sheridan opened the fridge and took out a bottle of wine, pouring them both a glass before flopping on to the sofa.

'You look exhausted. Are you okay?' Sam wrapped her fingers around Sheridan's hand.

'Anna's pregnant.'

'That's fantastic.'

'She's not keeping it.'

Sheridan told Sam how Anna had never wanted children and although Steve had tried to persuade her a handful of times during their relationship, Anna had never been swayed, and he seemed to have accepted they would never have children together. When Anna had told Sheridan that morning, she had made her promise that the subject was closed and she had already booked a termination. Initially, Anna had declined Sheridan's offer to go with her, but eventually agreed.

'Why is Steve not going with her?' Sam asked.

Sheridan ran her finger around the rim of her glass. 'Because he doesn't know.'

◆ ◆ ◆

Later that evening, Sheridan and Sam stood arm in arm, ready for the big switch-on of the Christmas tree lights. Its branches stretched out, holding up a hundred twinkly bulbs. Decorations of every colour, shape and size hung proudly, glistening like stars.

It was a Holler family tradition that every year, Sheridan's parents bought her a new ornament to hang from the tree. It was always special, always magical. There was the little robin they'd found at a Christmas market in Belgium, the wooden reindeer her father had hand carved, the little silver star they'd given her when she joined the police force. So many memories all around the branches. It was also Sheridan's tradition every year to add the final touch.

When she was a little girl, she had asked her mum why there was no snow on the branches of their Christmas tree. And so, the following year, Rosie bought the softest, whitest wool she could find and painstakingly wove it together. She then carefully draped it all around the tree, until it looked like snow had settled on the branches. Sheridan had kept the wool for all these years and as she placed the last of it around the bottom of their tree, she and Sam smiled at how beautiful it looked. And sat proudly at the top of the tree was Hylda the hippo.

As Sam tidied up the living room, Sheridan sat on the sofa flicking through Jennifer's file. She had promised to return it and wanted to check she hadn't missed anything. After she'd finished, she carefully put everything back in the box file before following Sam upstairs to bed. Leaving Maud to tap the baubles on the Christmas tree.

CHAPTER 67

Tuesday 11 December

Hill dropped her briefcase on the desk and stared at the amaryllis for a moment before opening the card that was tucked under the pot.

> *When I saw this on your window ledge, I honestly thought it was dead, so I took it home to try and revive it for you. Sam thought it was an onion. I always intended to return it, unless we'd managed to kill it off completely and then I would have totally denied all knowledge.*
> > *You're not allowed to be mad at me.*
> > *Merry Christmas,*
> > *Sheridan*
> > *x*

Hill swallowed and bit down on her lip so hard that it hurt. Picking the plant up, she touched the stem, which stood proud and tall, before holding it closer, noticing the first signs of a flower. Clearing her throat, she placed it back where it belonged, before spotting Sheridan by her car, looking up.

Hill smiled, nodded and put her thumb up.

Getting into the car, Sheridan smiled back, nodded and drove out of the back yard. As she sat waiting for the lights to change, her mind came round to Anna. The abortion was booked for the following week and Sheridan had arranged a day off so that she could take Anna and stay with her for a few hours after the procedure. If everything proceeded without complication, Anna would make a quick recovery and be able to return to work the next day.

Sheridan thought about Steve. *Would Anna ever tell him? Did he have the right to know? Would Anna ever regret her decision?* Sheridan was the only person Anna had told and the only person she would ever tell. Anna knew that Sheridan would tell Sam and she was fine with that. Anna had promised Sheridan that she would never keep anything from her again. She was her best mate. And best mates didn't have secrets.

CHAPTER 68

Rob Wills took a sip of his coffee and opened the envelope, pulling out the sheet of paper. He read it and then read it again, before looking around the office at his colleagues. A moment later, he stood up and made his way down the corridor towards Sheridan's office, peering round the door to find it empty.

'She's popped out.' Anna appeared behind him.

'Do you know how long she's going to be?'

Anna checked her watch. 'Not long. She's doing a briefing at one. Is everything okay?'

'She asked me to check the sperm sample again. The one that was found at the cottage after Daniel's murder.'

'The one that Jennifer said was from a one-night stand?'

'Yeah.' Rob looked at the sheet of paper in his hand.

'Have you got a result?'

'Yeah.' He turned the paper round for Anna to see the name written on it.

Anna's eyes widened. 'What the fuck?'

CHAPTER 69

Jennifer flipped the 'Open' sign over and stood in the doorway, watching streams of Christmas shoppers file past. She hadn't been to the shop for a while and the familiar smell of books comforted her. Turning her head, her eyes fell upon Daniel's poster. She walked over to it and carefully removed the tape holding it in place. Laying it flat on top of the counter, she began folding it up.

The bell above the door rang as a customer came in and she turned, smiling broadly. 'Hello.'

'Hi,' the woman replied. 'I thought you'd closed down. I noticed you haven't been open for a while.'

'I *am* closing down actually, everything's half price.'

Jennifer busied herself making 'Closing Down Sale' signs as the woman browsed the shelves. The shop began to fill as bargain-hungry shoppers snapped up Christmas presents. Several regulars asked Jennifer why she was closing the shop and she told them she was moving away. She could tell by their reactions that they only asked out of politeness and didn't really care why, as they filled their bags.

CHAPTER 70

Sheridan checked her watch as she reached the top of the stairs, debating whether to go straight into the briefing or risk another fight with the vending machine. Feeling in her pocket for some change and deciding she really did deserve a bar of chocolate, she headed for the machine and looked through the glass at the choices.

'Right, you little fucker,' she mumbled under her breath as she dropped the coins into the slot and pushed the button.

The mechanism started to turn. The chocolate bar edged teasingly closer to her, stopping just short of falling into the tray below.

'Bastard,' she said out loud and put her hands against the glass, pushing hard enough to rock the machine into submission. She smiled victoriously as two bars fell at the same time.

As she walked into the briefing, she threw the freebie bar at Anna.

'Bought you a present,' she said as she made her way to the front of the room.

'Sorry I'm late, everyone.' The silence in the room unnerved her for a moment. 'What?' she asked, quickly looking from face to face, before turning her attention to Anna.

'We've got a DNA hit on the sperm sample found at the cottage when Daniel was murdered.'

Sheridan smiled. 'Brilliant. So, we finally get to know who Jennifer's one-night stand was.' She looked to the ceiling. 'Go on then, hit me with it.'

'It belongs to Tony Harvey.'

CHAPTER 71

Jennifer's mobile rang. She saw it was Sheridan, but as she went to answer it, a customer appeared at the desk balancing an armful of books.

Two hours had passed by the time she had served the stream of shoppers, and grabbing the opportunity to call Sheridan back, she dialled her number. Sheridan told her there had been a development and she wanted to see her that evening. By the time Jennifer got home, Anna and Sheridan were already parked next to the cottage.

As they sat in the living room, Jennifer's chest tightened when Sheridan told her that the DNA sperm sample found in the cottage at the time of Daniel's death matched Tony Harvey's profile.

'How do you think it got there?' Sheridan asked, watching Jennifer's face intently for her reaction.

Silence.

'Jennifer?'

Silence.

'When we told you that Tony Harvey had killed your parents, you were adamant that he would never hurt *you*. How were you so sure?' Sheridan pressed, stealing a glance at Anna.

'I just didn't think he ever would.' Jennifer's voice was a whisper. 'I need a drink of water.' She stood up and walked slowly into the kitchen, staring at the tap; she swallowed hard and felt her hands shaking as she tried to hold the glass under the running water. When she returned a minute later, she took a sip before setting the glass down on the coffee table.

'I should have said something before.' She didn't look up. 'But I think I know how it got there.'

Sheridan and Anna waited.

'My mum and Tony flirted with each other a lot. I think I always knew there was something going on, I just didn't want to believe it. My parents had the perfect marriage, and to think that my mum would risk it all for a fling with a friend just didn't make sense.' She sat forward and took another sip of water. 'Anyway, I came home from work one day and saw Mum and Tony coming out of the cottage together. They didn't see me pull into the drive, so I backed up and sat on the road until they'd gone into the main house.'

'Why would they be in the cottage, rather than the house?'

'Obviously there was more chance of them being caught in the house if my father had come home.'

'Did you ever confront them?'

'No.'

'Did you ever tell anyone?'

'Only Daniel.' She looked up. 'I wanted to believe that it was innocent, that nothing was going on, but now I know it was true. I'm so sorry I didn't say anything before. I would never intentionally keep anything from the police.'

CHAPTER 72

Monday 17 December

Hailstones battered the window as Anna lay in bed, awake. She felt Steve turn over, and closed her eyes as his arm draped across her. She waited for a moment before sliding out of bed and stepping into the shower. She felt relief as the water hit her face and washed away the salty tears that stung her eyes.

By the time Steve woke up and came downstairs, she was dressed and ready, looking out of the window for Sheridan's car.

She had told Steve that the police station parking bays were being repainted and some officers were car sharing. He had offered to drive her in to the station, but she'd convinced him that it was easier for Sheridan to pick her up and drop her home as she had no idea what time she'd finish work.

Kissing Anna on the cheek before she stepped outside, he threw a wave at Sheridan. She waved back at him and leaned over to open the car door, just before hailstones started to bounce off the windscreen.

'You okay?' Sheridan asked as they pulled away. 'Forget that. Stupid question.'

Anna sighed. 'Do you think I'm a terrible person?'

'No. You're my mate and I love you.'

'That's not what I asked.'

'I don't think you're a terrible person, because if you were, you wouldn't be my mate.' Sheridan took her hand off the steering wheel for a second and squeezed Anna's shoulder.

They spent the rest of the journey to the hospital in silence and Sheridan sat in the waiting room while Anna went in. When it was over, they went to Sheridan's house and Anna lay on the sofa, finally falling asleep.

Sheridan made herself a coffee, trying to make as little noise as possible, and by the time she went back into the living room, Maud had nuzzled her way under Anna's arm and the two of them lay there together, eyes closed and peaceful. Sheridan quietly opened Jennifer's file, glancing at Anna and Maud as she did so. She knew that Anna would have barely slept the night before and had looked exhausted when she'd got into the car that morning. So, she let Anna rest while she settled down to reread the last notepad in Jennifer's file.

CHAPTER 73

Tuesday 18 December

Hill put the phone down and marched down the corridor to Sheridan's office, where she found Sheridan and Anna.

'Daniel Parks' finger has no other DNA on it, so we're no further forward. The search team at Crosby haven't found anything else and I'm thinking the chief will want us to wrap this up.'

'But we still don't know the motive for any of the killings,' Anna said.

'And we're probably going to have to accept that we never *will* know.' Hill plonked herself on the chair next to Anna.

Sheridan leaned back. 'It doesn't sit right with me. We haven't got to the bottom of everything.'

'That's not enough to keep going with it, Sheridan. I know it's frustrating but sometimes you have to accept that you don't always get all the answers.'

'That's not good enough for me.'

Hill stood up. 'I'm not arguing with you. It's just the way it is. Go and see Jennifer and let her know the case is being closed,' she snapped back as she left the room.

'Fuck.' Sheridan puffed out her cheeks and turned to look out of the window. 'We've missed something. I just know we have.'

At that moment, Dipesh Mois knocked on the door. 'Sorry to interrupt, ma'am, I've got the copies of the file you wanted.'

'Thanks, Dipesh.'

'What file?' Anna asked.

'Jennifer kept a file on Daniel's murder, and I've been reading through it. But I need to get the original back to her, so I've taken a copy.'

Dipesh placed the papers on Sheridan's desk before leaving.

Anna stood up. 'I've got a meeting with CPS. Shall we go and see Jennifer when I get back?'

'No, it's okay. I'll go on my own.'

CHAPTER 74

With Jennifer's file on the passenger seat beside her, Sheridan drove to the cottage. It was almost two months since Ronald and Rita Parks' bodies had been found, and the case had taken more turns than any other Sheridan had worked on.

She recalled the conversation she'd had with Jennifer, how her love for Daniel was tangible. Just like Sheridan's love for her own brother, Matthew. Both had been taken without the reason being known, and without the killer being brought to justice. Sheridan was now thirty years on from when Matthew was murdered. Would Jennifer have to suffer in the same way and for as long as Sheridan and her family had? Would she ever know what really happened? Was justice the luxury that would evade them?

Sheridan knew she was about to tell Jennifer that the chances were they would never find a motive for Daniel's murder, or the real truth behind her parents' deaths. Tony Harvey had taken his reasons with him.

Jennifer was in the front yard when Sheridan arrived. They went inside and sat next to the open fire. Sheridan went over the evidence in the case, explaining to Jennifer that the police were satisfied that Ronald had killed Daniel and Tony had killed her parents. The only thing still unanswered was why.

They talked about the possibility that Daniel knew about their mother's affair with Tony and perhaps he had told their father and that was what the argument between them was about. Perhaps Tony had killed Ronald and Rita because he thought the affair was about to come out and that could even have been the reason that Helen jumped.

The more Sheridan spoke, the more she felt uneasy. All her assumptions were simply that: assumptions. Because the truth of the matter was, no one really knew why any of it had happened and in Sheridan's eyes that wasn't good enough. But the order from above was that the case was to be closed and only reopened if new evidence came to light.

Looking at Jennifer, Sheridan felt she had let her down. 'I'm sorry that we don't have all the answers.'

'I'm going to be completely honest with you now. I sometimes had my doubts about whether my father was innocent.' Jennifer glanced at Daniel's file on the coffee table. 'I just never wanted to believe it. I stuck by him through the trial because he swore to me and Mum that he had nothing to do with Daniel's death and I had to believe him. Maybe it was a moment of anger, a moment of madness, even an accident. Maybe he never meant to kill him.' She looked straight at Sheridan. 'You said to me that we think we know someone, but do we really ever know them completely? Tony proved that to me.' She sighed heavily. 'So, that's it now?'

'Technically, yes. But I won't give up trying to find out *why* Daniel and your parents were murdered.'

Jennifer looked puzzled. 'So, you'll keep looking at the case?'

'Yes.' Sheridan nodded. 'I can't promise you anything, Jennifer, but I'll do whatever I can.'

'Thank you, Sheridan.'

'You don't have to thank me.'

'Do you have a family?' Jennifer asked.

'Partner, Mum and Dad. No kids.'

'What about brothers and sisters?'

Sheridan hesitated before she answered, 'I had a brother.'

'Had?'

'He died when he was twelve.'

'I'm so sorry.' Jennifer's voice was tinged with empathy. 'What happened to him, if you don't mind me asking?'

Sheridan inhaled. 'He was murdered.'

'Oh God. I'm so sorry. Did they catch who did it?'

'No. Not yet.'

Jennifer was clearly desperate to ask more questions but instead they sat in silence, momentarily lost in their own thoughts, and as Sheridan got up to leave, Jennifer put her hand out and Sheridan took it warmly.

'You've been amazing. Thank you and please thank Anna for me.'

'I will. I'll be in touch. I'm not giving up on this, not until I know why it all happened.'

CHAPTER 75

Christmas Day

Sam stood silently as Rosie and Brian Holler laid a Christmas wreath on Matthew's grave. The ground was still covered in a hard white frost and the grass crunched under their feet.

'Merry Christmas, Matthew,' Rosie said, resting her hand on top of the headstone.

Sam noticed she was smiling. She could feel the love for the boy she had never known, as she watched Sheridan and her parents pottering around the grave like they were tucking him into bed before kissing him goodnight.

Sam glanced around the cemetery, watching the other families that had come here today. All quietly grieving for their sons, their daughters, parents and grandparents, friends, husbands and wives. One woman, some distance away, stood with her head bowed, her outline softened by the mist of the morning light.

Sam watched as the woman turned and started walking towards the gates. To do so, the woman would have to pass them, and Sam felt intrusive watching her, so she turned back to Sheridan and her parents. Sheridan was crouched at Matthew's headstone, rearranging the ornaments that adorned his grave. She looked up as the woman walked past and immediately turned her face away.

She stood up and whispered to Sam, 'That was my boss.'

Sam frowned. 'You mean Hill?'

'Yeah.'

'She was visiting a grave over there.' Sam nodded her head in the direction that Hill had come from.

'Which one?' Sheridan asked, and after making sure Hill had left the cemetery, they made their way over to the grave she had been standing at.

Sheridan read the words engraved on the white headstone, before turning to Sam.

'Oh my God.'

CHAPTER 76

Thursday 1 May 2008

Over the next few months, Sheridan became embroiled in numerous other cases. CID were run ragged trying to keep up with the workload. There was little downtime, but whenever she could, she returned to the Parks case. She knew every piece of evidence and every statement practically by heart. It swam around her head whenever she let it in. Every two weeks she would religiously call Jennifer, trying to put her mind at rest that although she was no further forward, she would never give up. There had to be a reason for it all and, one day, Sheridan would figure it out. Whenever they spoke, she could hear it in Jennifer's voice, that trace of doubt that nudged its way in. But that only made Sheridan more determined to find the truth.

Jennifer had contacted several estate agents and had eventually chosen one who seemed less interested in the events surrounding her parents' deaths than actually selling the properties. Martin Pole didn't even mention the murders as he sat in the kitchen with Jennifer, sipping his cup of tea. He spent two hours with her, walking through the house and cottage, boasting about how he had a reputation for being the best in the business and he was confident he would sell it. When he had finished talking about himself and how fucking wonderful he was, Jennifer took the opportunity to mention that her whole family had been murdered and did he think this would affect the sale? Martin Pole told her that he had, many years ago, secured the sale of a property where the previous occupant had been found hanging from the loft and when police carried out a search, they found his wife buried in the back garden.

As they walked across the yard, Jennifer listened while he boasted about his twenty years in the business. They made their way through the brambles and stopped at the clearing beyond, where he admired the five acres of land behind the cottage.

'I'd buy this place if I could afford it,' he said. 'The fact that it has a bit of a history wouldn't bother me.' He carefully removed a thorn from his trousers.

'I don't want to be here when you show people around,' Jennifer stated, gazing up at the trees.

'No problem, leave that with me. I take it that the police won't need to come back here and start digging the place up, looking for your brother's body?' he asked nonchalantly.

'No. They did all that when he disappeared,' she responded, completely taken aback by the bluntness of his question.

'Good. Well, let's have a look around, shall we?' He smirked as he traipsed off into the woods with Jennifer in tow. 'Be a good place to hide a body though, eh?' he said, stopping for a moment to catch his breath.

Jennifer didn't respond, remembering how the land had been searched. A team of officers, scouring the area, had checked around fallen trees and rifled through the woodland, looking for any signs that the ground had been disturbed.

Martin Pole glanced at her. 'Sorry. I have a tendency to say things before I think. I'm sure there are no bodies here.' He grinned apologetically.

Jennifer turned and made her way back to the cottage, leaving him alone to take one last look around.

After walking across the land that surrounded the property, he ambled over to the large fallen tree at the back of the cottage and sat down on it. Breathing in the crisp fresh air, he inhaled the surroundings of this beautiful place. Feeling the tree's bark crumble under his touch, he absentmindedly broke a piece off and flicked it on to the ground.

What Martin Pole did know was that he would have no trouble selling this property.

What he didn't know was what was buried right under his feet. Wrapped in a white towel.

And neither did Jennifer.

CHAPTER 77

Sam quickly snapped her laptop shut as Sheridan walked into the kitchen, drying her hair with a towel.

'Do you know how suspicious that looks?' Sheridan shook her head as she put her cold coffee in the microwave.

'I'm chasing the delivery on one of your birthday presents. So, if any packages arrive, you're not allowed to open them.'

Sheridan wrapped her arms around Sam's neck. 'Is it a Porsche?'

'Yes, it is. That's it, you've guessed it, well done. Surprise ruined.' Sam raised her hands in the air and crossed her eyes.

Sheridan hugged her. 'Do I tell you enough that I love you?'

'No.' Sam grinned.

'I really do though. I *really* love you.'

'I love you too, but I actually haven't got you a Porsche for your birthday.'

Sheridan removed her arms and gently flicked the top of Sam's head, before replying, 'That's it, I take it all back, I might need to reconsider this love thing.'

Just then, she received a text from Anna: *Do you two fancy a drink after work tonight?*

She read out the text to Sam before typing back: *It's 7 in the morning and you're already thinking about alcohol, shame on you . . . Oh and yes, we would love to join you two for a drink*

Anna replied: *It'll just be me, Steve's working away for a couple of days*

Sheridan texted back: *No worries. See you at work in about an hour, you can leave a cup of posh expensive frothy coffee on my desk if you want. Please and thank you*

◆ ◆ ◆

By five o'clock, Sheridan had turned off her computer, zipped up her jacket and was walking down the corridor. Popping her head around Anna's door, she asked, 'You ready to go? Sam's meeting us there.'

'Absolutely.'

The pub was quiet when they walked in. Sheridan found a table by the window, and checked her phone while Anna went to the bar to get the drinks in. As they waited for Sam to arrive, the conversation turned to Hill.

'I take it we still don't know her real name?' Anna asked.

'Maybe Hill *is* her real name. You know, like when people call their kids River or Fountain.'

'I actually like those sorts of names. I always wanted to be called Storm.'

'Storm Markinson.' Sheridan laughed loudly, almost choking on her drink. 'Okay, what about a good name for me?'

Anna tilted her head to one side, eyeing her up and down before responding, 'Hippy.'

'Hippy Holler?' Sheridan put her drink down and they started laughing so hard that a young couple at the bar turned to stare at them.

Anna abruptly stood up. 'I need the loo. A little wee just came out.'

◆ ◆ ◆

She emerged from the toilet a few minutes later. As she walked past the main door, she noticed a commotion outside. Curious as to what everyone was looking at, she stepped outside to see people running into the road. A car had stopped at an angle and lying on the ground was a young woman. Anna quickly pushed her way through the small crowd, asking if anyone had called an ambulance, before kneeling down, gently moving a long strand of hair from the woman's face. Her eyes widened and she immediately got up. 'Don't move her!' she shouted before running into the pub, hurrying towards the table where Sheridan was now standing, peering out of the window, trying to see what was happening. She looked up as Anna came towards her.

'What's going on out there?' Sheridan asked her.

'Sheridan, quick! It's Sam.'

Anna ran, full pelt, back to the police station to pick up her car. Pulling out of the back yard, she drove as fast as she could through the traffic, taking every short cut she knew. Fifteen minutes later she swung into the hospital car park and ran into A&E, looking around for Sheridan.

'Anna.' She heard Sheridan call out behind her.

'What's happening? Is she alright?' Anna took hold of Sheridan's arms and pulled her close.

'I don't know yet, they took her straight through.'

An hour later they were sitting in the waiting area when a doctor emerged and called out Sheridan's name. She approached him with Anna by her side. 'I'm Sheridan Holler, how is she?'

'Are you her next of kin?'

'Yes, I'm her partner, is she alright?' Sheridan felt tears stinging her eyes.

'She's had a bang to the head and has a fractured wrist. A few bumps and scratches, too, but otherwise, she's doing okay.'

'Can we see her?'

The doctor looked at Anna. 'Are you a relative?'

Sheridan linked her arm in Anna's. 'Yes. She's my sister.'

The doctor gave a warm smile. 'Fine, come with me. She's a bit groggy but she's awake.'

As the doctor pulled the curtain to one side, Sam turned her head on the pillow and gave a sleepy smile. 'Hey, gorgeous.'

'Hey, you.' Sheridan stepped over to the bed and leaned over her, kissing her gently on the lips.

Sam's voice was croaky and slurred, and her eyes looked a little glazed over. 'Hi, Anna, how are you?'

Anna grinned. 'How am I? I'm fine. Glad to see you're doing okay. You had your missus worried there for a while.'

'Can you go and feed Maud?' Sam asked.

Sheridan shook her head at Anna and took Sam's hand. 'Sweetheart, don't worry about Maud, I'll ask Joni to go and sort her out. You just rest.'

'But we're going to the pub.' Sam lifted her head off the pillow, frowning.

'We'll go to the pub when you're better.'

'Yeah, okay.' Sam put her head back down. 'You get him though.' She closed her eyes.

'Get who, sweetheart?'

'The fucker who pushed me.'

CHAPTER 78

It was midnight by the time Sheridan arrived home. As she parked on the drive, she looked up to see Joni opening the front door, with the boy cat, Newman, in her arms.

'How is she?' Joni asked, her voice wavering a little.

Sheridan walked up the path. 'They're keeping her in, but she's going to be okay. So, this is Newman? Has Maud tried to kill him yet?' she asked, stroking his head as she stepped into the hallway.

They went into the kitchen, where Maud was sitting under the kitchen table, surrounded by the remains of a Jaffa cake.

'They actually seem to get on really well.' Joni set Newman down and put the kettle on.

'Thank you so much for sorting Maud out. Do you need to get home, or do you want to stay over?'

'I'd like to stay over, if that's alright, so I can go to the hospital with you tomorrow?'

'Sounds good.' Sheridan sat at the table and rubbed her face. 'You okay?'

'Not really. It was just so awful seeing her lying in the road like that.'

'I can imagine. How did it happen? Did she slip or something?' Joni put her hand on Sheridan's shoulder.

'She said someone pushed her. But then when some colleagues from the traffic unit went to speak to her, she couldn't remember saying it. Anyway, we're checking the CCTV, so hopefully we'll find out what actually happened.'

'Was it a drunk driver that hit her?'

Sheridan sighed. 'No. He was sober, and pretty shaken up by what happened.'

They sat talking while Maud and Newman became acquainted, chasing each other around the house at a hundred miles an hour.

Joni got up to make more coffee. 'Oh, a package came for you, I've left it in the cupboard under the stairs. Maud was trying to pull the tape off it, so I can only assume she thought it was for her.'

'That'll be something Sam's ordered for my birthday. Bang goes my hope that she'd bought me a Porsche.' Sheridan tried to smile but all she really wanted to do was cry. She had been assured by the doctors that Sam was going to be alright, but it didn't take away the image of her lying hurt and helpless in the road. When Joni noticed her face begin to crumble, she immediately wrapped her arms around her.

'I don't know what I'd do if I lost her.'

'Trust me, Sam's going to live forever, just to annoy everyone,' Joni said, making Sheridan smile.

◆　◆　◆

The next morning, they stepped out of the lift and made their way to the ward. As they reached Sam's bed, they found her sound asleep, so Joni went off to find some chairs. When Sheridan gently kissed Sam's forehead, she slowly opened her eyes, blinking the lights away.

'Sorry, I didn't mean to wake you.' She took Sam's hand.

'I'm glad you did. You okay?' Sam smiled. 'They've said I can come home today.'

'That's brilliant. Joni's here, she was desperate to see you.'

'I'm going to wind her up, play along with me.' She looked past Sheridan and spotted Joni coming over, carrying a chair.

Sam winked at Sheridan, before sitting up slightly and smiling at Joni. 'Thank you, nurse.'

Joni frowned as she set the chair down. 'Hi, Sam.'

'Sorry to be a pain, nurse, but could you get me some more water?'

Joni looked at Sheridan, then turned her attention back to Sam. 'I'll ask one of the nurses to get you some. How are you feeling?'

'Oh, sorry, I didn't realise you were a doctor. You were here last night, weren't you?' Sam flicked her head to one side and pulled a confused expression.

'Sweetheart, this is Joni.' Sheridan sat on the chair and tried to keep a straight face as she turned to Joni. 'They said she might get confused. It could be the bump on the head or the painkillers.'

Joni nodded. 'That's okay, I learned about this when I did my head injury course. I'll just grab another chair.' She walked off down the ward, leaving Sam and Sheridan hiding their grins.

'How long are you going to keep this up?' Sheridan whispered to Sam.

'As long as I can.'

Joni joined them and Sheridan sat there, watching the mock confusion on Sam's face as Joni talked about how they had met as children at school, how they had shared holidays and had lived together in Joni's flat in Crosby. Nights out in Liverpool, getting drunk and falling in and out of taxis. All the while, Sam slowly shook her head and rubbed her chin, until finally, she put her index finger up.

'I think I'm remembering something now.'

'Really? That's good. What are you remembering?' Joni asked eagerly.

'I remember how fucking gullible you are.'

Joni sat bolt upright and folded her arms. 'You twat. You total twat.'

CHAPTER 79

Later that day, Sheridan crept quietly downstairs, having checked on Sam, who was still sleeping. Maud hadn't left her side from the moment she'd arrived home, and was snoring loudly at the foot of the bed.

Sheridan made herself a coffee and settled in the armchair, quickly grabbing her ringing mobile from the coffee table and answering it in a whisper.

'Hi, is that you, Sheridan?'

'Yes, who's this?'

'It's Andy from Traffic. You wanted the CCTV pulled from the incident with Sam on Friday night. How is she, by the way?'

'She's doing okay, thanks, mate.'

'That's good to hear. Well, the bad news is the camera is quite a way back from the incident, but I've had a good look at it. Although the street is pretty packed. There's quite a few people walking past Sam at the time, it could be that someone bumped into her, but I can't see anything that would suggest she was pushed.'

'Can you tell if she slipped or anything, then?'

'Not really. From what I can tell, the crowd walk past her and . . . she's on the pavement one second and the next, she's in the road and the car hits her.'

Sheridan closed her eyes. 'Okay, thanks, Andy. Can I ask a huge favour? Can you get me a copy of the CCTV?'

'Will do. But keep it between us, eh?'

'Of course. Cheers, Andy.'

Sheridan ended the call just as the doorbell rang. Opening the door, she was surprised to find Hill standing there, holding a big bouquet of flowers. At that moment, Maud came down the stairs to investigate, stretching as she reached the bottom step.

'I won't come in,' Hill said. 'I just know that people are supposed to bring flowers at times like this.' She shoved the bouquet towards Sheridan. 'How is she?'

Sheridan smiled and stepped back. 'She's doing alright. These are lovely, thank you, Hill.'

'Good. Well, call me if you need anything.' She gave a thumbs up and turned to walk away.

'Hill.' Sheridan called after her. 'The kettle's just boiled.'

Hill followed her into the kitchen and stood with her arms crossed, ignoring Maud, who was busily sniffing her shoes.

'I can put her out in the conservatory if she's bothering you. I know you hate cats.'

'No, it's alright.' Hill pulled a chair out from the dining table and sat down, casually glancing around the kitchen and spotting a black and white photograph on the wall. She peered more closely at it and recognised Sheridan as a girl standing next to a young boy, with their parents smiling proudly behind them.

'I take it that's your brother?' Hill took the coffee from Sheridan as she nodded at the picture.

'Yes.' Sheridan took a Jaffa cake out of the cupboard and coaxed Maud into the living room with it before sitting down opposite Hill.

'He's buried in Birkenhead Cemetery.' Sheridan felt her cheeks flush. Although she had seen Hill there on Christmas Day, she hadn't mentioned it to her. But she had returned a few weeks later to reread the inscription on the headstone where Hill had been standing:

RALPH KNOWLES BORN 2ND MARCH 1956 – DIED AUGUST 17TH 1983

BELOVED HUSBAND AND FATHER

ALISON KNOWLES BORN 1ST MAY 1977 – DIED AUGUST 17TH 1983

ABIGAIL KNOWLES BORN 1ST MAY 1977 – DIED AUGUST 19TH 1983

NOW BOTH SAFE IN DADDY'S ARMS.

Hill's jaw tightened and she quickly stood up. 'Oh, right. Anyway, I'd better be off. Call me if you need anything.'

'We were there on Christmas Day.' Sheridan remained sitting, staring at her coffee and half expecting Hill to walk out without another word. Instead, Hill slowly sat back down and gently drummed her fingers on the table.

Neither said a word and the only sound was the ticking of the kitchen clock. Sheridan lifted her coffee mug and stole a glance at Hill, who was staring at her. Their eyes locked and then Hill spoke.

'They died in a car crash on my twenty-sixth birthday. Ralph was taking the girls to pick up a cake when he swerved to miss a cat and they were hit head on. Ralph and Alison died instantly. Abigail died two days later.' She swallowed. 'I never talk about it, and I'd appreciate it if *you* didn't.'

'Of course,' Sheridan replied, quietly stunned that Hill had told her anything at all.

'And please don't go thinking that we now have some sort of special bond, because we don't.' She got up to leave and just as she reached the front door, she stopped without turning around.

'You see, I'm angry, Sheridan. I'm angry at everything and I can't get past it. I should have been with them in the car, we should have all gone together. We were all so happy and now I wake up most mornings and think of a reason not to end it and the only thing that stops me is the job.' She opened the door and walked to her car without another word.

CHAPTER 80

Sunday 11 May

Anna felt his hand across her face and cried out in pain. 'Enough!' She instinctively shoved Steve away and walked out of the room.

'Anna, I'm sorry.' He followed her as she made her way upstairs, stopping halfway and turning to face him.

'I'm done, Steve. I want you to leave.' Carrying on up the stairs, she went into the bedroom, pulled the wardrobe door open and proceeded to hurl all his clothes on to the bed.

'Can't we just talk about this? I need help and you're chucking me out?' He went to take her by the arms, but she shrugged him off and threw a pile of shirts at him.

'You've hit me for the last time, Steve, and if you don't go right now, I'll call the police and report you. I fucking mean it.' Her voice trembled with anger.

Half an hour later, she watched out of the window as he slammed the boot shut, yanked the car door open, got in and drove off at speed. She remained standing there, shaking. For a second, she foolishly considered calling him but then her phone rang. It was Sheridan.

'Hi,' she answered, desperately trying to sound cheerful.

'Happy birthday to me, happy birthday to me, happy birthday dear Sheridan.'

Anna sat on the bed. 'Happy birthday, mate.'

'Sam's made a birthday cake and I need you and Steve to come over and help me flush it down the toilet.'

Anna managed a false laugh. 'Be there in an hour.' She put the phone down and her head in her hands.

Anna arrived at Sheridan's with a card and a bottle of champagne under her arm.

'Where's Steve?' Sheridan looked past her.

Anna knew that if she told Sheridan she'd thrown Steve out, the whole day would revolve around her, and this was Sheridan's day. She'd pick her moment, but now wasn't the right one.

'He had to go into work. He says he's sorry and happy birthday.' She followed Sheridan into the kitchen and hugged Sam, spotting the strangest-looking birthday cake on the table.

Noticing the expression on her face, Sam explained, 'It was supposed to look like a pair of handcuffs, but I fucked up the ingredients and it's risen too much. So now it just looks like a pair of boobies.' Her voice was etched with a mixture of disappointment and pride.

Anna grinned at Sheridan. 'You got a tit cake for your birthday.'

Joni arrived a short while later, followed by Rosie and Brian, and as they all settled in the living room, Sheridan opened her presents. Everyone tried Sam's cake, which she had cut into slices to hide its shape from Sheridan's parents. Maud was having a wonderful time, graciously accepting the lumps of tit cake that everyone was passing to her when Sam wasn't looking.

As Sheridan began clearing up, Sam came up behind her in the kitchen and kissed the back of her neck.

'Sorry about the cake. It tasted okay though, didn't it? Everyone seemed to be eating it.'

Sheridan turned and kissed her on the nose. 'It was delicious, darling.'

'Shall I give everyone a piece to take home?'

'No.'

Joni came into the kitchen, carrying empty plates and cups. 'So, what was in the package?' she asked, filling the washing-up bowl with water.

'What package?' Sheridan asked, scooping Maud up and picking cake crumbs off the top of her head.

'The one that arrived when old twat face here got run over.'

'Oh yeah. I'd forgotten about that.' Sheridan raised her eyebrows at Sam, who looked totally confused.

'I have no idea what you're talking about.'

Plonking Maud down, Sheridan made her way to the cupboard under the stairs and found the package that Joni had left there. She looked at the name on the front and noticed it was addressed to her and not to Sam.

'I didn't order that. You've had all your presents.' Sam frowned.

Taking a pair of scissors from the kitchen drawer, Sheridan carefully cut the thick brown tape that sealed the ends. Peering inside, she pulled out a piece of paper and read the words typed on it.

Anna came in to see what everyone was doing, leaving Rosie and Brian nodding off on the sofa.

Sheridan finished reading the note. 'Guys, can you give me and Anna a minute?' She smiled at Sam and Joni, not wanting them to think that anything was wrong.

'What is it?' Sam asked.

'Nothing. I just need a word with Anna.'

Joni and Sam went back into the living room, closing the door behind them.

'Grab me a pair of rubber gloves from under the sink. And you'll find some plastic sleeves in that drawer over there.'

'What's going on?' Anna asked a minute later, handing the gloves and plastic sleeve to Sheridan.

Sheridan carefully slid the note into the sleeve, handed it to Anna and waited for her reaction.

Anna read the note. 'Fucking hell. We need to call Hill and get to the nick.'

CHAPTER 81

Hill hurried up the stairs and headed straight into Sheridan's office. Sheridan and Anna quietly waited while she read the note.

> *I can't say who I am and it's not important, but inside this envelope is a disc. Please watch it. I was asked by Daniel Parks to keep it safe. He trusted me with it and instructed me to hand it to the police should anything ever happen to him. I have only just discovered that Daniel was murdered in January last year, so I apologise for the delay in getting it to you.*
>
> *I didn't want to post it to the police station as I was concerned it might not reach you, hence I sent it to your home address. I understand from the newspapers that you are the officer dealing with Daniel's case.*
>
> *I am not a danger to you, so please don't be alarmed that I know where you live.*
>
> *As far as I am aware, the disc is the original and there are no copies.*
>
> *I have not viewed it myself as Daniel asked me not to and I could never betray his trust.*
>
> *Regards*

'Get this to Forensics.' She handed it back to Sheridan and, pulling on a pair of gloves, she carefully removed the disc from the envelope. The three of them sat side by side as Hill slid the disc into the slot and pressed play.

They watched in silence, struggling to believe what was unfolding in front of them.

At one point, Sheridan hit the pause button and, for a moment, just stared at the horrific image on the screen, before playing it again. When it finally ended, she slumped back with her hands on top of her head.

'Jesus fucking Christ.'

Anna blew out her cheeks. 'So my guess? *This* is why Daniel was murdered.'

CHAPTER 82

Monday 12 May

The next morning, the CID team listened as Sheridan described the contents of the disc. From what she, Anna and Hill had seen, it was clear that the camera had been set up in the cottage. Judging by Daniel's apparent age on the recording, Sheridan estimated that it had been made approximately ten years earlier, when he was in his early teens.

His fresh and innocent face was wrought with pain and terror as Tony Harvey pulled his hands behind his back and secured them with cable ties. Before he raped him.

To the left of the screen Ronald Parks was visible, lying naked on top of Helen Harvey on a threadbare sofa, while Rita Parks was throwing back a drink and laughing.

She stood up and walked past the camera and out of shot momentarily. In the corner of the screen, her bare leg could be seen. Thirty seconds later she appeared again, sipping a glass of wine, and as she walked past her son, Daniel, she ran her hand through his hair, before sitting back to watch from the sofa.

When Ronald had finished with Helen, he stood up to take his turn at Daniel. While the two women sat, watching.

Tony joined them. Picking up another cable tie, he pulled Rita up by one arm and turned her around before securing her hands behind her back and bending her over. Helen looked on, smiling. At the end of the recording, Ronald was seen to walk across the bare wooden floors towards the camera. He quickly checked that the others weren't looking before he turned it off.

Sheridan's team were experienced officers, used to witnessing the horrors of what humans do to each other, but it was evident that they were all affected by what they had just heard.

Hill stood up. 'So, it looks like Daniel found this recording, possibly threatened to release it, and that was the motive for Ronald killing him. It's possibly what the argument was about the night Daniel was killed, which would explain why Ronald said he couldn't remember what they'd argued about. He couldn't say, because he couldn't admit that he'd raped his own son. As well as everything else we saw on the recording.'

Slow nods followed from everyone in the room.

Dipesh raised a finger. 'You said that when Ronald switched the recording off, he turned around to make sure no one else was looking, so it could be that they didn't know he was taping it. Maybe it was the only time he recorded anything?'

'Possibly.' Hill nodded.

'So, this is the disc that Tony Harvey was talking about at the cottage with Jennifer, before he was shot,' Rob said, rolling his pen between his fingers.

Sheridan was about to speak before Hill jumped in. 'It has to be. Tony wouldn't have known that Daniel had sent the disc to his friend. My question is, how did Tony find out that the disc even existed?'

'Maybe Daniel told him. Let's say for argument's sake that somehow Daniel finds the disc, views it and confronts Ronald and Tony before sending the disc to this friend of his. Ronald and Tony then plot together to kill him,' Sheridan said. 'When Tony went to the cottage, Jennifer told him that she had no idea about any recording, so I assume that Daniel never told her, which I admit I find odd.' Sheridan paused. 'Jennifer and Daniel were so close. They shared everything. Why would he trust someone else with the recording and not tell Jennifer?'

'Because he wanted to protect her?' Rob suggested. 'Maybe Jennifer knew nothing about Daniel's abuse. She's not in the video. Maybe it's the one thing he kept from her and that's why he never told her about the disc.'

'What doesn't make sense to me,' Sheridan said, 'is if Tony was as implicated as Ronald, then why did Ronald have to pay him fifty grand to dispose of Daniel's body?'

'Good point.' Hill did a thumbs up.

Dipesh raised his hand. 'We also have to consider the possibility that Jennifer was also abused.'

Hill looked at Sheridan. 'And that's a question you need to ask her.'

CHAPTER 83

Jennifer was walking across the yard carrying a box when Sheridan and Anna pulled up beside her. As they got out of the car, she put the box down and brushed her hands against her tracksuit top.

She smiled in greeting, but noticed immediately that their returning smiles were somewhat strained.

'How's it going with the house sale?' Sheridan asked as they walked towards the cottage and followed Jennifer into the living room.

'I've had two viewers so far. The estate agent said they both seemed keen, so I'll have to wait and see.'

She moved a pile of cushions from the sofa to make space for them. They declined the offer of a coffee and made idle conversation with Jennifer while she put the kettle on to make herself a drink.

'So, anyway, have you come with news or is this just a passing visit?' Jennifer came back into the room, blowing on her coffee before taking a sip.

Sheridan inhaled slowly, her mind trying to work out how to start the conversation about the recording.

'We know that Daniel didn't really have a lot of friends, but if he trusted someone, who would it be?'

Jennifer sat on the armchair, legs tucked under her, frowning. 'Just me. Why?'

'There's no one you can think of who he would confide in?'

'No. I mean, he had a few old school friends that he kept in touch with, but no one he was close to. Why do you ask?'

'I need to ask you a very difficult question.'

'Okay.'

'Was there ever a time that your parents were abusive towards you?'

'Abusive?' Jennifer screwed her face up. 'You mean like shouting at me?'

'I mean physically.'

'No. Never. They weren't like that.'

'Okay. How about any other form of abuse?'

'What do you mean?'

'I mean sexually.'

'You must be joking. My parents would never do anything like that. Where the hell has this come from?' She put her coffee down.

'What about Daniel? Did he ever talk about any abuse?'

'You need to tell me where this is coming from.' Jennifer's jaw tightened.

'We have evidence that Daniel was abused, sexually abused, by your parents.'

Jennifer stared at Sheridan as the atmosphere quickly turned palpably hostile. 'What the fuck are you talking about?'

'We have a recording that was made in the cottage, possibly around ten years ago. This recording . . . it shows Daniel being raped.'

Jennifer put her hand to her mouth.

'I'm sorry, Jennifer,' Sheridan said.

'Raped by who?' Jennifer's voice grew louder, tinged with anger.

'Your father and Tony Harvey.'

229

Jennifer put her face in her hands. 'There must be some mistake. Daniel would have told me. He would have told me.' She choked on her words.

'I'm so sorry.'

'Are you sure it's Daniel?'

'Yes. And the recording shows that your mother and Helen Harvey were there too.'

'Oh God. They were raped as well?'

'No. They were watching.'

Jennifer stood up and paced the room. The look of sheer horror on her face cemented it for Sheridan, that she knew nothing of Daniel's abuse. Jennifer's complete and total disbelief was too credible. Sheridan had interviewed thousands of victims and perpetrators over the years, and she could smell a fake response from a mile away. This was real. This was genuine. Jennifer didn't have a clue about what had happened.

'You can tell us the truth. Did they ever do anything like that to *you*?'

Jennifer shook her head. 'No. I swear to God.' She sat back down. 'I just can't believe it. Why wouldn't Daniel have told me?'

'Maybe he wanted to protect you.'

'Where did this recording come from?' Jennifer asked, her hands shaking as she clasped them together.

'It was sent to me.'

'By who?'

'We don't know. That's why I asked you if there was someone else Daniel would trust. He sent it to this person and asked them to release it to the police should anything happen to him.'

Jennifer shut her eyes tightly. 'Fuck.'

'I'm so sorry we had to tell you . . .'

'I don't want to hear any more.' Jennifer slowly shook her head. 'Please don't tell me details.'

'Okay.' Sheridan stole a glance at Anna.

'Do you think this is the reason my father killed Daniel?'

'Possibly.'

'He was so convincing when he told me and Mum that he hadn't done it.' She wiped her mouth. 'Now I *know* he was guilty. And my mum and Helen . . .' She burst out crying.

'Jennifer . . .'

'They were all evil. How did I not see it?' she screamed, clenching her fists.

'I think Daniel wanted to protect you from it all.'

'I fucking knew these people. My parents? And I thought of Tony and Helen as family. I can't believe they did this.' She lifted her head. 'I can't think about it. Please can we not talk about it any more?'

'Of course.'

The light was fading by the time they left. Jennifer was exhausted from the conversation and what had been revealed. After Jennifer had again declined a family liaison officer or referral for support, Sheridan told her to call if she needed anything. They made their own way out and walked across the yard back to their car, spotting the box that Jennifer had been carrying when they'd arrived.

'I'll take it in to her.' Sheridan bent down to pick the box up and puffed out her cheeks. 'Fuck me, that's heavy.'

Anna helped her and the two of them carefully carried it to the door, stopping twice to rest it on the ground and peeking inside to find it was filled with hardback books.

Jennifer gratefully and effortlessly took it from them and put her hand up as they drove away.

'You were very quiet in there, Anna. Are you okay?' Sheridan asked once they were a fair distance from the house.

'Yeah, I'm fine.' Anna turned her face away to look out of the window.

'I know you. Something's on your mind. No secrets, remember?'

'I threw Steve out yesterday.'

Sheridan pulled the car into a narrow lay-by and turned to face her.

'Why didn't you say? What happened?'

'He's just been an arsehole lately and I'm sick of his moody shit. It's over and if I'm honest, I'm glad.' She looked at Sheridan. 'I'm fine, honestly. I don't need to talk about it. It's been coming for a while.'

'Okay. But I'm going to ask you this once and only once.'

Anna looked at her. 'What?'

'You came into work once with a bruise on your arm. Was he hitting you?'

Anna shook her head. 'Do you think for one second I'd have stayed with him that long if he was violent?'

'No. But I just wanted to check.'

'Steve's an arsehole but he'd never hit me.'

Sheridan nodded, tapped Anna's hand and pulled away.

CHAPTER 84

The next morning Sam listened as Sheridan told her about Anna and Steve, and how she wasn't totally convinced that he'd never been violent, so was quietly relieved that he had gone. Although she worried that this wasn't the end. In her experience, the perpetrator usually found a strategy to wheedle their way back into the victim's life.

As she drove to work, her mind turned back to Jennifer. Although the case was technically closed, there were still so many questions that she didn't have answers to. She had asked Rob Wills to check the details of Ronald Parks' will and he confirmed that everything had been left to Jennifer and Daniel, the conclusion being that he hadn't updated it after Daniel's murder.

As she came out of the Kingsway Tunnel and headed for Hale Street nick, she wondered about the disc that was sent to her house. Whoever sent it had found out where she lived. *Had she been followed? Had someone discovered that Sam was her partner and followed her from school?* They had talked about the risks this person might pose to them and Sam was unfazed by it. She agreed, however, to be cautious when she was at home on her own and promised to stay vigilant. Sheridan's stomach flipped when she thought about anyone hurting Sam.

Arriving at work, Sheridan was just about to head up the stairs to her office when the public enquiry officer called her back.

'A package came for you this morning. I'll just grab it.'

Sheridan stopped in her tracks, waiting at the bottom of the stairs. A moment later the PEO handed her a brown envelope. The same shape and size as the one that had been delivered to her house.

'Was it handed in at the front counter?' Sheridan asked, taking the package carefully by its corner.

'No, it came by internal mail.'

'Okay, thanks.' Sheridan smiled and made her way upstairs, placing the package on her desk before heading to CID to get an evidence bag and a pair of gloves. Anna looked up as she came in.

'Morning. You okay?'

'Morning. Yeah, fine. Have you got a sec?' Sheridan asked, tilting her head towards the door.

A few moments later they stood in her office, staring at the package.

'Do you think it's another disc?' Anna asked.

'I don't know,' Sheridan replied, carefully opening it and immediately spotting the note and disc inside.

'It's another one, isn't it?' Anna said, perching on the edge of the desk.

Sheridan nodded. 'Yeah.'

Half an hour later, Hill walked in, frowning at the sight of them both staring closely at Sheridan's computer screen.

'What's so interesting?' she asked.

'Nothing much. Just going over some stuff.' Sheridan exited out of her screen. 'What are you doing for lunch?'

'I thought I'd order some truffles and have them delivered to my office by a unicorn,' Hill answered sarcastically.

'How about Anna and I take you out for a bite to eat?' Sheridan asked brightly.

'How about not?' Hill replied, before she turned and walked out.

'Why did you invite her to lunch?' Anna shook her head.

'Because I knew she'd say no and then leave.' Sheridan reopened her screen and pressed play. They watched closely before sitting back.

'What do you think?'

'She wasn't pushed, mate.' Anna shoved her chair away and stood up.

Sheridan looked again at the screen and felt her stomach turn over as the image of Sam being hit by the car played out in front of her. Her thoughts were only broken when her phone rang.

'DI Holler.'

'Hi, Sheridan. It's Andy from Traffic. Just checking you got the disc with the recording of Sam's accident. You know what internal mail's like.'

'Yeah, I got it this morning, I've just watched it and I agree with you, I don't think she was pushed.'

'Cool. How's she doing anyway?'

'She's fine, thanks, mate. And cheers for the disc. I owe you one.'

'No worries. Take care.'

Sheridan put the phone down, noticing Anna looking sheepish. 'What?'

'I used to have a thing with him, years ago.' Anna smiled. 'We went out a few times.'

'Andy from Traffic?' Sheridan raised her eyebrows. 'You've never told me that.'

Anna's smile broadened. 'He was lovely. But you know what the job's like. Everyone knows your business and it all gets a bit too much.'

'Well, maybe I'm talking out of turn here, but you've broken up with Steve – maybe you should get straight back on the horse. Give Andy a call. Just invite him out for a drink. Have you still got his number?'

'Maybe.' Anna winked.

'You've already thought about calling him, haven't you?'

'No. Of course I haven't, you muppet.' She stood up, amused at Sheridan's expression. 'You're so gullible. I promise I haven't still got his number.' She swiped a finger diagonally across her chest. 'Scout's honour.'

Sheridan shook her head. 'I don't believe you.'

Anna laughed and left the office, calling out, 'You can check my phone if you don't believe me, Detective.'

When she was gone, Sheridan's eyes remained on the empty doorway, Anna's words ringing in her ears.

And then it came to her.

She stood up and walked out of her office, spotting Rob Wills coming out of the gents' toilet. Without a word, she linked her arm in his and marched him back to her office, closing the door behind her.

'Am I in trouble?' He pouted.

'I've just had an idea, and I need a favour.'

Rob paused. 'Go on.'

Sheridan quickly wrote out a note as Rob tried to see what she was writing. Tearing the sheet off, she read it to herself before handing it to him.

'I need you to dig out Jennifer Parks' phone records from the file. But only the ones specifically between these dates. Her mobile, landline and the bookshop.' She hesitated. 'And I need you to find out everything you can about *him*.' She pointed at the name.

'Hill will do her bollocks if she finds out about this. The case is closed.'

'I know. So, it's just between you and me.' Sheridan pulled a face.

He folded up the piece of paper, shaking his head. 'Okay,' he said.

CHAPTER 85

Anna sipped her water as she pushed her half-eaten plate of salad to one side.

'You not hungry?' Sheridan asked, biting into a massive chunky chip that she'd covered in tomato sauce.

'I'm on a diet,' Anna replied, aimlessly gazing out of the café window.

'There's nothing of you, why do you want to lose weight?' Sheridan wiped her mouth with a tissue and took a swig of coffee.

'I feel fat.' Anna sighed, poking her own stomach.

'Fuck off. You're the same size as me and I'm not fat,' Sheridan replied, dipping another chip into the mountain of ketchup.

Anna nodded towards the window. 'Look. There's Jennifer.'

Jennifer's bookshop was situated just along the road from the café they were sitting in. They watched as she stopped to hand a coffee to a homeless guy who was sitting in the doorway of a disused charity shop.

'We could pop in and see her before we go back to the nick, see how she's doing?'

Sheridan nodded in agreement before cursing as a blob of sauce landed on her crisp white shirt.

They left the café and made their way to the bookshop, the windows of which were now covered in 'Closing Down' signs.

Jennifer looked surprised as they walked in. 'Hi. Is everything okay?' She looked gaunt and tired.

'We were just passing by and thought we'd pop in to see how you are,' Sheridan replied as Anna ambled around, scouring the shelves for diet books.

'I'm doing okay, just feels so strange to be closing this place down and selling up.' There was a tinge of sadness in her voice as she looked around her shop.

A customer came in and she quickly feigned a smile. The customer hesitated in the doorway, his tall frame awkward as he looked from Sheridan to Jennifer. Sheridan pretended she hadn't noticed him and turned to join Anna, who had picked up a book on how to lose weight in a week.

Sheridan browsed the shelves, keeping a discreet eye on the man as he followed Jennifer towards the back room. Their voices were too low for Sheridan to catch what they were saying. She tried to inch closer but then he reappeared, face flushed as he headed for the exit. He pulled the door open with such force that he almost hit himself in the face with it before he left and disappeared down the street. Jennifer reappeared a moment later.

'Everything okay?' Sheridan asked.

'Yeah, fine.' She waved her hand as if to dismiss what had just happened.

'Problem customer?' Sheridan pressed, trying to sound disinterested.

'Not really, just a guy who keeps asking me out,' she said. 'It's fine.'

Anna appeared and handed her the book she'd chosen.

'Please take it, call it a thank you from me.' Jennifer popped the book into a bag and gave it back to Anna.

'I really can't, I have to pay for it. We're not allowed to accept gifts.'

'Oh. Sorry, of course.'

They stood talking and Jennifer told them how she'd accepted an offer on the house and was hoping it would all go through quickly.

'What about the bookshop?' Sheridan asked.

'It's sold. There's a good market for properties like this in Liverpool.'

'Where will you go?'

'I haven't decided yet.'

They both noted the lack of energy in her demeanour and voice; her words seemed empty and pointless, as if she had lost the will to even speak.

As they strolled back to the nick, Sheridan told Anna about the man in the shop.

'Did you see him? He looked really familiar, but I can't place him,' Sheridan said, holding the door open.

'I noticed a guy come in, but I didn't pay much attention.'

'It'll come to me.'

'I'm sure it will. Anyway, I'd better go, I've got a witness coming in for a GBH job,' Anna said as she headed off.

CHAPTER 86

Rob Wills frowned as Sheridan walked in. She instantly remembered she had tomato sauce down her shirt.

'Ketchup,' she explained, raising her eyes to the ceiling and sliding into the seat next to him. 'You got anything for me?'

'You make it sound like a drug deal.' He opened his drawer and slid a thick printout towards her that contained Jennifer Parks' phone records.

Sheridan picked it up, glancing around quickly to make sure no one was listening. 'What about the other thing?' she whispered.

'I'm a police officer, Sheridan, not a magician,' he whispered back. 'I'm working on it.'

'Sorry, I know you're busy with other jobs and I've already asked you for—' She stopped.

'What's wrong?' he asked.

'Where's the CCTV from when Jennifer Parks met that guy at Lime Street?'

Ten minutes later, they were watching the recording and Sheridan paused it. 'That could be him,' she said, pointing to the screen.

She told Rob about Jennifer's visitor at the bookshop earlier that day.

'So, he's a guy who fancies her, and who happened to be at Lime Street when she was on her way to Cornwall. They have a coffee together. She gets on the train. And he leaves. You really do suspect everyone, don't you?' Rob grinned.

'Yeah, I guess I do.' Sheridan pursed her lips. 'But you said before that you couldn't find an image of him *arriving* at Lime Street, so where did he come from?'

'I could have missed him, it's a busy station.'

'You don't miss anything.' She stood up. 'Anyway, keep me posted on the other thing.' She winked at him and went back to her office to scrutinise the printout he'd given her.

CHAPTER 87

Sheridan came home to find Joni in the kitchen with Sam. Newman and Maud were at their feet, ever hopeful of catching anything that might fall from the worktop. She kissed Sam and gave Joni a hug.

'We're making pizza,' Joni said, beaming.

'Sounds divine. You staying over?' Sheridan asked as she opened the fridge to take out a bottle of wine.

'Yeah, is that okay?'

'Of course.' Sheridan poured out three glasses and took a large gulp of her own, instantly feeling the stresses of the day dissipating. Peering over Sam's shoulder, she watched her placing layers of cheese over the pizza base and suddenly let out a thunderous involuntary burp, making Sam jump.

'Pardon me.' Suddenly finding it highly amusing, she started giggling uncontrollably. Sam and Joni looked at each other, shook their heads and continued with their pizza creation.

Sheridan went off for a shower and while getting dressed, she thought of Anna and had an overwhelming urge to call her. She dialled her number.

Anna answered, 'Hi. You okay?'

'How do you fancy coming over? We've got a shit-load of wine.'

'Sounds good. I'll be there in an hour.'

Three bottles of wine later, the four women were settled in the living room and by midnight the conversation had turned to relationships, with Joni and Anna agreeing rather drunkenly that they were going to abandon their sexuality and try the lesbian thing.

'I'd make a cool lesbian,' Joni piped up. 'I've got the short hair, the boyish but feminine good looks . . . And I've spent enough time with Sam to know the basic rules.'

They all agreed that Joni had a point. Kind of.

'*You*, on the other hand, would be a rubbish lesbian.' Sheridan pointed at Anna.

'Why? All I need to do is get a haircut like Joni's, buy a pair of boots and kiss a few girls.'

'Not all lesbians have short hair,' Sam said, pointing out that she and Sheridan had long hair. But she agreed that being a lesbian did require a certain amount of same-sex kissing.

'I kissed a girl once,' Joni announced.

Three heads turned to look at her, awaiting the details.

Joni rested her head back, cradled her wine glass and continued, 'She was beautiful. Her mother was Indian, and she had the darkest brown eyes and really soft lips. I don't know if it was love, but I still often think about her and wonder what she's doing now.'

'How old were you?' Anna asked.

'Six,' Joni replied.

Sam was the first to burst out laughing, to the point of choking, followed by Sheridan and Anna. The room erupted with snorts and tears and for several minutes, no one could speak. When they'd recovered, Sam and Sheridan listened in total amusement while Anna and Joni engaged in a deep and meaningful conversation about whether they were compatible as a couple, finally deciding they probably weren't and would just remain friends.

As they all climbed the stairs, rather unsteadily, Anna stopped on the landing and before opening her bedroom door, she gave Sheridan a hug and whispered, 'Thank you for tonight. I needed this.'

Sheridan squeezed her tightly. 'I know you did,' she replied, kissing her on the cheek.

CHAPTER 88

Monday 2 June

Hill pushed three files across her desk and leaned back in her chair. She had spent the morning with Sheridan discussing several cases that had come CID's way in the last few weeks. The Ronald Parks case had taken a lot of time and resources, but now Hill needed the team to knuckle down and concentrate on other work.

As Sheridan stood up, there was a knock on the door, and Anna's face appeared. 'Sorry to bother you. There's a guy at the front counter to see you, Sheridan.'

'Who is it?' Sheridan scooped up the files.

'He says he's Ronald Parks' solicitor.'

Sheridan introduced herself to the man in the worst suit she had ever seen. Beads of perspiration sat above his top lip and his breath reeked of cigarettes and caffeine.

'I'm Nicholas Shackleton. I was Ronald Parks' solicitor.'

'How can I help you?' Sheridan asked, crossing her arms in an attempt to avoid touching his nicotine-stained fingers.

'I found something this morning that I believe you need to see.' He opened his brown leather briefcase and pulled out a large white envelope, handing it to Sheridan.

'What's this?' she asked.

'It's Ronald Parks' last will and testament.'

'We've already obtained a copy of his will.'

'Not *this* copy.'

Sheridan opened the envelope and read the contents before thanking Nicholas Shackleton and seeing him out of the station. Then she turned and took the stairs two at a time, racing to CID to grab Rob Wills before heading to Anna's office.

'What's going on?' Anna put the phone down as they stood in her doorway.

'Ronald Parks made two wills. We were only ever aware of *one*.'

'And?'

'And it could change *everything*.'

The three of them stood at Hill's desk waiting for her to read the contents of the envelope, which contained Ronald Parks' last will and testament and two letters.

The first letter was dated 14 November 2006:

> *Ronald.*
>
> *It's taken me a few years to put pen to paper and write to you.*
>
> *My mum has told me all about you and your relationship and although she never wanted me to make any contact with you, I decided to anyway. Life has been tough for her and for me and I believe you have a duty to at least try to put that right. I*

am your son and I think you owe me at least some of the life you have had, in that, I mean financially. I don't think it's too much to ask that you help me out.

If you are willing to meet with me, please ring me on the number below.

Your son,

Jason

The second letter was dated 20 December 2006:

Ronald,

As you haven't responded to my first letter, I decided to write another one. I'm not asking for much. I don't want you in my life, I just want some of what is rightfully mine. I just want you to help me and my mum build a better life for ourselves. I've seen my mum struggle for years to make ends meet, I've seen her go hungry so that I was fed. I don't want much, just enough money to maybe find me and my mum somewhere nice to live. Surely, you owe us that?

I am your son.

Please call me on the mobile number below so that we can arrange to meet. I could have just turned up at your house, but I'm not going to do that, so please just ring me.

Your son,

Jason

'How the fuck did we not know about this?' Hill dropped the papers on her desk and folded her arms, looking to Sheridan for an answer.

Sheridan explained that up until that morning, even Nicholas Shackleton was only aware of the original will made by Ronald

Parks back in 1999. Shackleton Solicitors was a small firm, situated down a tiny back street in Liverpool. Nicholas worked alone and only employed a part-time secretary. In September 2006, he had been persuaded by a family friend to take on their son, Damien, who was training to be a solicitor, and Nicholas had reluctantly agreed. A decision he had almost immediately regretted. In Nicholas's own words, he was 'a fucking liability'.

Then, on Friday 22 December 2006, Nicholas was away on business in Kent. Unbeknown to him, Ronald Parks visited the office, where he was seen by Damien. That was the day that Ronald Parks changed his will. It was also the day that Damien sealed the envelope and misfiled it. When Nicholas returned from his trip, the office was in total chaos, and he dismissed Damien on the spot. It was only when Nicholas Shackleton was in the process of closing down his business and retiring that he found the second will. And the two letters attached to it.

'Ronald didn't have to make a new will, he could have just added a codicil, surely?' Hill asked.

'Yes, but this Damien didn't know what he was doing, hence him being a fucking liability.' Sheridan raised her eyebrows.

'So, the will was never even registered?' Hill asked.

'Nope. It basically sat misfiled the whole time,' Sheridan replied.

'Surely Ronald Parks spoke to his solicitor about it at some point though?'

'He probably didn't get a chance to. The second will is dated two weeks before he was arrested for Daniel's murder. And after his arrest, I suspect he had other things on his mind, like a potential life sentence. Then, he gets released from prison in the September of 2007 and is killed two months later.'

'I guess this is the only copy as well? We searched his house thoroughly. If he'd kept a copy for himself, we would have found it.'

'Exactly.'

'Do we think Jennifer knows about these letters?' Hill asked.

'Possibly.'

Hill chewed her bottom lip. 'We need to find Jason. We need to make sure he wasn't involved with Ronald and Rita's murders.' She looked at Sheridan.

'Rob's already looking into it,' Sheridan replied a little coyly.

'Since when?' Hill snapped, throwing a look at Rob, who suddenly looked more like a sheepish schoolboy than a detective with over fifteen years' experience.

'Since I asked him to, a couple of weeks ago.' Sheridan waited for the retort from Hill.

'What the fuck are you talking about?' Hill said. 'This case was closed. So why were you getting Rob to make further enquiries?' She folded her arms.

'I remembered from the original file into Daniel's murder that Ronald had a son from a previous relationship. He couldn't be located, and neither could Ronald's ex-partner. So, I just asked Rob to make a few enquiries to see if he could find them.'

'What the fuck for?' Hill's voice was still raised.

'Because I'm not satisfied that we've got all the answers yet.'

'Oh, *you're* not satisfied? The chief bloody constable is, but Sheridan Holler isn't. Is there anything else I should know about?'

Sheridan put her hands on her hips. 'No.'

'So, that's it? You tasked Rob to find Jason and his mother, nothing else?'

'Well, there is one other thing.'

'Go on.'

'I'm going through Jennifer's phone history to see if I can work out if she's been contacting Jason. Up until now, I didn't have a number for him so I've been working blind, but now I've got a number, I can check it against her phone records.'

Hill put her hands in the air. 'Right. Well, I might as well go home, because clearly I don't need to be here at the Sheridan fucking Holler show.'

She ordered them out of her office, and they all left without another word. As Rob made his way back to CID he turned briefly to stick his tongue out at Sheridan, who replied with her middle finger before heading for the vending machine, with Anna in tow.

'What made you come up with the idea to check Jennifer's phone records?' she asked.

'It was what you said when we were talking about you keeping Andy from Traffic's number. We've always thought that Jennifer would have to have been working with someone and I figured maybe she was in touch with Jason.'

'So, why didn't you tell me about Rob making those enquiries?' Anna asked, folding her arms as Sheridan studied the chocolate selection.

Sheridan looked around and whispered, 'I never meant to keep you out of the loop, but you'd just broken up with Steve, been through an abortion and—'

'That's bullshit. I'm fine about breaking up with Steve. And we never keep anything from each other, Sheridan.'

'Okay. Look, I thought maybe you had your head somewhere else. And if I'm honest, I didn't want you to worry that I was breaking a couple of rules. Like Hill said, the case was closed when I asked Rob to do those checks and you had a massive workload to concentrate on. Just because *I* go off on one doesn't mean I have to take *you* with me. Do you want a KitKat?'

'No, I don't want a bloody KitKat.' Anna dropped her arms to her sides. 'And I don't want you to keep stuff from me again.'

'Okay. I'm sorry, it won't happen again. Do you want a Twix?'

'Yeah.'

CHAPTER 89

Jennifer had been sitting on the bench for over an hour, staring at the headstones. She looked down at the pot plants she'd brought with her, then reached inside the bag by her feet, pulling out the trowel and weighing it in her hand.

A woman with a tiny dog smiled at her as she walked past, tugging on the dog's lead as it stopped to sniff Jennifer's leg. As the woman disappeared through the gates, Jennifer stood up and, picking up the plants and the bag, walked over to her parents' grave.

Resting a hand on the headstone and using one of the plastic carrier bags to kneel on, she pushed the trowel into the earth and began to dig. Once the first plant was in place, she moved along to the foot of the grave and again pushed the trowel deep into the soil.

When she'd finished, she eased herself up, thinking as she brushed a patch of dirt from her jeans that the plants looked rather pathetic now. The evening sun was setting behind the houses that lined the back of the cemetery and a chilly wind blew across her face. She read her parents' names, engraved on the white marble headstone. Then she closed her eyes, inhaling the cold air deep into her lungs. She felt her jaw tighten as she zipped her jacket up and made her way back towards the bench, where she sat for another hour. Thinking.

CHAPTER 90

Jennifer's car wasn't on the drive when Sheridan turned off the lane.

She parked in front of the main house, switched off the engine and got out. She walked slowly to the front door, where she stood, thinking, imagining, before walking back to her car and then repeating the process. Then she made her way across the gravel drive towards the cottage, passing the door and stepping around the side.

As she squeezed through the small gap in the bushes, her sleeve caught on the thick brambles. Beyond the bushes was a small, grassy patch of ground that led to a woodland. She'd been here before but this time she took a long moment to take in her surroundings before continuing, carefully ducking under the hanging branches of trees that stood tall above her, blocking out the light. Out of the corner of her eye, she caught a glimpse of a squirrel as it leapt expertly from branch to branch, before disappearing with a swish of its tail.

Eventually, she found herself in a clearing and realised she was at the far end of the lane. Removing a twig that had become entangled in her hair, she turned and made her way back through the trees and as she reached the bramble bushes by the side of the cottage, she made a mental note that anyone could walk down the lane, through the trees and watch the cottage without being seen.

Someone could so easily have sat up in the darkness and watched Jennifer. From where she was crouched, she could see the cottage, the yard and the main house and as the light began to fade, she climbed back into her car, started the engine and drove slowly away, glancing up at the house with the CCTV as she passed, before making her way to Crosby Beach.

Twenty minutes later she was next to the Iron Man statue, feeling its rusty coldness against her fingers. As the wind blew her hair across her face, she made her way over to where Ronald Parks' body had been found and stared down at the sand. Then, taking the spade she had put in her car that morning, she began to dig.

◆ ◆ ◆

Lying in bed that night, unable to sleep, Sheridan could hear the rain on the windowpane and Sam breathing beside her. Squinting at the clock, she carefully pulled the duvet back and got out of bed, making her way downstairs, followed by Maud, who assumed she was going to be fed.

As she waited for the kettle to boil, she could hear Sam coming downstairs and took another mug from the cupboard.

'You okay?' Sam asked, yawning and wrapping her arms around Sheridan's waist.

'I'm fine. Just can't sleep.'

They sat at the kitchen table and Sheridan told her about the woods at the back of the cottage and how she had driven to Crosby Beach.

'But I thought the case was closed?' Sam asked, yawning into her coffee.

'It is, sort of, but I wanted to go through everything in my head and get a clearer picture of how Tony Harvey did what he did.'

'Did you dig a hole the same size as the one that Ronald's body was found in?'

'No. I gave up after about half an hour, I was fucked.'

'This case has really got to you, hasn't it?' Sam rested her hand on the back of Sheridan's neck.

'A bit. It's just that all the pieces don't fit together, and you know I hate that.'

They talked until it was time to shower and get ready for work. As they kissed goodbye at the front door, Sam held Sheridan's face in her hands.

'I love you, and I worry when you don't sleep.'

'You haven't slept either.'

'Yeah, but I'm a lot younger than you.' Sam pulled a face.

'Cheeky cow.'

Tuesday 3 June

Sheridan arrived at work to find everyone outside taking part in a fire drill, the smokers among them taking the opportunity to have a crafty cigarette.

Once they were allowed back in the building, Rob Wills returned to CID and pulled a sheet of paper from the printer.

Sheridan looked up as he appeared in her doorway. 'I've just tried that mobile number for Jason. The one on the letter he sent to Ronald.'

'And?' Rob asked.

'It's out of service. Can you do a check on it? See if we can find out if it's registered?'

'Will do.'

'Thanks. Anyway, what's up?'

'I think I've found Ronald Parks' ex-partner, Tanya Harris.' He smiled, waving the sheet in front of her, and she quickly grabbed it out of his hand.

Her eyes widened as she read it. 'Caroline Smith? Are you sure this is her?'

'Pretty sure. She's been off radar for a while, looks like she's moved around a lot and changed her name.'

'And she's living in Cornwall?'

'Looks that way.'

CHAPTER 91

Within ten minutes of eventually persuading Hill to allow her and Anna to travel to Cornwall, Sheridan had booked the hotel. At six o'clock the next morning, she picked Anna up and they headed south with the radio blaring as they bombed down the motorway.

After they checked in to their hotel, Anna dropped her overnight case on the floor and inhaled the view from her hotel window.

'Bloody lovely, eh?' Sheridan exclaimed as she walked in, immediately jumping on to Anna's bed and lying there with her arms and legs spread out in a star shape.

'It's gorgeous.' Anna grinned as she turned to watch Sheridan bouncing up and down before swinging her legs off the bed and standing up.

'I'll have a quick shower, give Sam a call and then we'll head out.'

◆ ◆ ◆

Sheridan and Anna could taste the sea air as they got out of the car and looked up at the tall Victorian house. They climbed the concrete steps and pressed the buzzer to Caroline Smith's flat. She opened the door, but immediately stood back as Sheridan introduced herself and Anna.

'Has something happened to Jason?' Caroline Smith put her hand to her mouth.

'No. We're here about your ex-partner, Ronald Parks. Can we come in?'

The tiny flat was immaculately clean and smelt as fresh as the vase of flowers that stood in the middle of the kitchen table, which they all sat around.

'Sorry to just turn up like this.' Sheridan took out her pocket notebook.

'If you're here to tell me Ronald Parks is dead, I already know.' Her response was polite and yet guarded.

'What can you tell us about him?'

'He was evil and I'm glad he's gone.' Caroline looked Sheridan straight in the eye as she spoke.

'Why do you say that?' Anna asked.

'Because he ruined our lives, and I hated him for it.' Her eyes filled with tears. She quickly got up to grab a tissue.

She told them how, soon after they had moved in together, Ronald Parks began to hit her. He controlled everything in their relationship, and she was rarely allowed out of the house. He would give her just enough money to buy food for herself, while he spent hours, often days, in the pub with his friends. When she became pregnant with Jason, he accused her of having an affair and always denied the child was his, refusing to support her. He threatened her almost every day that if she ever left him, he would find her and kill her. And not one day went by that she didn't think he would.

One evening, when Ronald came home from the pub, Jason was crying and Caroline was standing at the window, rocking him in her arms, trying to settle him. And that was the night that Ronald came up and punched her in the back of the head. Managing to keep hold of Jason, she fell to the floor and lay there while Ronald kicked her. All she could do was try to protect the innocent child in her arms, wrapping herself around him while Ronald's boots smashed into her body. That was the night she knew that she had to escape.

And so she did just that, finding sanctuary in a women's refuge in Liverpool before moving to one in Manchester where she stayed for three months. She changed her appearance and her name. In the years that followed, she moved from county to county, never settling and never staying too long in one place, picking up cash-in-hand jobs as she went, earning just enough to pay the rent and put food in Jason's belly and clothes on his back, often going hungry herself.

Then, a few years later, she found herself on a train to Cornwall, spending two nights in a hostel before finding a bedsit for herself and Jason. As he grew older, Jason often asked about his father and Caroline would make up stories about him, stories that weren't true. That he was a nice man but had moved abroad and she didn't know where he was.

One day, Jason told her that he wanted to find Ronald; that he wanted to meet him. That was when she sat him down and told him the truth. She told him of her guilt for not providing the start in life she had always wanted for him. And she lived with the fear that, one day, Ronald Parks would find her.

'When I found out that he'd been murdered, I realised I could finally live in peace and come out of the woodwork. I hadn't really existed up until then.' She gripped her coffee mug tightly. 'I always knew he'd kill someone one day. I just always thought it would be me.'

'You said that Ronald accused you of having an affair and didn't believe that Jason was his son. Please forgive the question but is there any chance Jason was someone else's?'

'No.' Caroline traced her finger along the table. 'I was faithful to him. Ronald always wanted me to sleep with other men. And he wanted to sleep with anybody he could.'

'Anybody?' Sheridan asked.

'He had a very high sex drive, and that was what literally dominated our relationship. He liked to invite other couples round that he knew from the pub. He'd make sure everyone was drinking. Then he'd start flirting and joking, suggesting that we could all have sex.'

'And did you?'

'No. I don't drink, and I wasn't into anything like that. But he'd talk about it constantly, calling me a prude and saying that if I loved him then I'd do whatever he wanted. I knew that he was sleeping around, and I knew that he wasn't fussy. Ronald always got what he wanted. I think people were afraid of him. He was very forward and confident, but he had a quick temper.' Caroline looked up. 'When I left him, I knew that one day he'd probably look for someone that was willing to get involved in his sex games.'

Sheridan didn't respond.

'Did he?' Caroline asked and then immediately put her hand up. 'Sorry, I know you can't tell me anything.'

'No need to apologise. So, can I ask . . . ? Did you ever have contact with Ronald's other children? Jennifer and Daniel?'

'No.' She shifted in her seat. 'No, I didn't.'

'Did you not think to come forward when Ronald was arrested for Daniel's murder?'

'No. I just couldn't. I was terrified that if I did, he'd find a way to come after me. I didn't want anything to do with the investigation, I'm so sorry.' She blew her nose and put her head down.

'Did you know that Jason wrote to Ronald?'

By Caroline's stunned reaction, it was clear she had no knowledge of this. 'No. I didn't.'

'We've recently discovered Ronald Parks' will. Attached to it are two letters that Jason wrote to him, asking for money.'

Sheridan waited for a moment for Caroline to absorb the information before continuing.

'Ronald made a specific stipulation in the will that Jason was not to inherit anything. He didn't believe that Jason was his son.'

Caroline stared at Sheridan. 'I had no idea.'

'Where does Jason live now?'

'I don't know. I haven't seen him for a while, he comes and goes.'

'Do you have a picture of him?'

'Only from when he was a kid. He never liked having his photo taken.' Caroline fetched a photo album and handed one of the pictures to Sheridan.

Sheridan studied it, immediately noticing the Parks' family resemblance. The dark hair and eyes, the striking and chiselled looks she'd seen in Jennifer and pictures of Daniel. Deciding not to mention her observations to Caroline, she slid the photograph towards Anna. 'He's a good-looking lad,' Sheridan commented. 'Has he changed much?'

'Not really, just got taller.' She smiled and closed the album. 'He's not in some sort of trouble, is he?'

'No, he's not in trouble, we just want to make sure he's okay. Do you have any idea how we could contact him? A phone number or last known address?'

'No. I'm sorry, I don't.'

'Does he live in Cornwall?'

'No. I don't know where he's living. Like I said, he comes and goes.'

'When was the last time you saw him?'

'Months ago, maybe even a year. We hardly have any contact. He just turns up and then he's gone again.'

'Does he work?'

'Yes, he does a bit of everything, odd jobs, that sort of thing.'

Sheridan pressed with more questions. Caroline told them that Jason never stayed in one place for too long. As far as she knew, he didn't have a current partner. The last girlfriend she could recall was several years ago. She couldn't remember the girl's name or where she lived. Jason had no children and few friends, none she believed he was still in touch with and the names of which she couldn't remember. Jason worked mainly cash-in-hand jobs all over the country. He rarely called her, and regularly changed his mobile number. As Sheridan tried to surreptitiously establish Jason's whereabouts around the time that Ronald and Rita were murdered, Caroline remained vague with her answers.

'I'm really not trying to be unhelpful, but I honestly don't know where Jason is the majority of the time.'

'If he does contact you, can you let him know that we just want to speak to him?'

'Of course.' Caroline took Sheridan's card.

'Has he ever been in trouble with the police?' Sheridan asked.

'No, I don't think so. Jason's not like that, he's a good lad.'

'And his date of birth is the eleventh of June 1976?'

'That's right.'

'And what surname does he go by?'

'Smith.'

Ten minutes later, Caroline was holding the front door open as Sheridan and Anna stepped outside.

'Thanks for your time, Caroline.' Sheridan smiled and was about to walk away. 'Oh, sorry, one other thing, does the name Izzy mean anything to you?'

Caroline shook her head. 'No. Why?'

'It was just a name that came up, that's all.'

◆ ◆ ◆

After they had left, Caroline went back inside and sat at the table, flicking through the photo album, running her fingers over the pictures of Jason as a child. She'd never noticed before how sad he looked, his dark hair flicked across his forehead, hiding what seemed like a permanent frown. She looked at his eyes and felt her own sting with tears.

Picking up her mobile, she scrolled through her contacts and pressed the dial button.

'Hello?'

'It's me. Two police officers from Merseyside were just here, looking for you.'

'What did they want?'

'They found letters that you wrote to Ronald, asking for money. What the hell were you thinking?'

'I wasn't. I'm sorry. Why are the police looking for me?'

'They said you weren't in any trouble, and they just wanted to make sure you're alright. I told them I hadn't heard from you for a while and had no idea where you are.'

'Why did you say that?'

'I just get paranoid about people knowing where we are.'

'I know you do. Anyway, are you alright? Did you get the money I sent you? I know it wasn't much, but I should have some overtime coming up soon, so we can put it away in our savings.'

'Yeah, I got the money. You're not working too hard, are you?'

'No, I'm fine.'

'You don't have to work so far away, you know, there are jobs here. I miss you.'

'I miss you too. But I can earn good money here.'

'I just hate the thought of you being in Liverpool.'

'Not much longer, I promise. Once I've finished *this* job, I'll be home.'

CHAPTER 92

Sheridan followed Anna's directions to the address that Jennifer had given them for her friend, Izzy, who she had stayed with while the house and cottage were being searched. Her only friend, by all accounts.

'What did you make of Caroline?' Anna asked.

'I think she was lying through her back teeth. She knows exactly where Jason is.'

An hour later, they pulled up outside. 'What do you reckon?' Anna asked as they sat in the car, looking up at the house.

'I reckon that Izzy doesn't exist. I think Caroline is Izzy. When Jennifer told me she was going to stay with a friend in Cornwall, she was actually coming to see Caroline.'

'You think they know each other?' Anna frowned.

'It wouldn't surprise me. This case is so fucking complex that I'm starting to doubt everything and everyone. But I bet your arse we don't find an Izzy at this address.'

Before they had the chance to ring the bell, the door flew open and a tall, heavily built man with thick blond hair jumped back at the sight of them on the doorstep.

Sheridan smiled. 'Sorry to startle you. I don't know if you can help us? We're looking for someone called Izzy.'

He smiled broadly. 'I'm Izzy.'

Fuck, thought Sheridan. 'Ah, great,' she said. 'That's great.'

'What's this about?' he asked, opening the straps of his crash helmet.

'We were just in the area and wanted to introduce ourselves. You're a friend of Jennifer Parks?'

'That's right. Is she okay?'

'She's fine. She might have mentioned me, DI Holler.'

'Oh, of course, Sheridan and Anna?'

'Yes. So, your name's Izzy?'

'It's a nickname. My middle name's Isambard and everyone calls me Izzy.' He smiled. 'So, what brings you to Cornwall?'

'Strangely enough, we've got a case where there's a witness living in the area and we thought while we were here, we'd pop and see you before we head back to Liverpool.'

'Oh, what a shame you didn't come earlier, I'm literally heading out to work and I'm already late. I'm so sorry. How's Jen doing?' he asked, closing the front door and hitching a small rucksack across his back before pushing the crash helmet on to his head.

'She's doing fine. Izzy, can I take your mobile number?' Sheridan took out her pocket notebook. 'And just your full name and date of birth.'

'Sure. Can I ask what for?'

'It's just that I know Jennifer sometimes comes to stay with you and if I can't get hold of her, I can try *you*.' Sheridan handed Izzy a pen and he wrote his details down:

Rufus Isambard Haughton 15/04/78

'And you're going to run my name through PNC to check I haven't got a criminal record.' He grinned as he handed the pen back to Sheridan. 'It was nice to meet you both, but I really have to go. I'm on a late shift and I really can't be late. Pardon the pun.'

'No problem. Can I quickly ask, how did you meet Jennifer?'

'At a book fair in Newquay, couple of years ago,' he replied, climbing on to his moped, his large frame almost swallowing it up. 'Why do you ask?'

'No reason. Were you ever in a relationship?' Sheridan pressed on with her questions as he turned the key.

'With Jen? No.' He winked through his visor. 'I'm not into girls,' he said, before riding off down the road.

They got back into the car. 'Shut up,' Sheridan said without looking at Anna, who was grinning in the passenger seat.

'We were just in the area, three hundred miles from Liverpool, and thought we'd pop in,' Anna mimicked Sheridan, who slapped her leg.

'Well, I wasn't expecting *that*.' Sheridan shook her head.

'Neither was I. Why are all the really fit guys always gay?' Anna sighed.

Sheridan pulled her mobile out of her pocket and dialled Rob Wills' number, asking him to carry out a PNC check on Rufus Isambard Haughton and Jason Smith. Ten minutes later he called back, confirming that there was no exact match for Jason Smith, but hundreds of possibles, which the PNC bureau would check through and update him if they found anything. They confirmed that Rufus Haughton was no trace on the system.

◆ ◆ ◆

After a rather heavy night in the local pub, Sheridan and Anna enjoyed a lie-in, before showering and heading back to Liverpool. Pulling out of a petrol station, Sheridan threw Anna a packet of crisps.

'They only had pickled onion flavour.'

'They'll do.' She tore the packet open and shoved a handful into her mouth.

'What happened to your diet?'

'Got bored.' She stuck the crisp packet under Sheridan's nose. 'Want one?'

'No ta. I'm on a diet.'

It was just before 10 p.m. by the time they pulled up outside Anna's house, having been held up by an accident on their way back. As she got out to retrieve her overnight case from the boot, Sheridan hugged her and watched her walk up the path, turning back at the front door.

'See you tomorrow.'

Sheridan smiled. 'See ya, mate.'

Once she was inside, Anna set her case down, leaned back against the wall and kicked her shoes off. Opening the living room door, she didn't see him in the darkness. Not until she turned the light on.

'Jesus.' She stepped back, gripping the door frame as he came towards her.

'No, Steve. No!' She screamed as she felt the weight of his hands on her shoulders, the force of his body against hers causing her to fall backwards and hit her head against the radiator.

'I'm sorry.' His words echoed in her ears as she slumped to the floor.

CHAPTER 93

Friday 6 June

Sheridan arrived at work at the same time as Hill, who parked next to her.

'I need a full update on your Cornwall trip. My office, with Anna, straight away. I've got a meeting to get to,' Hill said sharply as she locked her car.

'I need a quick wee first,' Sheridan replied. She hurried up the stairs, only to be met by Rob Wills.

'Morning, boss, how was the trip?'

'I'll tell you shortly. Hill wants to see me and Anna, can you let her know?'

'Anna's not in yet,' Rob called out as Sheridan disappeared into the toilets.

A few minutes later, Hill listened as Sheridan briefed her on their meeting with Caroline Smith, every now and then checking the time and wondering where the hell Anna was.

Hill agreed that Rob Wills could continue trying to locate Ronald's estranged son, Jason Smith, as long as it didn't interfere too much with his other cases. She made it very clear that the Parks case was not a priority. CID was swamped with work and so it had to be on the back burner.

'Let's face it, we know what happened in this case.' She put her hand up. 'And before you say it, Sheridan, yes, there are some discrepancies that don't add up, but I can't afford for you and the team to sit around scratching your heads over them. I will say this though. We *do* need to locate Jason, if only to eliminate him from the enquiry, and then we'll put it to bed once and for all.'

'Fair enough,' Sheridan agreed, sneaking another look at her watch.

'I take it Anna decided she didn't need to be here?' Hill sniffed.

'Sorry, boss, I forgot to tell her,' Sheridan lied.

'Well, I've got a meeting to get to.' Hill stood up, swiped her briefcase from her desk and left without another word.

Sheridan put her head around Anna's door before checking in at CID. She wasn't there either, so she rang Anna's mobile. The call went straight to voicemail. She left a message before logging on to her computer and going through her emails.

An hour passed. Still no sign of Anna. She tried her number again. Voicemail. Sheridan didn't leave another message, and instead decided to drive to her house. Something was wrong. Anna was never late for work.

As she got into her car, she spotted something in the passenger footwell and leaned down to pick it up. Anna's mobile.

She pulled up outside Anna's house and was surprised that her car wasn't on the drive. Maybe she was on her way to work? Maybe she'd passed her?

Sheridan called Rob Wills and he confirmed that she hadn't turned up at the office yet.

'That's not surprising, she was shattered when we got back from Cornwall last night. I'm off out on a quick enquiry, so I'll pop by her place on the way and drag her arse out of bed.' Sheridan tried to sound casual but inside she felt very uneasy as she left her car and walked slowly up the path to Anna's front door. It was already open. Now she was really worried.

She tentatively pushed the door even wider and the first thing she noticed were the spots of blood on the hallway carpet. Carefully stepping over them, she turned into the living room and paused in the doorway.

'Anna?' she called out, straining to hear any sound in the deafening silence of the house. Nothing but the ticking of the clock on the wall. Her eyes scanned the room, a smear of blood on the arm of the sofa, the lamp next to the house phone on its side. Her heart began to pound as she walked slowly, deliberately, into the kitchen, where a blood-soaked tea towel lay on the worktop and pieces of a smashed mug were scattered across the floor. Gripping her radio tightly, she made her way upstairs, continuing to call out Anna's name. Her bed was still made, and the other rooms appeared undisturbed. Sheridan stood on the landing, conscious that her hands were shaking, and her mouth was bone dry.

Back downstairs, the feeling of panic began to creep over her. She breathed in and out slowly, calming herself as she looked at the house phone. Pulling her sleeve over her hand, she picked it up to check the last dialled number and 99 screamed back at her. *She tried to call for help but didn't get the chance to call 999.*

'Shit,' she said aloud, wiping her mouth, putting the phone back in its cradle and pressing down on the talk button on her radio.

'Charlie Delta six-six.'

The control room operator replied, 'Charlie Delta six-six. Go ahead.'

'I'm at the address of—' She fell silent as the living room door suddenly flew open.

CHAPTER 94

Rob Wills pulled a home-made flapjack from the sealed bag his wife had put into his lunchbox.

'What's that?' Dipesh asked as he came into the office carrying a steaming bowl of soup.

'Flapjack. You want some?' Rob broke a piece off and handed it to him.

'Cheers. You want some soup?'

Rob wasn't aware that Hill had walked in. 'Yeah, go on then. Can I dip my flapjack in it?'

'There's a law against that.' Hill had leaned down to Rob's ear, making him jump. He almost fell off his chair when he saw her standing behind him wearing the biggest grin. He couldn't remember ever having seen her smile. It completely softened her face.

'Where's Sheridan and Anna?' Her face reset back to its usual snarl and the beautiful moment was gone.

'I don't know, boss,' Rob replied, dipping his flapjack into Dipesh's bowl.

'What's that?' Hill pointed at the report on Rob's desk.

'It's the forensic results from the disc in the Daniel Parks case.'

'Anything found?'

'A partial print on the Sellotape, not enough for a match and no DNA on the disc, envelope or the note.'

'Anything back on the mobile phone number for Jason Smith?'

'Nothing. It's a pay-as-you-go phone.'

'Okay.' Hill thumbed up and walked out.

Rob turned back to Dipesh. 'That was weird.'

Dipesh shrugged his shoulders. 'Says the man who just stuck his flapjack in another man's soup.'

CHAPTER 95

'What the hell is going on? Your front door was open and there's blood everywhere.' Sheridan followed Anna into the kitchen and watched as she picked up the blood-soaked tea towel and dropped it into a bin liner, before pouring bleach across the worktop. Opening the cupboard under the sink, she took out a dustpan and brush and swept up the remains of the smashed mug, tossing them into the bin.

'Anna,' Sheridan snapped at her. 'What happened?'

Anna suddenly burst into tears and Sheridan instinctively held her, gripping her tightly and feeling her body heave as she wept.

'Steve was here when I got home last night.'

She went on to tell Sheridan how she had come in to find him sitting on the sofa, his bare arm outstretched and a large cut across his wrist. He'd got up and staggered towards her, seemingly semi-conscious, and had fallen on to her, forcing her to stumble backwards on to the radiator, hitting her head. She had managed to help him up and wrap his arm in a tea towel before grabbing the phone to call an ambulance.

'As soon as I started dialling 999, he fucking miraculously snapped out of it, and begged me not to call an ambulance. But he did agree to let me drive him to the hospital. I couldn't remember your mobile number, so I tried calling your office number first thing but there was no answer and I tried again before I left the hospital. I had to use a payphone because, to top it all, I've lost my bloody mobile.'

'I've got your mobile, it was in my car. So, how is he?' Sheridan put the kettle on and leaned back on the worktop.

'He's fine, it wasn't a bad cut. The psych team are seeing him this morning.'

'Did he say why he'd done it?'

'He said he's struggling with the break-up.'

'Does he know about the abortion?'

'No.'

'Then do me a favour.'

'What?'

'*Never* tell him.'

'I wouldn't. He'd never forgive me.'

Sheridan nodded, wanting to say more but deciding to keep her concerns to herself. She knew that what Steve had done was for attention, to make Anna feel guilty and beg him to come home. She knew it wouldn't end there. Over time, he'd try different ways to pick away at her, until she gave in. This was just the beginning. The thought went through Sheridan's head again that Steve might have hit Anna in the past. Anna had denied it every time she had broached the subject, but Sheridan's instinct told her that Anna was hiding the truth. What Sheridan didn't want to do was push too hard. If she did, Anna would likely clam up and shut Sheridan out.

Anna rubbed her face with her palms. 'I need to shower and get to work. Has Hill asked where I am?'

'Don't worry about Hill, she had to go to a meeting. Why don't you take the day off?' Sheridan inspected the lump on the back of Anna's head.

'It's just a bump, the doctor checked me out.' She refused the offer of taking the day off and after they'd cleaned the place up, they made their way to Hale Street in Sheridan's car, agreeing on the way to tell Hill that Anna's car had broken down, hence her reason for being late for work.

When they arrived in the office, Rob Wills updated them about the forensic results from the disc and confirmed that Jason Smith's mobile was a pay-as-you-go. Anna's head was thumping. She threw two paracetamols into her mouth, swallowing them down with a cup of water.

By mid-afternoon, she was feeling better, helped by the massive cream cake Sheridan had brought back from town. Just as Sheridan was wiping jam off her shirt, they were summoned to Hill's office and knocked on the door to find her furiously tapping away on her keyboard.

'Take a seat,' she barked, not looking up, continuing to type with one hand while answering her phone with the other.

'I'll be there shortly, sir.' She slammed the phone down and stood up. 'I wanted to go over an aggravated burglary job that Rob's dealing with. We'll have to do it next week. I've just been called to another fucking meeting and then I'm off for a few days. I want all three of you back in my office first thing Wednesday morning.' She grabbed her briefcase from the desk and walked out. 'Nine o'clock sharp,' she shouted from the corridor.

Anna rolled her eyes. 'She is so fucking blunt. She's got a face like a slapped arse and talks to people like they're shit. Why do you think she's like that?'

'She's angry.'

'At what?' Anna raised her hands in the air.

Sheridan told her about the car accident that had wiped out Hill's husband and children. Anna listened, open mouthed.

'Jesus' was all she could say, looking at the door as if Hill was still standing there.

'So, I guess we should cut her a bit of slack.'

'How do you ever get over something like that?'

'She's *never* got over it,' Sheridan replied.

◆　◆　◆

After work, Sheridan drove Anna home and together they listened to the answer machine message that Steve had left on the house phone, apologising for his behaviour and promising not to contact her until she was ready. He'd been referred for support with his mental health and swore that he would never try anything like it again.

'Why didn't he leave a message on your mobile?' Sheridan asked as Anna deleted the message and walked into the kitchen.

'He did. I ignored it.'

Sheridan sat at the kitchen table, running her finger around the edges of a placemat while she watched Anna put the kettle on and make them both a cup of coffee. They sat talking about Steve and how Anna currently had no intention of resuming the relationship, and certainly not while he was unstable.

'I've seen it too many times in the job. He's acting like a controlling DV perp and although he's never hit me, I can see all the signs.' Anna blew on her coffee. 'I know he had no intention of killing himself – he obviously waited until I got home to cut his bloody wrist, then hoped I'd feel sorry for him and take him back. But trust me, that's not happening.'

'You need to change your locks.'

Anna nodded. 'Yeah, I'll sort it.'

CHAPTER 96

Tuesday 10 June

Sam dialled Sheridan's number as she walked out of the school gates.

'Hello, you,' Sheridan answered.

'Am I allowed out to play this evening?'

'That depends on who you're playing with.' Sheridan grinned as she locked her filing cabinet.

'A few of us are going out for a drink. It's Alison's birthday and I forgot all about it, so now I have to go and get her a bloody card and present. She likes Dolly Parton, but she's probably got all of her CDs. I was going to pop out at lunchtime . . . but someone set fire to a toilet roll in the girls' loo, so we had to evacuate the whole bloody school. Anyway, I won't be late home. How was your day?'

A huge smile had spread across Sheridan's face as she listened to Sam rambling on. 'My day was fine. You go and play. I'll see you later.'

'Okay. I love you.'

'I love you too.'

As she ended the call, Anna came into her office.

'You off home?' Sheridan asked, reaching under her desk for her bag.

'Yeah.'

'Fancy grabbing a takeout and keeping me company? Sam's out for the evening.'

'Sure. As long as we don't talk about the Ronald Parks case. Because my head's in my other jobs right now, and my brain is fried.'

'Deal.'

An hour later they were in Sheridan's kitchen, tucking into their food, deep in conversation about the Ronald Parks case.

'So, do you think that Jason could really have been involved?' Anna asked, putting her fork down.

'It's possible, but would he kill Ronald and Rita in that way, just to inherit some money? And then we've got Tony and Helen in the mix. I just wonder if somehow Jason and Daniel had been in contact, maybe Daniel told Jason about the abuse and when Daniel was murdered, Jason decided to take revenge on Ronald and Rita. Or maybe he thought he would inherit some of the estate.'

'Unless Jennifer and Jason were in touch and planned the murders together – that way, they'd split the inheritance?'

'Possibly.'

They went over the evidence, bouncing theories off each other until they were going round in circles.

Finally abandoning the dinner table, they settled down in the living room. Anna shifted a cushion to make herself more comfortable.

'Do you think you're a bit obsessed with this case?' she asked, wiping her mouth and taking a sip of water.

'No more than any other case. Why?'

'I think this one's really got to you.' Anna eyed Sheridan. 'It's not a criticism, by the way, just an observation.'

'I see where you're going with this. You think I'm obsessed with it because Jennifer lost *her* brother, and I lost *my* brother to

278

murder too.' Sheridan pursed her lips. 'You also think that because we don't have an actual motive for Daniel's murder, it reminds me of Matthew's case and the fact that we don't know all the answers to *his* killing.' Sheridan raised an eyebrow.

'That's *exactly* what I think. I know losing Matthew must have been unbearable for you and your parents . . .' Anna's voice trailed off as she noticed Sheridan had closed her eyes.

'Matthew's been gone for thirty years.' Sheridan opened her eyes and blinked. 'He'd be forty-two now, possibly married with kids, maybe he'd have gone to university and studied, made a life for himself. Maybe he would have joined the job like I did and become a detective.' She looked at Anna. 'Maybe he'd have become a scientist and found a cure for cancer.'

Anna didn't respond, just listened carefully.

Sheridan continued, 'You see, we can only wonder what he might have done with his life. We can only wonder what he might have become. Because the fact is, he never got the chance to become anything other than my little brother. And then someone took him from us. We know where he died, and we know how he died. What we don't know is who killed him and why. I'm thirty years on from where Jennifer Parks is right now, and I don't want her to spend her life not knowing the truth about her brother's death. Because I know how that feels and I can't bear the thought of someone else going through what my family have been through. There's no pain like it.'

In that moment, Anna realised that Sheridan had never really talked to her about Matthew in this way before. Whenever she mentioned her brother, it was always clinical, always about the evidence . . . or lack of it. Never had Sheridan talked about him as a little boy, whose body was found in a park. Her brother. Her parents' son. Matthew was real, not just a name in a thirty-year-old cold-case file.

'I'm so sorry,' she finally said.

'What for?' Sheridan got up.

'For saying that you're obsessed.'

'I *am* obsessed. I'm going to put the kettle on and then we're going to go through the Ronald Parks case again.'

Anna slumped her shoulders. 'Seriously?'

Sheridan kissed the top of her head as she walked into the kitchen. 'No. I'm kidding, you numpty.'

CHAPTER 97

Wednesday 11 June

It was 5.30 a.m. and Sheridan lay awake with her arm draped across Sam, watching her chest gently rising and falling. Sam suddenly let out a loud snore, waking herself up just as the phone rang. She turned, wiped her mouth and squinted at the clock before spotting Joni's number on the screen.

'It's stupid o'clock. You'd better be in some sort of mortal danger to be ringing at this time,' Sam said croakily.

Joni's voice was a whisper. 'When I went to bed last night, Newman came in the room and fell asleep on my pillow. I've just woken up and he's still there. He's never done that before.'

'That's nice.' Sam yawned just as Maud launched herself on the bed, meowed loudly and tramped across the duvet. She stopped momentarily to knead it with her huge paws before collapsing dramatically on her side, flicking her tail across Sam's face.

'I couldn't wait to tell you. I'm gonna ring my mum now and let her know.'

'Good.'

'Okay, bye. Love you.'

'Love you too.' Sam dropped the phone on the duvet and relayed the revelation to Sheridan, who decided that as she was now wide awake, she might as well make an early start.

◆ ◆ ◆

When Sheridan arrived at work, she was surprised to see Anna already there.

'Blimey, did you shit the bed?' Sheridan asked as she walked in and perched herself on the edge of the desk.

'I've got to prepare three files for CPS and thought I'd get them ready before our meeting with Hill. Typically, she's just texted me to say she's now moved our meeting to this afternoon. How come you're in so early?'

Sheridan told Anna about the phone call from Joni.

Anna laughed. 'And she *absolutely* had to tell you at five thirty in the morning?'

'Apparently so. It's quite sweet, actually.' Sheridan smiled and promptly left. She wanted to take advantage of the early start by continuing to go through Jennifer Parks' phone records. After making herself a coffee, she sat at her desk, studying them.

◆ ◆ ◆

It was gone 6 p.m., and Rob and Anna were in Sheridan's office when Hill put her head around the door.

'Sorry about the late meeting. Good to see you're all here. My office please, five minutes.' She thumbed up, and was gone.

Rob went back to CID to grab his file while Anna and Sheridan popped to the ladies' toilets. Anna emerged first and leaned against the sink, pulling a face as she listened to Sheridan in the cubicle.

'Sorry about that,' Sheridan called out.

Anna smiled. 'Farty fucker,' she said as Sheridan came out and started washing her hands.

'Thanks for last night, mate. Sorry if I got a bit heavy talking about Matthew and I know I keep banging on about the Parks murders, but talking it through with you really helped.'

'No worries. I bet you were up all night thinking about it though, weren't you? You look knackered.'

'I'm fine. It's just been a long day.' Sheridan looked at her watch. 'Could have done without Joni's early morning wake-up call.' She grinned.

'Yeah, but surely the first time your cat sleeps on your pillow is a big event. It needs shouting about from the rooftops. Anyway, I'll see you in a couple of minutes.' Anna dashed off to CID to pick up a notepad and pen. She spotted Rob, already heading to Hill's office.

'Tell Hill we'll be there in two minutes.'

'Will do.' Rob put both thumbs up.

Sheridan checked herself in the mirror, staring at her own reflection.

And then it hit her.

She flew down the corridor into her office, where she ran her finger down the pages of Jennifer Parks' phone records, checking and rechecking the numbers against the dates.

'Fuck,' she said out loud, immediately dialling Jennifer's mobile. No reply. She tried her home and the bookshop. No reply. Grabbing her jacket, she ran down the corridor, bumping into Anna on the way.

'What's up?' Anna asked.

'We need to speak to Jennifer. She's not answering her phone.'

'Why do we need to speak to her? What about our meeting with Hill?'

'It'll have to wait.'

'What's so important?'

'I'll explain on the way.'

CHAPTER 98

Hill sat with a face like thunder, drumming her fingers on the desk, making Rob Wills feel *very* uncomfortable. She suddenly stood up and marched out of her office. Rob sighed and got up to stretch. Looking out of the window, he spotted Sheridan and Anna driving out of the back yard.

'Oh shit, Sheridan, where the bloody hell are *you* going?' He put his hands on his hips and then, feeling his mobile vibrating in his back pocket, he fumbled with it before answering. 'DC Wills.'

'It's Anna. We need you to do something right *now*.'

Hill burst into CID and scanned the room, before checking Anna and Sheridan's offices. Finding them both empty, she went back to her office, catching Rob Wills on his mobile.

'Okay, I'm on my way.' He ended the call and turned to find Hill standing in the doorway.

'What the fuck is going on, Rob? Where's Anna and Sheridan?'

Five minutes later, Rob Wills pulled out on to the main road and put his foot down, weaving through the evening traffic, taking the back roads that he knew so well. Hill was in the passenger seat beside him.

Twenty minutes later, at the Parks property, he pulled up next to the removal van. Hill was out of the car before Rob could even get his seatbelt off.

Anna peered through the bookshop window and noticed all the shelves were empty. Piles of boxes were stacked in one corner and a 'Sold' poster was stuck across the window. Sheridan was on her mobile, still trying to get hold of Jennifer, when Anna's mobile rang.

'Yes, Rob?'

'She's gone.'

'Gone?'

'Yeah, the sale was completed this afternoon and she's gone. We missed her by an hour. The new people said she had a train to catch.'

The streets around Liverpool Lime Street station were rammed with cars. Sheridan had been driving around for ages now, hopelessly trying to find a parking space.

'Fuck this.' She pulled over. 'Can I leave you to find somewhere to park? I need to get in there.' She got out of the car and raced into the train station. Once inside, she quickly made her way to the rows of seats that faced the departure boards. She immediately spotted Jennifer, sitting at the far end of the concourse, unzipping her suitcase. Feeling her heart thumping, she walked slowly towards her and stopped as Jennifer looked up, clearly startled at the sight of Sheridan standing there.

'Sheridan? What are you doing here?'

'I had to catch you before you left. I did try to call you. So, where are you going?' She sat down next to Jennifer, gradually catching her breath.

'I'm taking some time out. Thought I'd travel a bit around Europe.' She stretched out her fingers, before crossing her legs and resting her hands on her lap.

'That's a shot out of the blue. Are you travelling on your own?'

'Yeah. And I'm sorry I didn't say goodbye. I was going to call you, but it's been a bit hectic. I can't thank you and Anna enough for everything you've done. I'm glad I've got to see you before I go.'

Sheridan rested her head back. 'You know, I've dealt with hundreds of cases in my time but this one gave me the most sleepless nights.'

'I'm sorry.'

'Don't be. I just wanted to get to the bottom of everything and give you some closure.' Sheridan took a piece of paper out of her pocket and handed it to Jennifer. 'It's a paragraph from the diary you kept. I've read it so many times. I never wanted to lose sight of how you felt and how much you wanted us to solve Daniel's case.'

Jennifer read the note.

Monday 5th November – Two police officers, DI Holler and DS Markinson, came to the bookshop to tell me they're reopening Daniel's case. I'm going to the police station tomorrow morning to go over my statement.

I pray they'll find out who really killed him. Maybe then we'll finally get some peace and the three of us can try to move on.

'You're an amazing person, Sheridan.' Jennifer handed the note back and looked straight ahead, clasping her hands tightly together, before separating her fingers, uncrossing her legs and then crossing them again.

And that was when Sheridan saw it: the tattoo on Jennifer's ankle.

Out of the corner of her eye, she saw Anna coming through the main doors with Rob and Hill in tow. They were all scanning the station and when they spotted her, she discreetly put her left hand out in a gesture to let them know to stay back. And with her other hand, she took her mobile out and sent Anna a text.

Anna looked at her mobile and showed the message to Hill and Rob, who immediately made the call.

Sheridan continued talking to Jennifer. 'I'm not amazing. I just do the job the best way I can. When I read that entry in your diary, it made me realise how much it meant to you that we were reopening Daniel's case.'

'It meant everything. I suppose a part of me always thought my father *did* kill him, but another part of me always wondered if the police had maybe got it wrong.' She turned to look at Sheridan.

'We didn't get it wrong. Your father killed Daniel and Tony Harvey helped him get rid of the body.'

'I know that now.'

'But in the case of your parents' murders, I think there was someone else involved. The way they were killed just doesn't make sense. Why would Tony Harvey leave them like that?'

'I don't know.'

'Did you ever have contact with your half-brother, Jason?'

'No,' Jennifer replied, frowning at the question.

'He never tried to contact you or Daniel?'

'No. We knew about him, but we never met. Why?'

'I just wonder if he was involved in the death of your parents.'

'Why would *he* be involved?' Jennifer shifted in her seat.

Sheridan was about to answer but her phone pinged in her hand. Turning away, she read the response from Anna before quickly texting back: *Are you sure?*

Anna responded: *Positive*

Sheridan closed her eyes and, feeling her jaw tighten, she continued.

'I can't prove that Jason was involved. But I'd really like to speak to him.'

Rob watched closely, taking a step forward to get a better view of Sheridan and Jennifer. His eyes grew wider, and he turned to Anna and Hill.

'She's signing.'

'What?' Anna and Hill replied in unison.

'Jennifer's using sign language.' He looked back and stared at Jennifer's hands. The slow, subtle movement of her fingers would have gone completely unnoticed by most people. But Rob knew what he was seeing because he used it every day to communicate with his wife.

'Who's she signing to?' Hill asked, looking around at the sea of faces drifting past.

'We need to get closer. Anna, you stay here. Jennifer knows you but she's never seen me or Hill.' Rob took Hill by the hand and casually walked across the concourse, stopping at the destination board. They both pretended to study it before Rob turned around to face Hill, using her to hide the fact that he was watching Jennifer.

'Can you make out what she's saying?' Hill asked, trying to scan the crowds.

'Not yet.'

Sheridan had seen Rob and Hill and knew something was wrong; she let her eyes wander towards Anna, who was on her mobile, texting. Sheridan looked down as the message came:

She's signing to someone

Sheridan didn't text back, but kept talking to Jennifer, facing forward, not giving her any indication that she knew what she was doing.

'If we could find Jason, then if nothing else we could eliminate him from the enquiry.'

◆ ◆ ◆

Rob was looking over Hill's shoulder, focused on nothing but Jennifer's hands. And then he saw it.

'Run.'

Hill looked up at him. 'What?'

'She's signing the word "run".'

'Keep watching her, don't take your eyes off her.' Hill dialled Anna's mobile number and she answered it immediately.

'Yes, Hill.'

'She's telling someone to run, you watch that side, I'll cover this side.'

Anna sent a text to Sheridan: *She's telling someone to run*

Sheridan responded: *Jason*

Anna replied: *Keep her talking*

Hill walked slowly and purposefully among the crowds, looking for anyone who appeared focused on Sheridan and Jennifer. Her mobile rang. Anna informed her that Jason had to be here somewhere. As Hill watched, she spotted a young man rising from his seat, lifting his backpack and walking towards the exit. He glanced back at Jennifer for a split second before heading out of the door. Hill could see that Rob was still watching Jennifer and that Anna had approached the uniformed police officer who was on patrol in the station. Dialling Anna's number, Hill quickened her pace, reaching the doors just in time to see the young man disappearing down the steps.

Anna answered, 'Yes, Hill?'

'He's just left, front entrance, going down the steps, crossing the road towards St George's Hall. He's wearing jeans, a white T-shirt, thin brown jacket and he's carrying a dark-blue backpack.'

'Uniform are right behind you.' Anna quickly relayed the information to the uniformed officer, who immediately called for assistance on his radio as he ran towards the exit doors. Anna raced over to Rob and grabbed his arm. 'We think he's just left. Hill's following him with uniform backup. Is Jennifer still signing?'

'No,' Rob replied.

'You stay here, keep watching them, let us know if she starts signing again. That way we'll know if we're following the wrong guy.'

Rob nodded and saw that Sheridan was discreetly watching them. Sheridan's mobile rang and she listened as Anna explained what was happening. Noticing Jennifer watching her, Sheridan ended the call.

'Sorry about that. I've got a big case on and everyone's trying to get hold of me,' she explained.

◆ ◆ ◆

He crossed the road and, glancing back, he spotted Hill following him. And then he ran.

'Bollocks.' Hill started running after him, quickly realising he was so much faster than her. She could feel her heart racing as he turned into a side street and as she turned the corner, she spotted him swing into an alleyway. He was gaining pace, so she kicked off her shoes, mentally waving them goodbye. At the end of the alleyway was a main road and she made it out in time to see him running across it, way ahead of her. At that moment, the uniformed officer caught up with her, still relaying information into his radio as he flew past and disappeared around another corner. Hill struggled to keep up. She turned into an alleyway to try and cut him off, but as she neared the end, she suddenly felt excruciating pain and cried out. Looking down, she could see blood pouring from her foot. She slipped and instinctively put her hand out to break her fall, landing heavily as she smacked her head on the pavement.

◆ ◆ ◆

Anna was breathing hard as she ran, her eyes scanning the alleyways and streets for any sign of Jason. Just as she was about to ring Hill, she spotted her lying on the ground. Anna ran over and crouched down.

'Jesus. What happened?' she asked as Hill tried to get up.

'I'm alright. Uniform are chasing him. They went that way,' Hill said, pointing. 'Go, I'll be fine.'

'I'm not leaving you. You're bleeding.' Anna noticed a large sliver of glass sticking out of Hill's foot.

'Just go. I'll be fine,' Hill snapped, wincing as the pain shot up her leg.

'Oh, for once, will you just shut the fuck up.' Anna dialled 999 on her mobile and cradled Hill's head in her arms.

◆ ◆ ◆

Jennifer reached into her bag for a bottle of water. 'If you find Jason, what will happen to him? Will he be arrested?'

'Possibly.' Sheridan saw Rob answering his phone and put his thumb up, slowly nodding to her as he walked towards them.

Sheridan stood and took a deep breath.

'Are you going?' Jennifer asked, looking up at her, smiling.

'Yes. I'm going now,' Sheridan replied.

Jennifer stood and went to shake Sheridan's hand. 'Thank you again, for everything.'

Sheridan dropped her head and then raised it before she replied.

'Jennifer Parks, I'm arresting you on suspicion of conspiracy to murder.'

◆ ◆ ◆

Anna was sitting in A&E when Hill came out, supporting herself on a pair of crutches.

'How you feeling?' Anna asked, getting up.

'Pissed off. I bloody loved them shoes. What's happening?'

'Sheridan and Rob have booked Jennifer into Hale Street custody and uniform have booked Jason in at Potters Road. Jason took a swing at the arresting officer, so for now he's just been nicked for assaulting police. We're all going back to the nick to write up our interview plans, so they've been bedded down for the night, and they'll be interviewed in the morning.'

'Good.'

'Anyway, what have they said about your foot?'

'It's fine. They've stitched it up.'

'And your head? Any concussion? Memory loss?'

'I know what you're doing, Anna. My memory is fine. So, no, I haven't forgotten that you told me to shut the fuck up.'

'You're going to put me back in uniform, aren't you?' Anna asked as she held the door open.

'Yes, I am. And then I'm sending you out on the streets to find my bloody shoes,' Hill replied as she shuffled outside.

CHAPTER 99

Early the next morning the briefing room was buzzing when Hill limped in, having impatiently discarded her crutches.

'Morning, everyone. I know we were all here until gone midnight, but we're pretty much ready to go this morning. Jennifer Parks has been arrested for conspiracy to murder, and uniform nicked Jason for assaulting a police officer. Sheridan spoke to Potters Road custody last night, to let them know the circumstances around the arrests, and Rob and Dipesh will head over there shortly to interview Jason. Anna and Sheridan will be interviewing Jennifer.'

She paused. 'Good teamwork yesterday. Right, keep me fully updated.' She hobbled out of the room and back to her office.

Sheridan and Anna made their way down to the custody suite and having checked through Jennifer's custody record, they noted that she'd waived her right to legal advice. She had slept through the night but had declined breakfast, accepting only water.

'Are you ready to interview her?' Custody Sergeant Buckland asked, as the detention officer stood waiting with the cell keys in her hand.

'Yes. We'll set up in interview room one. Can you bring her through?' Sheridan asked.

'Sure.' The detention officer nodded, looking up at the camera that displayed Jennifer's cell. She was sitting up, her legs tucked under her chin, and Sheridan noted just how small and vulnerable she looked.

◆ ◆ ◆

Rob and Dipesh had arrived at Potters Road custody suite and, likewise, read through Jason Smith's custody record. He had also slept through the night, hadn't eaten and declined legal representation.

'How's he been since he was brought in?' Rob asked the custody sergeant.

'He seems okay. He was on fifteen-minute checks up until a couple of hours ago.'

'Is he suicidal?' Rob asked.

'No. Not according to his risk assessment, but we wanted to keep an eye on him. It's his first time in custody and he could be looking at some hefty offences.'

'Has he said anything?' Dipesh asked.

'Not had a peep out of him, just nods or shakes his head. He did speak briefly when he was being booked in, apparently, so he *can* talk.'

'This'll be interesting then.' Rob looked at Dipesh, who raised his eyes to the ceiling and tutted.

'We'll go and introduce ourselves and then we should be ready to interview him.' Dipesh took the cell keys from the custody sergeant and Rob followed him down the corridor. Before opening the cell door, they looked through the wicket and noticed the blanket covering his whole body and face.

'Jason?' Rob spoke, stepping over to the bench. No response. No movement.

'Jason?' he repeated, glancing at Dipesh before slowly pulling back the blanket. He was lying flat on his back with his arms crossed over his chest. Rob leaned in for a closer look, and immediately stepped back.

'Oh, shit.'

CHAPTER 100

Sheridan put a cup of water on the table in front of Jennifer while Anna put the tapes into the machine.

'Are you ready?' Sheridan asked and Jennifer nodded.

There was a knock on the interview room door and Anna stopped, just as she was about to hit the record button. Sheridan got up and answered it.

'What is it? We're about to interview,' she snapped.

'Sorry. There's a call for you.'

'Well, it can wait.'

'Apparently it can't.'

Sheridan shook her head and marched into the custody suite, picking up the desk phone.

'DI Holler.'

'Sheridan, it's Rob.'

'Yes, Rob, I'm just about to interview Jennifer. How's it going with Jason?'

'You need to get over here, Sheridan. We've got a massive fucking problem.'

◆ ◆ ◆

Three hours later, Sheridan and Anna were back at Hale Street, still reeling from what had happened at Potters Road. Jennifer was brought back into the interview room and seemed to sense that something was wrong. Sheridan indicated to her to sit and pushed a cup of water towards her. Jennifer pulled the chair back and sat down, her hands folded in front of her, resting on the table.

As the tapes began to record, Sheridan led the interview, with Anna sitting next to her taking notes. She found herself unable to take her eyes off Jennifer, waiting for the *exact* moment when they told her why her interview had been delayed.

After the formal introductions and caution, Sheridan asked Jennifer to confirm her name.

'My name is Jennifer Parks.'

After confirming that Jennifer was still happy to be interviewed without a solicitor, Sheridan started her questioning.

'When we came to the bookshop to tell you that we were reopening Daniel's murder case, how did you feel?'

'I was pleased. You know I was. I wrote it in my diary.' She directed her response to Sheridan.

'Yes, you did.' Sheridan shifted her papers and read the entry out loud:

> *'Monday 5th November – Two police officers, DI Holler and DS Markinson, came to the bookshop to tell me they're reopening Daniel's case. I'm going to the police station tomorrow morning to go over my statement. I pray they'll find out who really killed him. Maybe then we'll finally get some peace and the three of us can try to move on.'*

She looked at Jennifer before continuing. 'How do you think your parents would have reacted? Bearing in mind that your father spent nine months in prison for a murder he said he didn't commit. Do you think they would have been relieved?'

'Yes. Of course they would have.'

'Unfortunately, you never got to tell your parents about us reopening Daniel's case. As we all now know, your parents were murdered on Friday the second of November and formally identified on Tuesday the sixth of November. So, when we came to the bookshop on Monday the fifth of November, none of us knew that your parents were already dead.' Sheridan looked up from her notes.

'No. We didn't.'

'Except, you *did*, didn't you, Jennifer.'

'What are you talking about? How could I have possibly known that my parents were dead?'

Sheridan sat back and crossed her arms. 'A couple of days ago, a friend of mine called at five thirty in the morning to tell us that her cat had slept on her pillow all night and she was *so* happy about it that she felt the need to ring.'

'What's that got to do with me?'

'I'm making a point.' Sheridan uncrossed her arms and leaned forward slightly. 'You get told that your brother's murder case is being reopened, and who do *you* call?'

'I can't remember.'

'Well, I'll tell you. We checked your phone records, and you didn't call *anyone*. Not a soul. Do you see where I'm going with this?'

'Not really.'

'You didn't call your parents to tell them. From the moment myself and DS Markinson left the bookshop that day, you didn't call your mother, your father. No one. Why was that?'

'I was probably busy at the shop and was going to tell them when I got home.'

'Except, when you got home, you didn't go into your parents' house. You instead went straight to the cottage, where you stayed all evening. According to your initial account. Why *was* that?'

'I don't know.'

'You told us that you and your parents didn't live in each other's pockets, that you often went for days without seeing each other.'

'That's right.'

'But we tell you that we're about to reopen your brother's murder case and you don't ring your parents or go to the house to tell them.'

'So?'

'So, I think the reason for that was because you knew they weren't there. You knew your parents had been taken from the house on the Friday and were dead by the Saturday morning. You knew they were dead when DS Markinson and myself came to the bookshop that Monday. That's why you didn't try to call them. And that's why you didn't go into the house. Am I right?'

Jennifer sat back, shaking her head. 'No. You're wrong. And none of this proves that I had anything to do with their murders.'

Sheridan turned the page of her interview notes.

'You have a half-brother. Jason?'

'Yes. But I've never met him.'

'Have you ever had any kind of contact with him?'

'No.'

'Did you know that Jason wrote to your father on two occasions, asking him for money?'

Jennifer's eyes widened and she put her hands on the table, palms down. 'No. I didn't know that.'

'Your father ignored the letters but changed his will to ensure that Jason inherited nothing. Did you know *that*?'

'No.'

'I'm going to move on. Now, remember that you can stop this interview at any time. If you need a break, just tell us and we'll stop. I understand how hard this might be for you, Jennifer, but I'm going to talk about the video that showed your brother, Daniel, being raped. When we first told you about the recording, you said you didn't know that Daniel had been abused.'

'That's right.'

'And we asked you if your parents had ever sexually abused *you* and you said they hadn't.'

'That's right.'

'Did Tony Harvey ever sexually abuse you?'

'No.'

'Did Helen Harvey ever sexually abuse you?'

'No.'

'Before we told you about the recording, were you aware that Daniel had been raped by Tony Harvey and your father, Ronald Parks?'

'No.'

'Are you sure?'

'Positive.'

'If you *had* been sexually assaulted, would you have told Daniel?'

'Yes. But I wasn't. My parents never laid a finger on me.'

'I know it's the hardest thing to talk about, Jennifer. No one finds it easy.'

'I wasn't raped or sexually assaulted by anyone, ever.'

'How long have you had that tattoo on your ankle?'

'Since I was about thirteen.'

'Who did it for you?'

'Daniel did it. We both had one.'

'What's the symbol?'

'It's supposed to mean strength and courage.'

301

'In the recording of Daniel's rape, there are five people. Your parents, Tony and Helen Harvey and Daniel. At one point, your mother, Rita Parks, gets up and walks off camera. She returns a short while later. On the recording, it shows a glimpse of someone's leg. At first, we thought it was Rita, but whoever it was had a tattoo on their ankle. We checked and your mother didn't have any tattoos. But you do. And it's exactly the same as the one in the recording.'

Sheridan waited as Jennifer took it in, giving her time to absorb her words. Jennifer closed her eyes and put her head down.

'Do you need a break?' Sheridan asked.

'No.'

'It's *you* in the recording, isn't it?'

Jennifer looked up. 'Can you see my face in the recording?'

'No.'

'Then how do you know it was me?'

Sheridan held Jennifer's stare before continuing.

'Yesterday when I was talking to you at Lime Street train station, were you alone?'

'Yes.'

'Were you planning to travel alone?'

'Yes.'

'Where did you learn to use sign language?'

'I don't know how to use sign language.'

'You were signing to someone.'

'No, I wasn't.'

'My colleague saw you. He uses sign language, and he saw you signing to someone. Who was it?'

Jennifer put her head back and stared at the ceiling. 'I'm tired, Sheridan.'

'You need a break?'

'No. I'm tired of these questions. Look, I wasn't abused, I had nothing to do with what happened to my parents, I have no idea how to use sign language and I don't think you have a shred of evidence to prove otherwise. So, please can I just go?'

'You used sign language to tell someone to run. You see, what we figured is that your half-brother, Jason, had a motive for killing your parents. We thought that maybe he'd made contact with Daniel and that Daniel told Jason about the abuse. Then, when Daniel was murdered, Jason planned to kill your parents, partly out of revenge and partly for the money. Then at some point you and Jason were in contact and from there, you continued the plan together. So, when you were signing to someone yesterday, we figured that you must be signing to Jason and telling him to run.'

'No.'

'And he *did* run.'

'I don't know what you're talking about.'

'And we caught him.'

Jennifer's shoulders dropped and her head went down. The room fell silent while they waited for her response.

Finally, she asked, 'Is he okay?'

Sheridan put her notes down and leaned forward to take a sip of water. She stole a brief glance at Anna, whose eyes were fixed on Jennifer.

CHAPTER 101

Rob was making a final check of his notes when Hill rang.

'You and Dipesh okay?' she asked. Rob sensed a genuine concern in her voice.

'Yeah, we're fine. Still a bit shocked though, to be honest.'

'I'm not surprised. Let me know when you're done there, and we'll have a debrief.'

'Okay, no probs.' He ended the call and puffed out his cheeks before taking a last sip of cold coffee.

Just as Rob stood up, Dipesh came up from behind and put a hand on his shoulder. 'You ready to interview him, mate?'

'Yeah, let's go.' Rob scooped up his paperwork and they headed down the corridor.

In the interview room, they waited for the buzzing of the tape machine to stop before Rob spoke.

'For the tape, can you please confirm your name?'

'Yes. My name is Daniel Parks.'

CHAPTER 102

Jennifer's dark eyes fell on Sheridan.

'It's over, isn't it?'

Sheridan nodded. 'Yes. It's over.'

'Is Daniel okay?'

'He's fine. Are you okay to continue, or do you need a break?'

'Is he saying anything?'

'I don't know. He's at another police station, being interviewed by my colleagues.'

'He won't tell you anything until he knows I'm alright. Can you tell him that I'm fine? And just say to him to tell nothing but the truth. You have to say that, because then he'll tell your colleagues everything.'

Sheridan and Anna stopped the interview and Jennifer was taken back to her cell. As expected, Daniel had refused to speak until he knew that Jennifer was alright. He had asked to speak to her, but his request was declined. Rob called Sheridan and it was no surprise to her that Daniel had said the exact same thing.

'Tell Jennifer that I'm okay and say nothing but the truth.'

◆ ◆ ◆

When they went back into interview, Sheridan asked her first question.

'So, Jennifer, are you ready to tell us from the beginning what really happened?'

'Yes. I'll tell you everything.' She sat back, took a deep breath and began recounting the full story.

◆ ◆ ◆

Daniel and Jennifer moved into the cottage when they were in their late teens. They had always loved to play in there together as children, pretending that the thick stone walls and tiny windows were the rooms of their castle. They spent hours in there, playing hide and seek, Jennifer squeezing herself into the tiny space under the old kitchen sink and trying to hold her breath so that Daniel wouldn't hear her. And it was while they were in there playing one day that they found the tunnel.

They had no idea if anyone else knew it was there, but decided to keep it a secret anyway. Their father had used the cottage for storage and the place hadn't been lived in since after the Second World War. The tunnel started under a kitchen cupboard behind a heavy wooden board and was big enough to fit an adult. When they first crawled through it as children, they didn't know where it would take them, and Jennifer remembered the excitement of their new discovery. As it happened, the entrance to the tunnel brought them out at the far end of the lane, hidden under thick bramble bushes.

As children, they had no idea that the tunnel would play such a big part in their lives. The place where they would hide and feel safe. A place where no one would find them. A place where, after Daniel had set up his own murder, he could hide, and no one would know he was there.

'We found out later that there are a lot of properties like ours, with tunnels that were used during the Second World War. People were smuggled in and out of them.' Jennifer was calm as she spoke, with an air of peace about her.

'So, after Daniel disappeared, he could go to and from the cottage without anyone knowing?' Sheridan asked.

'Yes. But he had to be careful that no one was around. At first, when the police were coming back and forth, he didn't come very often. I had to let him know when it was safe.'

'How did you communicate?'

'I was going to buy cheap mobiles for us to use, but Daniel didn't like that idea. He thought the police might have a way of tracing them.' She paused, taking a sip of water from the polystyrene cup in front of her.

'So, he let his beard grow, wore a hat and gloves and went to live on the streets. He used to sit in the doorway opposite the bookshop so I could see him. Sometimes I'd buy him a cup of coffee and leave a message inside wrapped in plastic. He needed to know what was going on during the enquiry and that's how I kept him updated.'

Anna wrote a note and nudged Sheridan's leg, prompting her to look at it.

We saw her give a homeless guy a coffee when we were in the café. That was fucking Daniel!!!

Sheridan bit her lip and continued. 'How else did you and Daniel communicate?'

'We used to sign to each other when there were no customers in the shop. And when he could, he'd come to the cottage and have a shower and a good night's sleep.'

'So, he lived like that throughout the investigation into his own murder and your parents' murders?'

'Yes.'

'Tell us what prompted Daniel to set up his own murder.'

Jennifer took another sip, settled back in her seat and began.

When they were children – around the age of six or seven – Jennifer remembered her father touching her when he came into her bedroom. She knew it was wrong. She told Daniel, who said their father touched him too. And so did their mother.

That was how it began. And it carried on throughout their early years. Then came the night of the first party. The party that would change their lives forever.

Tony and Ronald had been drinking for most of the afternoon in the main house. Rita and Helen were outside talking and joined the men when the music started up, throwing back glasses of wine. The four of them began dancing drunkenly and swapping partners, their laughter wafting through the house and up the stairs to where Jennifer and Daniel lay in their beds. It was later that evening when they decided to go over to the cottage to get away from the noise.

And it was *that* evening when the four adults had joined them.

Rita instigated the first dance with Daniel, grabbing him from the sofa and pulling him close to her, kissing his cheek while the others watched in hysterics. Then Tony wrapped his arms around Jennifer, lifting her up and dancing around the room.

Helen took Daniel by the hand and pulled him up the stairs, with Rita following behind. And while they were with Daniel, Ronald and Tony were downstairs. With Jennifer.

Jennifer went into detail about the horrors that she and Daniel were subjected to that night.

'How long did the abuse go on for?' Sheridan asked gently.

'A few years. Every time they had a party, Daniel and I knew what was coming. Then as we got a bit older, it stopped.'

'And you never told anyone?'

'No.'

'So, if the abuse had stopped, what prompted Daniel to plan his own murder?'

'It was the day that Tony came to the cottage. We thought that it was all over. As we got older it was like they weren't interested in us any more. There was the odd occasion that my father tried to touch me, but I avoided him as much as I could. My mother would get drunk a lot and if we were in the cottage, she'd come over and try to do things to Daniel. But like me, he tried to stay out of her way.'

Jennifer swallowed and rubbed her hand over her forehead.

'It was mainly when Tony and Helen came round. They'd all get drunk and come over to the cottage. They'd tie our hands behind our backs with cable ties.' She looked up. 'You've seen the recording, so you know what they did to us.'

Sheridan felt her stomach turn over. 'How did it make you feel?'

'Like I wasn't human. But we got used to it, I suppose, it became something that just happened. And when it was over and they all left, Daniel and I would just sit on the floor together, holding hands.'

'This is a really difficult question, Jennifer, but did they ever make you and Daniel do anything to each other?'

'No. It wasn't like that.' She looked down at the floor. 'Daniel and I have never had sex with anyone. Other than our parents, and Tony and Helen.'

Sheridan tried not to react as Jennifer's statement hung in the air.

'I have no feeling inside. I can't get aroused, and neither can he. Neither of us have ever had a partner. We just can't be intimate with anyone.'

'Did your father and Tony always use protection?'

'Yes. I think so.'

Sheridan flicked a look at Anna. The horror of what had happened to Jennifer and Daniel made her want to scream. She waited for a moment before she spoke.

'So, you said that Daniel planned his own murder after Tony came to the cottage one day. Tell us what happened.'

◆ ◆ ◆

Jennifer stepped out of the shower and wrapped a towel around herself. As she went into the living room, she spotted Tony Harvey coming across the yard towards the cottage. He tapped on the kitchen door and walked in to see her standing there.

'Hello, Jen, I was looking for your dad.'

'They've gone out for the day.' Jennifer held the towel tightly around herself as Tony looked her slowly up and down.

'You've grown into a beautiful young woman, Jen. We had some good times, didn't we?' He stepped towards her.

'I think you should go.'

'Don't be like that, Jen. I just want to have some fun.' He undid his belt and let his trousers drop to the floor. His eyes on her face.

'Please, Tony, just go.'

'I'm not going to hurt you, Jen.' Touching himself as he spoke, he smiled and carried on, aroused by the fact that she was watching him. 'You always liked to watch, didn't you?' He stepped forward and at that moment, he came, groaning loudly.

'We'll always be close, you and me, Jen. Always.' He zipped himself up and left.

◆ ◆ ◆

'So, Tony's sperm sample that we found in the cottage was from *that* incident, and not from the time you saw him and your mother coming out of the cottage together?' Sheridan asked.

'I made that up. I never saw them coming out of the cottage. I just had to think of something to explain how his sperm got on the carpet.' She looked up. 'I'm sorry I lied.'

'So, what happened next?' Anna asked.

Jennifer continued with her story.

When Daniel came home that night, Jennifer was still curled up on the sofa. Her face was red, and her eyes bloodshot from crying. She told Daniel what had happened. It hadn't happened for so long, and they had both thought naively that it was over. But now Daniel knew it wasn't and he had to put a stop to it. Once and for all. He started pacing around the cottage, swearing and hitting the walls, before falling to his knees and sobbing. He sat up all night, while she slept, thinking and planning what he was going to do. Then, when she woke in the morning, he told her that he had it all worked out.

He told her how he wanted them all to suffer. How he was first going to set their father up for murder and once he was locked up in prison, he was going to kill their mother and make it look like Tony and Helen had done it. But to make it work, he had to be invisible.

Daniel had gently taken Jennifer's hands in his. 'I'm going to make sure that you have an alibi for everything that happens from now on, Jen. I'm going to set him up and then once he's in prison serving life for killing me, I'm going to get the others.'

It was that night that Daniel told her about how, six months before, he had walked into the house one evening and found their father watching the recording of himself being raped by Tony and Ronald, while Helen and Rita looked on, laughing. Daniel had crept out of the house, crouching down and peering through the window. Feeling the bile rise in his throat, he watched his father smiling at the scene unfolding on the screen. When it was over, Daniel kept watching as Ronald stood up, removed the disc and slid it inside the pages of a book on the top shelf of the wooden bookcase. The third book from the left.

When his parents were out one afternoon, he retrieved the disc and took it back to the cottage. As he watched it, the hatred inside him boiled over and he knew that one day he would get them all. He'd get them all for what they had done to him. And for what they had done to his beautiful sister. What he hadn't noticed was that Jennifer's ankle could be seen momentarily. The ankle with the tattoo on. He had no idea if that was the only recording, so he had to assume it was and made a copy, returning the original back inside the book.

'Why did Daniel watch the recording?' Sheridan asked.

'Because he had to make sure that all their faces could be seen, to prove that they were all involved. And he wanted to make sure that I wasn't in the recording.' She slowly shook her head. 'I can't imagine how he felt, having to relive what they did to him.'

'Did you ever see the recording?' Sheridan asked.

'No. Daniel didn't want me to watch it.' Jennifer's eyes filled with tears again and she quickly wiped them away.

'Did you know that your father recorded what they did to you?'

'No.'

'Are you okay to continue?'

'Yes. I'm fine.' Jennifer pulled a tissue from the box on the table and blew her nose. 'Daniel told me exactly what to do and what to say after that. He was convinced that the way he planted the evidence would ensure that our father was convicted. While I was at the hotel on the first day of the book fair, he texted me about our father being in a bad mood, and he'd already told me what to say in the reply.'

'So, Daniel was the one that planned everything?'

'No. We planned everything together.'

'Why didn't Daniel just plan to kill them all in the house?'

'Because he wanted them to suffer. And *I* wanted them to suffer.'

'Did you want them all dead?'

'Yes. I wanted them to die. In the worst way possible.'

'So, tell us how Daniel set up his own murder.'

Daniel looked at the text message from Jennifer and took a deep breath. She had responded just as he had told her to. Finally, this was it. This was the beginning of it. He had to get it right. He'd meticulously planned every detail. It had started.

Walking across the yard towards the house, he could feel his legs shaking. As he stepped into the kitchen, he heard his parents talking to each other, their words slurred and loud. They were both drunk. And that worked well for Daniel.

'Alright, son?' Ronald said as Daniel entered the living room.

'Look at the state of you both,' he said, before turning to his mother. 'You're just a couple of fucking pissheads.'

Ronald got up and pushed his face against Daniel's. 'What did you fucking say?'

'You heard me. You're embarrassing, the pair of you, sitting here night after night getting pissed out of your minds.'

'What the fuck has it got to do with you?' Ronald pushed Daniel against the wall.

'That's it, push me around like you always did, you fucking pervert.'

'Who the fuck do you think you're talking to?' Ronald's face flushed with anger.

'You! You fucking child rapist,' Daniel bellowed, before storming out and returning to the cottage. *Was it enough? Had he enraged his father enough to come over to the cottage so that Daniel could start the fight?* He closed the door and left the light off, watching as Ronald came staggering across the yard and burst through the door.

'Where are you, you piece of shit?' he shouted, banging his fist against the kitchen door.

Daniel came out of the living room and walked straight towards Ronald, his fists clenched.

Ronald grinned as Daniel went to throw a punch. He caught his son's hand and twisted it up behind his back. Daniel swung his free arm around and, as hard as he could, drew his nails down Ronald's face, leaving a row of deep scratches across his cheek. Ronald pushed Daniel away and threw a punch that caught him clean on the nose, causing a flow of blood. Daniel wiped his hand across his nose and then grabbed Ronald's shirt, ensuring he transferred some of his own blood on to it, before dropping to his knees.

'I'm sorry. I'm so sorry, Dad,' Daniel cried out. 'I didn't mean what I said, I know what you and Mum have done for us. I'm so sorry.'

Ronald put his hand on top of Daniel's head and grabbed his hair, forcing him to look up.

'You're pathetic. Look at you. Call yourself a man? You embarrass me.' Ronald slapped his hand hard across Daniel's face and then left.

Daniel sat on the floor for a moment. It was working. The plan was working. He opened the kitchen drawer and grabbed the secateurs and tea towel. He rolled the tea towel up and pushed it into his mouth, biting down hard on to it before stretching out his hand. He couldn't hesitate, he couldn't back out now. Pushing his little finger between the jaws of the secateurs, he felt the agony as they sliced through skin and bone and almost vomited at the sight of his finger lying on the kitchen counter.

◆ ◆ ◆

Sheridan stopped writing her notes for a moment. 'Why did Daniel do that?'

'If there was no body, he always knew the police would question if he was really dead. So, he thought a body part would be enough for you all to think that he'd been cut up and disposed of. Daniel learnt a lot about police procedures.'

'From where?'

'We owned a bookshop. You can learn a lot from books,' Jennifer remarked, before continuing.

'Daniel let the blood pour all over his duvet and smeared it around the place. Then he stopped the bleeding by wrapping a towel tightly around it, before he bandaged his hand up. Then, after our parents had gone to bed, Daniel took my father's boots and coat, got the keys to the truck, put the spade and duvet in and drove to Crosby Beach, where he buried his finger. Then he threw the duvet in a field where it would be found easily, giving the police the evidence they'd be looking for.' She stretched out her fingers. 'Then he scrubbed the spade clean to make it look like our father had used it to maybe kill or bury Daniel and then cleaned it to hide any evidence.'

'That's a hell of a thing to do, cutting his own finger off.'

'He felt he didn't have a choice if he was going to convince the police that he was really dead.'

'Was that the same towel that you told the police was missing when Daniel disappeared?'

'Yes. He wanted you to think that maybe our father had used it to wrap his body in.'

'What happened to it?'

'Daniel bagged it up and left it in the tunnel.'

'Why didn't he just throw it away with the duvet?'

'He thought the police might be able to tell from the way the blood had congealed on it that it had been wrapped around a wound and you'd think that was suspicious. He needed to make sure it was never found.'

'What did he do with the boots and coat?'

'He put them in the tunnel with the towel.'

'Why did Daniel bury his finger at Crosby Beach?'

'Because that was where he'd planned for our mother to die. The original plan was for my father to be locked up for Daniel's murder. Daniel thought he was only killing our mother at Crosby. But when my father was found not guilty and released, he had to change the plan so that they both died there. He figured that when you found our mother's body, you'd search the area for other evidence and hopefully find his finger, which you did eventually. He knew the police would be able to tell how long the finger had been there and that you'd know it was put there around the time he was murdered.'

'Yes, but why Crosby?'

'It was a place we went to as kids. On one occasion, our parents took us there with Tony and Helen. I remembered Tony taking me by the hand and we went to buy ice creams. On the way back I dropped one of them and Tony told me to stay where I was while he went back to the ice cream van. There was a man that came up to me and asked if I was alright and if I was lost. I remember his face to this day. He had soft, kind eyes and for some reason I felt like I could trust him. I wanted to tell the man what Tony and my parents were doing to me and Daniel. I wanted to scream it out loud, but then I saw Tony coming back and I said nothing. It was the same day that my father tried to coax my mother into the sea, just to put her toe in the water. She was panicking and getting really upset.'

'What was she upset about?'

'She was terrified of water.'

Sheridan had advised Jennifer that now would be a good time for a break. Anna watched the detention officer escort Jennifer back to her cell, before making her way upstairs for a quick briefing with Hill and Sheridan.

'Can I get you a drink?' the detention officer asked.

'A cup of tea would be lovely. What's your name?' Jennifer asked, as the detention officer was about to close the cell door.

'Eve.'

'Do you enjoy your job, Eve?' Jennifer said, standing in the middle of the cell.

'It's okay.'

'Is the money good?'

Eve smiled. 'It pays the bills. Just.'

'It's ironic, isn't it?'

'What is?'

'You're out there, free as a bird and just managing to scrape by. And I'm locked up in here with a shit-load of money in the bank.'

Eve hesitated in the doorway. 'What's your point?'

'Just food for thought.' Jennifer shrugged her shoulders and smiled.

'I hope you're not hinting that I could be bribed into letting you escape.'

'Of course not.'

'I've been doing this job a long time. Trust me, I've been offered all sorts over the years and there isn't enough money in the world that would tempt me to let a prisoner go.'

'I think you'd be surprised, Eve. People do strange things for money.'

'Do you want sugar in your tea?'

'Yes, please.'

Eve closed the heavy cell door, briefly glancing back at Jennifer through the wicket before snapping it shut.

Half an hour later, they were back in the interview room. Sheridan reminded Jennifer that she was still under caution before continuing.

'Did Daniel know that the house down the lane had CCTV?'

'Yes. We knew Mr and Mrs Atherton from when we were kids, and we knew they had the cameras installed a few years ago. Then my father had some building equipment stolen out of the yard and Daniel was there when the police came to take the details. They told us that they'd checked the CCTV and although there was a dark image of someone lurking around on there, it wasn't clear enough to make out anyone's face. So, when Daniel drove our father's truck out of the yard and back that night, he knew you'd see it on the camera, and you'd think it was my father driving.'

'So, moving on to when Daniel set Tony up for killing your parents, he wouldn't have known that the CCTV was fifteen minutes fast,' Sheridan said, unconsciously tapping her thumb on the table.

'Yes, he *did* know. It was him that changed the time on it to make it look like the texts that he sent between my father's phone and Tony's phone were made *before* Tony arrived at the house.'

'How did Daniel get into the Athertons' property?'

'They were visiting their son in Germany, and we knew they kept a key in the back garden. So, while they were away, Daniel got into the house and changed the time on the cameras.'

Sheridan tried not to react but knew Anna was probably thinking the same thing. *Very clever.*

'During your father's trial, you supported him. Why?' Anna asked.

'It was purely pretence. I had to convince my parents that I was on their side. I needed to be able to stay in the cottage because Daniel needed a place that he could come and go to safely and not be seen. If I'd turned against my parents, then my father might have thrown me out of the cottage, in which case Daniel's plan would never work.'

'So, during the time your father was on trial, Daniel was living on the streets?'

'Yes, but he came to the cottage whenever he could. I'd let him know when it was safe, and he'd come and spend the night. We'd talk about what was happening in the trial. Daniel was confident that he'd set our father up perfectly and the jury would find him guilty. So, when we managed to spend time together, we'd talk through his next plan, which was to kill our mother and set Tony and Helen up for it.'

'What was the plan?'

'He was going to wait until we knew that Tony and Helen were coming over, then he would tie our mother up before they got there. When Tony and Helen arrived, he'd tie *them* up too, before making them all watch the recording of what they did to him. Then, leave Tony and Helen tied up in the house, put my mother in the boot of Tony's car, drive to Crosby Beach and strap her to the Iron Man. Then drive back to the house and tell Tony and Helen that if they ever told the police what had happened, he'd release the disc to the police. He was going to tell them to disappear. He wanted them to run so that it looked like they'd killed my mother. Daniel knew the CCTV would show Tony's car arriving at the house and leaving a short while later. He also knew that there would be sand in the car, which the police would match to the sand at Crosby.'

'Why not just kill Tony and Helen?'

'Because then the police wouldn't have a suspect. This way, Tony and Helen were the suspects, and they were going to spend their lives running, terrified that the police would catch up with them and arrest them for our mother's murder. They were never going to get away with it. And they were never going to tell the police that Daniel was alive because then the disc would be released, and they'd be fucked anyway.'

'So, when your father was found not guilty, Daniel had to change his plan.'

'Yes. But the basic plan was the same, except that Daniel had to work out how to get them all together and overpower them one by one. So, a week or so before, my parents told me that Tony and Helen were coming over for the evening and Daniel knew that was the perfect opportunity. On the day he did it, he waited until my father went out, which gave him the chance to get into the house and tie our mother up. Then when our father came home, he tied *him* up. Then he made my father ring Tony on the pretence that they were going to turn the evening into one of their sessions and asked him to pick up the cable ties on the way. Of course, when Tony arrived on his own, Daniel had to rethink the plan again. Once Tony was there and they were all tied up, Daniel sent the texts between my father and Tony, talking about the money my father had paid Tony and asking where Daniel's body was. He even put a clue in the text messages for the police to see, about where parts of Daniel's body could be found.'

'Another place.' Sheridan nodded, putting her head down, making a mental note to remind Sam what a genius she was.

'Yes. He knew someone would work it out and probably search near to where you would find my parents' bodies. Then you'd assume that Daniel's body was cut up into bits and scattered across Crosby Beach. He also figured out that because of the tides, it would be almost impossible for the police to search the whole beach, but as long as you found the finger, then you had a body part.'

Sheridan sat back and put her pen down, gathering her thoughts.

'Why did your father pay Tony thirty thousand pounds?'

'It *was* actually money he already owed him from a few years back, a loan. So that bit was actually true. Daniel knew about the loan, and he also knew that our father had paid Tony back, so when Daniel sent the texts between my father's phone and Tony's phone, he worded it so that you would think Tony had been paid to get rid of Daniel's body.'

'How did Daniel manage to get everyone to comply, once they were in the house?'

'He threatened them with a knife.'

'Tell us exactly what happened.'

◆ ◆ ◆

Daniel stepped into the kitchen and silently watched his mother at the sink, her back to him. She turned and gasped at the sight of him standing there, silent and motionless.

'Daniel?' She took a step towards him, clasping a hand to her mouth in shock.

'Hello, Mother.'

'What the fuck . . . We thought you were dead.' She hadn't noticed that his hands were behind his back, gripping the lorry straps he'd taken from the shed. Lunging towards her, he whipped the first strap over her head and pulled it down, securing her arms tightly by her sides.

'What are you doing?' she screamed, looking down in confusion at the strap as he dragged her into the living room and quickly secured her legs with a second strap. All the while she was screaming his name.

When he pulled duct tape out of his pocket and tore a strip off, she began to shake her head violently from side to side.

'Please, Daniel . . . please no,' she begged him.

'Stay still or I swear I'll slit your fucking throat.' He knelt on her legs and used the weight of his own body to hold her there, while he stuck the tape across her mouth to drown out a final scream.

'We're going to wait for my father now.' Just as he stood up, he could see Ronald's car pull on to the drive. As soon as Ronald entered the living room, Daniel jumped him from behind and wrestled to get his arms strapped up before shoving him roughly on to the sofa. Ronald was kicking out as hard as he could. He stopped kicking when Daniel suddenly held a knife to his face.

'Daniel? What's happening?' Ronald's voice was broken, brittle with terror.

'Stay still and I'll let you live.' Daniel grabbed Ronald's legs and secured the second strap around them, ignoring his father's pathetic cries.

Once he'd tightened the straps, Daniel stood back, taking in the sight before him. It was the first time he had ever seen fear in his father's eyes. Leaning forward, with the knife in his hand, he smiled. 'Well, look at the two of you. All strapped up. Isn't this fun?'

His wild eyes focused on Rita for a moment. Taking a step towards her, he tapped the knife against her face. She shrank back in horror, trying to recede further into the sofa. But there was nowhere to go.

'Calm down, Mother,' Daniel said as he ran his hand through her hair. 'What time are Tony and Helen coming round for dinner?'

'In about an hour. What's going on, son? Please let's sort this out,' Ronald pleaded.

Daniel leaned into his father, their faces just inches apart. 'We *are* going to sort this out and you're both going to live. But first, you're going to call Tony and Helen. And if you don't say exactly what I tell you to say then I will kill my mother right in front of you and then I'll kill *you*. Father.'

Ronald listened as Daniel told him the exact conversation that he was going to have with Tony and Helen. Daniel made him recite the words over and over again, until he had it verbatim.

And then, taking Ronald's mobile, Daniel rang Tony's number and put the call on loudspeaker.

'Ron, how's it going?' Tony answered cheerfully.

'Hello, Tony. All good, thanks. Looking forward to tonight, just checking you're still coming?'

'Yes, absolutely. We're just getting ready, should be there in an hour or so.'

'Perfect. Me and Rita were actually wondering if you fancied some fun tonight. Like the old days? Just the four of us.'

Tony laughed. 'Bloody hell, I wasn't expecting *that*. Sounds good to me. Getting a fucking hard-on already.'

'Me too. Can you do us a favour, stop on the way and pick up some of those cable ties we like?' Ronald asked, feeling the tip of the knife against his neck.

'Consider it done. Looking forward to *this*.'

'Us, too. See you both soon.'

'Okay.'

Daniel ended the call and pulled off another strip of duct tape.

'Daniel, please just stop for a minute.' Ronald began to cry. 'You can have whatever you want, just don't hurt us.'

'There's nothing you have that I want. You took everything from me and Jennifer and now I'm going to put that right. Stop crying, you piece of shit. I'm not going to kill you. I'm just going to have some fun.' Daniel wrapped the duct tape across Ronald's mouth.

Turning to the DVD player, he slid the disc inside, ready to play.

They sat in muffled silence as they waited for Tony and Helen to arrive. When their car pulled up, Tony was alone.

'Shit,' Daniel said under his breath. *Where the fuck is Helen?*

He watched as Tony got out of the car and noticed a carrier bag in his hand. *He brought the cable ties. That's good.*

As Tony stepped into the living room, Daniel grabbed him and held the knife to his throat.

'Hello, Tony.'

'God. What the fuck?' Tony dropped the carrier bag and froze, as he slowly registered that Ronald and Rita were strapped and gagged before him.

'Turn around and face the wall or I'll kill you here and now,' Daniel said calmly.

Tony immediately complied and turned around, unable to resist as Daniel threw the strap over his head and pulled it tight around his torso, securing his arms at his sides before strapping his legs together. He then slipped Tony's mobile out of his back pocket, pushed him to the sofa and placed his phone on the coffee table next to Ronald's.

'Where's Helen?' Daniel asked abruptly.

'She's gone into town. What's fucking happening here? Everyone thought you were dead, Daniel. I can't believe—'

'Is Helen joining us later?' Daniel cut in.

'No. She changed her mind about coming.'

'Why?'

'She didn't fancy it.'

Daniel burst out laughing. 'She didn't fancy one of your sessions. Is that what you mean?'

No reply.

Quickly checking the time, Daniel picked up Ronald and Tony's mobiles and began sending the back-and-forth texts between them:

Ronald: *You're not getting another penny until you tell me where Daniel's body is*

Tony: *You said you didn't want to know what I did with him*

Ronald: *The police were supposed to have found him by now, this needs to be put to bed, it needs to end, where is he?*

Tony: *Most of him is in one place and a bit in another place*

Ronald: *Did you cut him up?*

Tony: *I tried, I'll tell you everything, but I want the other twenty, I'm just around the corner, get on to your bank.*

Daniel set the mobiles down on the coffee table. 'Right then, let's watch a little home movie that my father made a few years ago, shall we?'

When Ronald closed his eyes, Daniel stepped over to him. 'I'll cut your eyelids off if I have to. You *are* going to watch. I know you enjoy reliving what you did, Father. I know you watch this when Mother's gone to bed. So now we can all watch together.'

Ronald obediently opened his eyes before Daniel continued.

'I want you all to see what you did. I want you to always remember that you destroyed me and Jennifer. I wanted to kill you all, but that would be letting you off too easily. If I let you live, then you'll spend the rest of your lives never knowing when I'm going to appear again. I want you to live with the same fear that Jennifer and I have lived with all our lives.'

The room was silent apart from the sound of Rita sobbing through the duct tape. She looked absolutely terrified. And so did Ronald and Tony. Daniel knew he had to play it right. He had to make them believe that he wasn't going to kill them. He needed Tony to drive them to Crosby and if Tony thought he was going to die, then he would never comply.

At that moment, he pressed play on the DVD player.

Daniel watched their faces distort with fear as the recording played out in front of them. The horror of what they had done, right there on the screen. When it was over, he removed the disc before turning to his father.

'How many times did you record what you all did? Was it more than once? Are there any more discs?'

His father shook his head from side to side as Daniel leaned over him. 'I don't believe you.'

Ronald shook his head again, his eyes streaming with tears.

Daniel turned to Tony. 'You're going to make a call to Helen and I'm going to tell you exactly what to say.'

Just as he did with Ronald, Daniel made Tony go through the conversation he was about to have with his wife. Word by word. Sentence by sentence. Until he had it right.

When he was ready, Daniel put the call on loudspeaker and held it up to Tony's face.

Helen answered, 'Hiya. How's it going? You having fun?'

'Where are you?'

'Right now, I'm treating myself to a rather nice meal in The 180 Restaurant. Oh, and flirting with a rather handsome married man.' She laughed.

'You're missing out on all the fun. Come over to the house.'

'I don't want to, I'm really not in the mood.'

'Please come over, we've got a fantastic surprise for you, you have to come.'

'What surprise?'

'You'll see when you get here.'

'Tony, I really don't want to come. I've just ordered some food. You stay and enjoy yourself though.'

'Please, Helen.'

'No, Tony. I'm not coming. End of.'

There was a silence as Daniel held up the piece of paper. The note he'd prepared for Tony to read out, should Helen not be tempted to join them at the house.

'Are you still there? You sound weird, what's going on?' Helen asked.

'Helen, listen to me. We're all in the shit. There's a recording of what we did to Jennifer and Daniel, when we raped them. The police are on their way. You need to come to Ronald and Rita's right now.'

'What the fuck are you talking about? What recording?'

'Ronald taped us. The video shows what we did to Daniel and Jennifer. We're all fucked. You need to come to the house.'

327

'Jesus fucking Christ, what are we going to do? Are we going to be arrested?' Her voice was muffled as she whispered down the phone.

'Yeah, I think so. We're all going to get nicked. You need to run, Helen. Either run or come to the house.'

They could all hear Helen breathing, short, sharp breaths. There was a silence before she answered.

'No. I'm not coming to the house, Tony.' And then she abruptly ended the call.

◆　◆　◆

Daniel carefully studied each of their faces in turn. Did they truly believe that he wasn't going to kill them? Had he played it right? He had to go through with the plan, but what about Helen? He knew she'd never go to the police and hand herself in. She would run, and that was part of the plan anyway. He tried to focus. He had to keep everyone calm. Because the calmer they were, the easier it would be to get them in the car.

'I'm not going to kill any of you, but we *are* going for a little ride.'

Daniel hid the spade behind the seats of Tony's car before going back inside the house. Then, after he had dragged his parents across the yard, he took a last glimpse at their faces as he closed the boot. He stood Tony up and removed the straps before crouching into the footwell of his car, the knife pressed against Tony's groin.

When they arrived at Crosby, the darkness of the beach gave Daniel the perfect cover. He threw the spade to Tony.

'Dig.'

Once the hole was deep enough, he pushed the knife against Tony's back and marched him to the car, ordering him to pull his father out of the boot. Tony heaved Ronald out and dragged him towards the hole. Ronald was struggling the whole time, every now and then letting out a muffled cry. He tried desperately to dig his feet into the sand, turning his body in all directions to avoid the inevitable. Finally, Tony managed to drag him to the edge of the hole, rolled him on to his side and swung his legs over the edge. With a slight push, gravity did the rest and Ronald slid into his sandy tomb.

Daniel then ordered Tony to lie face down on the sand before wrapping straps around his body and legs. 'Stay here. There's a good boy,' Daniel whispered in his ear. 'And if you make a noise, I'll probably kill you.'

That was when Daniel started refilling the hole. Packing sand tightly around his father. He desperately tried to free himself, but the more sand Daniel shoved into the hole, the harder it became to resist. He was going nowhere. Except to hell.

Then it was Rita's turn.

Daniel opened the boot and, coldly ignoring his mother's muted screams, he hauled her tiny frame out and headed off across the sands. Dragging his mother by her feet. When he reached the perfect spot, he looked back to make sure he was in full view of his father, just as he'd planned.

That was when he strapped his mother to the Iron Man statue.

'You were always terrified of water. Now you'll have a good reason to be. You're going to drown here. You're going to watch as the water slowly rises up and consumes you. And my father is going to watch. He likes watching. But this time, he's going to watch you die. Right, would love to stay and chat but I've got to strap these to Father's face. Bye, Mother.'

Daniel hurried back across the sand and, after checking Tony's straps were still secure, he roughly taped the binoculars to his father's face.

'Now you can watch *her* suffer. Like you watched me and Jennifer suffer. I know you used to watch Jennifer in the cottage.

I've seen you looking through these binoculars at her, watching her getting dressed. I'll let you into a little secret. I always knew I was going to kill you both.'

For a moment, he was lost in thought as he gazed towards the sea and the iron silhouette. 'The tide's coming in soon. I hope that when you take your final breath, the last thing you think about is what you did to your own children.'

With the plan almost complete, Daniel turned his attention to Tony. Cutting the strap away from his legs, he pulled Tony to his feet, shoved him in the back and made him walk towards the car.

'You said you weren't going to kill them,' Tony said, struggling to walk, partly through fear and partly because his legs were so numb from being tightly bound.

Daniel coolly responded, 'I lied.'

'What happens now? Are you going to kill *me*?'

'No. Today's your lucky day. You get back in your car, go home, grab that bitch of a wife and disappear. Let's hope for your sake that she hasn't turned herself in. And remember, I've still got the recording of what you both did. So, if Helen hasn't gone to the police and you decide to later, then I'll give them the disc and you and Helen will spend a very long time in prison. Do you know what they do to child rapists in prison?'

'But the police will find evidence that I was involved in this. They'll think I killed Ronald and Rita.'

'Yeah, I know. Just like I planned. It's a fucker, isn't it? Best you start running.'

'I could tell the police that you forced me, you held a fucking knife to my bollocks. That you killed your own parents.'

'Yeah, you could, but then I'll give them the disc. If I get caught, I don't care. I just need you and Helen to suffer, and either way, you will.'

'You little cunt.' Tony spat his words out as he took a step towards Daniel but stopped abruptly when faced with the knife.

Cutting the final strap from Tony, Daniel smiled. 'Off you run. I'm going to stay here and watch the sun come up. And watch my parents slowly drown.'

Tony, now resigned to the total mess he was in, put his hand out. 'Can I have my mobile back?'

'No.' Daniel shook his head and watched as Tony turned, walked back to his car and drove off into the darkness. Then he took Tony's mobile out of his pocket and sent Helen a text message: *I've sorted them both. We need to run, start packing, I'll be home soon.*

◆ ◆ ◆

Jennifer took a sip of water. 'Obviously, when Daniel sent that text, he didn't know that Helen had killed herself. So when you told me what she'd done, I panicked for a second. I remember asking you if she'd left a suicide note and you said you didn't know. I was so worried that she'd written something down that would reveal the disc.'

'So, when we found Tony's mobile phone strapped to the lorry in Southampton, it was Daniel who put it there?' Sheridan asked.

'Yes. Daniel knew that Tony's only way out was to get the disc and destroy it. Then Tony could tell the police that Daniel was alive and that he'd been set up for helping to kill our parents. We figured there was a chance that Tony would come to the cottage, maybe even threaten to kill me.'

'You said to me all along that Tony would never harm you.'

'I said that because I didn't want all the safety measures at the cottage. I didn't want the police car parked outside. I wanted Tony to come, and I knew that if he was watching the cottage then he wouldn't come anywhere near it if he thought the police were around.'

'You *wanted* him to turn up?'

331

'Yes. I wanted him to come to the cottage. I was hoping that I could kill him and make it look like self-defence. Even though it was unlikely, there was always the worry in the back of our minds that Tony might just tell the police what really happened. So, once Tony became the prime suspect, we needed him dead. If Tony was dead, then the investigation would probably be closed.'

'What made you think you could kill Tony?'

'I keep myself fit. I might not look it, but I'm exceptionally strong.' Jennifer smiled.

'And you think you could have overpowered him?'

'Absolutely. I was confident that if I was alone in the cottage and he turned up, I'd be ready for him. I know I could have grabbed a knife and stabbed him. Easily.'

'So the day you texted me saying Tony was there with a gun, why didn't you just stab him then?'

'Because when he turned up, I was in my parents' house, looking out of the upstairs window. I saw him come through the bushes and go into the cottage. I realised then that if I walked into the cottage, there was a chance that he had a knife or gun and might have killed me before I got the chance to do anything. So, I texted you to say he was there with a gun, knowing that armed police would turn up. All I had to do then was hope that he was shot dead. And it worked out perfectly, because that's exactly what happened,' Jennifer said, shrugging her shoulders.

'You said that Tony asked you for the recording, and that he'd written a note, which he then threw into the fire. Was that true?'

'It was, yes. I had to tell the truth because I didn't know if Tony had recording equipment on him. Or maybe he had a mobile phone in his pocket that was recording and if he did, then you lot would have found it. So, I had to be careful. The note actually said, *I know Daniel is alive and I know the police think I killed your parents, I know that the things we did to you were recorded and I want the disc, give me the disc and any copies and I'll say nothing to the police about what I know.'*

'When he walked out of the cottage that day, you shouted to him, "Please don't, Tony." What did you really mean by that?'

'Before he left, I told him that the police outside believed he had a gun. I could see it in his face that he knew it was all over. I think at that moment, he made the decision to get shot. When I shouted "Please don't, Tony", I meant please don't tell the police the truth about Daniel being alive. When he turned around to look at me, he knew what I was doing and what I was saying to him. But he also realised that his only way out was to get shot and I guess that's why he pretended to go for a gun in his pocket.'

'So, with Tony dead, it was all over. All you had to do was to sell the house and bookshop and move away.'

'Kind of. Except *you* told me that you'd never give up trying to work out *why* all this happened. You needed a motive. So, we worked out that if we sent you the disc, then you *had* your motive. You'd conclude that our father had killed Daniel because Daniel had maybe found the disc and threatened to take it to the police.'

'How did you find out where I live?'

'I hired a moped and Daniel followed you home from work one day.'

'Why did you keep a diary about the events around Daniel's . . . murder?'

'Because there was so much to remember, and I had to keep track of what was being said at the trial. I had to keep Daniel updated and make sure that he hadn't missed something. Also, because it made it look more authentic. I wrote everything very carefully because I guessed that at some point, the police would want to look at it. And you did.'

'Why did you keep pressuring the police to find Daniel's body?'

'I had to keep up the pretence. And if I'm honest, I felt absolutely terrible when all the volunteers showed up to help me search. But I didn't have a choice, I had to make everyone believe that Daniel was dead.'

'How did you know about your half-brother, Jason, and his mother?'

'We heard our parents talking about Jason and Tanya over the years. My father would get really angry about them, always claiming that they left him and simply disappeared. He always said none of it was his fault. We figured Jason and Tanya had probably been through what we were going through. Our father was evil and had been evil all his life.'

'But you never met Jason or his mother?'

'No.'

'When did you learn sign language?'

'We had a regular customer who used to come into the bookshop who was deaf. So, Daniel and I learned the basics, so that we could communicate with her and make her feel more comfortable. Sometimes, when Daniel was sat in the doorway opposite the shop, he'd sign to me, and I'd sign back.'

'Is that how you always communicated when he wasn't able to get to the tunnel?'

'Yes, but we'd also meet up. There's an alleyway that leads to the car park at the back of the shop and he'd follow me down there and we'd talk. Hardly anyone ever uses it, so it was pretty safe and there's no CCTV there.'

'Did Izzy know about any of this?'

'No. Izzy knew nothing. It was only ever me and Daniel. Izzy's just a friend I met at a book fair. He was safe because he's gay.'

'Who was the guy that came into the bookshop when Anna and I came to see you that time?'

'His name's Edward, he's just a customer who has a thing for me.'

'You met with him at Lime Street station before you went to Cornwall.'

Jennifer frowned and slowly shook her head, before smiling, realising that they had been watching her.

'He works there, he's a ticket inspector and happened to see me after he'd finished his shift. We had a coffee together. But I guess you already know that.'

Sheridan nodded. 'What happened to the other disc?'

'I got rid of it after we knew you'd received the original.'

'How did Daniel get the original disc in the first place? You said that he put it back in the book after he made a copy.'

'I took it two days before I went to the book fair in Cardiff, before Daniel disappeared.'

'One last question. Why didn't you and Daniel just come to the police in the beginning and report the abuse? With the disc as evidence, they would have been charged.'

'Because one day they would have been free. They would have had a second chance at life. Maybe they would have moved away and started again somewhere. They would have been free to hurt other children and we couldn't let that happen. We wanted them to suffer and the only way to make them suffer was to carry out the plan. Now, they're all gone. Daniel and I can sleep easily.'

'Before we end the interview, have you got any questions?'

Jennifer sat in silence for a moment before she answered, 'What would *you* have done? If you were me and it had all happened to you. What would *you* have done?'

Sheridan took a moment before she answered. 'I would have reported it to the police.'

Jennifer nodded and looked at Anna, who stood up.

'Interview terminated at 16.43.' Anna turned off the recorder and left, closing the door behind her and making her way down the corridor into the adjoining room, where Hill had watched and listened to the whole interview.

'Good job.' Hill sat back.

'Yeah, it went well.'

'We'll have to get the tunnel searched.'

Anna nodded in agreement. 'I bet the new owners will be chuffed to fuck about that.'

Sheridan remained sitting opposite Jennifer. She put her hands together and looked at the floor. The interview had left its mark on her. The abuse that Jennifer and Daniel had suffered and the way they'd planned everything, so meticulously, left her feeling an uncomfortable mixture of emotions. Relief that it was over, and she finally had all the answers. But also a sense of sadness at what those answers were. Two children, innocent and vulnerable, abused by those whose duty as parents was to protect them from evil. Not to inflict evil upon them.

'Are you alright?' Jennifer asked.

Sheridan frowned, a little astonished by the question. 'Am *I* alright?'

'I don't want you to hate me.'

'I don't hate you, Jennifer. I just wish none of this had happened to you and Daniel.'

'We can't change it, it's just the way it was. But it's over now and we can live out our days in peace.'

'Are *you* going to be alright?' Sheridan asked.

'I'll be fine. I know Daniel and I are going to prison. Maybe we'll never be released, but we made our peace with that a long time ago. We always said that if we got caught, we'd take the consequences.' She leaned forward and shrugged her shoulders. 'Daniel and I love to read. We're happy in our own company. We don't need anything. Prison is just going to be a place where we get to read our books.'

'But you won't be able to see each other.'

'We know. And we made our peace with that too. He knows I'll be okay, and I know he'll be okay. Prison won't be any worse than what we've come from. We've been in prison since we were children, it's just the walls will be different.'

Sheridan felt her jaw tighten as she stood up. 'I've never met anyone quite like you, Jennifer Parks.'

'So, you'll write to me?' Jennifer smiled, taking another sip of her water. 'I'm joking.' She put the cup down and stood up.

'The same,' Sheridan whispered.

'What?'

'You asked me what I would have done if it had been *me*.' She looked Jennifer in the eye.

'I would have done the same.'

Once Rob and Dipesh were back from interviewing Daniel, they all sat in Hill's office. Daniel had answered every question put to him and his story matched Jennifer's exactly. He hadn't faltered, he hadn't wavered and had fully admitted everything he had done.

Hill sat with her arms crossed and raised an eyebrow. 'I'd love to have seen your faces when you realised it was Daniel Parks we had in custody and not Jason Smith.' She shook her head slightly and put her palm up. 'I'm not blaming anyone, by the way.'

Rob went on to explain that when the uniformed officer, PC Jenkins, had finally caught up with Daniel, he'd turned around and thrown a punch, his fist glancing the officer's chin. PC Jenkins had no knowledge of Daniel Parks and assumed he had arrested Jason Smith. When he placed the handcuffs on him, he'd noticed the missing finger, but with no one from the CID team present at the time, he thought little of it. When asked his name, Daniel had simply replied, 'Jason.'

'When I was talking to Jennifer, she was signing to Daniel. She managed to tell him that we thought Jason could be involved,' Sheridan explained. 'So, in a last-ditch attempt to hide who he really was, he just pretended he was Jason.'

'And he only said his first name, because he didn't know what surname Jason was using,' Anna added.

'So, the first we knew that we actually had Daniel Parks in custody was when you two saw him in the cell and spotted his missing finger.' Hill looked at Rob and Dipesh, who both nodded.

'Right then.' Hill stood up. 'Let's see what CPS have to say.'

Sheridan presented the case to the Crown Prosecution Service. It was agreed that Jennifer would be charged with conspiracy to murder and perverting the course of justice, while Daniel would be charged with murder, perverting the course of justice, conspiracy to murder, kidnapping and assaulting a police officer.

The next day, the siblings appeared together at Liverpool magistrates' court and were both remanded in custody, with a date set to appear at the Crown Court. They spoke only to confirm their names and showed no emotion during the short hearing.

As Sheridan drove back to the station, Anna turned to her.

'Did you ever think during the investigation that Daniel could be alive?'

'To be honest, no. Did you?'

'Not for a minute.' Anna looked out of the window. 'They were very clever, weren't they?'

'Yeah. It was almost the perfect plan.'

CHAPTER 103

Anna poured herself a large glass of wine and threw her shoes into the hallway. Her body ached as she knelt on the floor next to the CD player and flicked through her collection. The doorbell rang and she got up, stretching out her back as she looked through the blinds to see Steve standing there.

'You can't just turn up like this, Steve. What do you want?' she said as she opened the door, her hand on her hip.

He put his hand up. 'I've got a job in Glasgow. I leave in the morning.'

'Oh. Well, that's good. I mean, you look happy.'

'I am. I really am. So, do I get a goodbye hug?'

As Anna stepped aside, Steve wiped his feet and followed her into the kitchen.

They talked about how he'd been to counselling and felt that he needed to move on with his life. He knew their relationship was over and he was so sorry for what he had put her through. He was ashamed of how he'd hurt her and wished he could turn the clock back to when they'd first got together. Anna patiently listened, studying his face for signs of the remorse he now spoke of. The face of the man she had loved so deeply, the man she had planned to spend the rest of her life with. She saw the face of someone who had once made her feel safe and loved, who made her laugh, who made her excited about the future. Then she saw the face of the man who had beaten her as she pleaded with him to stop. And that was the man she waved goodbye to that night as he drove away, his arm stretched out of the window, waving back.

As she went inside and closed the blinds, she didn't see his car stop at the top of the road, turn around and drive slowly past her house.

CHAPTER 104

Sheridan and Anna sat at the back of the court, listening to the judge as he prepared to pass sentence in the case of Jennifer and Daniel Parks.

They had both pleaded guilty to all charges and the judge took this into account, along with the mitigating circumstances that had no doubt led to the murders. He also considered that the victims, Ronald and Rita Parks, were not random strangers and had actually committed rape upon two innocent children. Their own children. It was unlikely that the defendants posed a risk to the general public, as their crimes had only targeted those who had perpetrated abuse upon them. However, the crimes themselves were totally premeditated and intricately planned. The defendants had ensured that their victims suffered from the moment they were tied up in the house to the moment they took their last breath. Even accounting for the defendants' subsequent admissions and early guilty pleas, the court could not ignore the fact that the defendants in the dock were calculating individuals.

Sheridan glanced at Jennifer and Daniel standing in the dock, separated by two dock officers. Separated and unable to speak to each other. Except through sleight of hand. Carefully timed signs, slowly formed words.

The message.

The message that no one saw.

Daniel: *Is the money in place?*

Jennifer: *Yes. Forty grand in two packages. Twenty each*

Daniel: *She knows what time to be there?*

Jennifer: *Yes. Does he?*

Daniel: *Yes. You sure she'll do it?*

Jennifer: *Yes. Will he?*

Daniel: *Yes*

Jennifer: *Do you trust him?*

Daniel: *Yes. Do you trust her?*

Jennifer: *Yes*

Daniel: *I'll see you tomorrow then*

Daniel turned his head to look at Jennifer and smiled. She smiled back. Everything was in place. Then they turned their attention to the judge.

Daniel showed no emotion as he was handed a life sentence, with a recommendation that he served a minimum of twenty-five years in prison.

Jennifer was also sentenced to life, with a recommendation that she served a minimum of twenty-three years' imprisonment.

As they were being led from the dock, Jennifer turned to Sheridan and signed to her, before disappearing down the steps back to the cells.

CHAPTER 105

The CID office erupted in applause as Sheridan and Anna walked in.

'Cheers, everyone.' Sheridan put her hand up, acknowledging her team's delight at the result. She smiled, but inwardly didn't share their feelings. 'The judge wanted to pass on his gratitude for all the work that went into the Parks case. And so do I. In all the years I've been in CID, I've never known an enquiry to be such a head fuck. It was a tough one. I want to thank you all for the hours you put in and for your determination and support.'

At that moment, Hill appeared in the doorway with an actual smile on her face.

Sheridan continued, 'I'm honoured to work with such a great team of detectives, and I hope you know that I appreciate every one of you and the job you do.'

'Yeah, fuck all that . . . where's the cream cakes?' Rob called out, setting off another round of applause.

Hill joined Sheridan at the front of the room.

'I also want to thank everyone. Bloody good job.' Hill gave a thumbs up and turned to Sheridan. 'Really great result today.'

'Thanks, Hill.'

'One last thing. The search team have found Ronald's boots and coat in the tunnel, along with the towel. So, that's it. No more loose ends.' She smiled.

As everyone went back to their desks, Sheridan tugged on Rob's arm.

'Jennifer signed something to me as she was walking out of the dock. What does it mean?' She showed Rob the sign.

'It means sorry,' Rob replied.

'Oh. Right.' She was about to turn and leave.

'You okay?' Rob whispered, tilting his head to one side.

'Mixed emotions if I'm honest, mate. I'm glad it's all over but hearing their sentences . . .'

'Doesn't sit right, knowing what they went through?'

'Kind of. They only did it because of what those fuckers did to them.' Sheridan bit her bottom lip.

'How did they seem in court?' Rob asked.

'They didn't show much emotion. They even smiled at each other at one point.'

'I don't think the sentences came as much of a surprise to them. Daniel was always one step ahead. He'd have been fully prepared to get life and I'm sure he prepared Jennifer for it as well. They probably even discussed it back when they were planning the murders.'

'You're probably right. Like you say, he was always one step ahead.'

By the end of the day, Sheridan was exhausted and ready to head home, tempted to ignore the phone ringing on her desk as she grabbed her jacket from the back of the chair and switched off her computer. As tired as she was, she couldn't ignore it.

'DI Holler.'

'Hi, Sheridan, it's Ruth Manning from the cold-case team. We've tracked down another witness from the photographs and he's given us a possible name. Stephen Tubby.'

'S. Tubby, Stubby.' Sheridan tapped her hand on the desk.

'Yep. The witness said he'd only seen him at a few football matches but also knew him from the local pub. Although he hasn't seen him for years.'

'What have you got on him?'

'There's a Stephen Tubby on PNC. Similar age, born in Liverpool. Last known address was 28 Gladstone Road, Sefton.'

'What has he got previous for?'

Ruth hesitated.

'Ruth?'

'Indecent assault on a twelve-year-old girl in 1989. There was no further action taken, it never got to court.'

Sheridan closed her eyes, reminding herself that there was no evidence to show that Matthew had been sexually assaulted before he was murdered. It was the one thing that had kept her parents going since he died. They had taken some comfort from the fact that Matthew had died instantly from a single blow to the forehead. In their eyes, he hadn't suffered, hadn't been molested and wasn't in pain when he took his last breath. If Stephen Tubby was the man who had killed him, had he tried to molest him? Had Matthew fought him off? Sheridan's head was spinning. Her first instincts were to go to Stephen Tubby's last known address and face him herself, but she knew the cold-case team would follow up on this new information and she had to trust them.

'We're going to visit him tomorrow and I'll let you know how we get on.'

'Thanks, Ruth.' Sheridan put the phone down and sat back, turning her head to look out of the window. Was this it? Was this what her family had been praying for all these years? Was the man in the photograph who was watching Matthew playing football the same man whose door would be knocked tomorrow? Deep in her own thoughts, she didn't notice Anna walking into her office.

'You off home?' Anna asked.

Sheridan told her about Stephen Tubby and how she was literally considering driving to his house there and then to confront him, to see if he was the man in the photograph.

'You know you can't do that,' Anna said, perching on the edge of Sheridan's desk.

'I know I can't, but what if it is him? We could be so close to solving Matthew's murder.'

'And you turning up at his house isn't going to help the cold-case team, is it?'

Sheridan put her jacket on.

'Where are you going?' Anna stood up.

'Home.'

'Straight home?'

'Yes, straight home. Via Stephen Tubby's house.'

Anna drove slowly down the road and parked up opposite the address. The house was one of six in a terrace, all in need of attention. The front garden was overgrown, with long grass and weeds almost covering the pathway that led to the front door. A wheelie bin lay on its side by the broken gate and a greying net curtain flapped in and out of an open window upstairs.

They sat for a few minutes, watching a group of lads coming down the road, one kicking a football and another kicking an empty beer can. Sheridan scanned the house, looking for any sign of movement from inside. Then her eyes fell on a child's bike propped up against the wall by the front door.

'He's too old to have children.' Sheridan shook her head. 'I don't think Stephen Tubby lives here any more. It doesn't feel right.'

'Shall we go?' Anna started up the engine and went to pull away, noticing the steering was overly heavy. She got out of the car and walked around it, before quickly getting back in.

'I've got a puncture.' She pulled a face.

'You're joking. Can you change the wheel?' Sheridan asked.

'Oh yeah, I'll just get my spanners out of the boot and we'll be ready to roll in a jiffy,' Anna replied, shaking her head and seeing the grin spread across Sheridan's face.

It was getting dark by the time the recovery truck arrived and they both got out of the car while the mechanic changed the wheel. As they stood waiting, Sheridan noticed an old man walking along the opposite side of the road towards them. She nudged Anna's arm and as he got closer, Sheridan could see his face.

'I think that could be him,' she whispered, watching as he looked over at them. Taking his keys out, he turned into the house where Stephen Tubby was believed to be living. Stepping inside, he quickly glanced back at them before shutting his front door.

'That *really* could be him,' she said, her eyes fixed on the house. The living room light went on and they watched him close the curtains.

'What's he doing with a child's bike in the garden?'

CHAPTER 106

Friday 17 October

The next morning, Hill was sitting in the CID office plucking watercress out of her sandwich when Anna walked in.

'Why do they put this shit in food? Does anyone actually ever eat it?' She tutted.

'Is that your breakfast?' Anna asked, making her way over to the water machine.

'No. It's my lunch. I had crisps for breakfast.'

Anna grinned and poured herself a cup of water, just as Sheridan came in carrying a huge box of cream cakes.

'Dive in, folks.' She opened the box and Hill leaned forward, immediately throwing her sandwich in the bin and grabbing a chocolate eclair before Rob could get to it.

'You've got to be quicker than that, DC Wills.' Hill bit into her cake, squirting cream all down her jumper. 'Bollocks.' She put the eclair down and swiftly made her way to the ladies' toilet.

Busily grabbing at the cakes, everyone ignored the desk phone ringing. When Anna finally took the call, she practically threw the phone at Sheridan, announcing, 'It's for you. It's the prison calling about Daniel Parks,' before rejoining the cake-grabbing frenzy.

They were all too busy to notice the look on Sheridan's face. Then she suddenly stood up.

'You're bloody joking,' she bellowed down the phone.

Everyone's attention was now locked on Sheridan.

'When was this?' She shook her head. 'Jesus Christ. How the hell did he manage *that*?'

No one breathed and it was only when Sheridan slammed the phone down that Anna spoke.

'What's wrong?'

'Daniel Parks is dead.'

'Shit.' Anna sat down. 'What happened?'

'He hanged himself in his cell last night. His cell-mate woke up and found him this morning.'

The room fell silent, and no one moved, all feeling rather awkward with their half-eaten cream cakes poised mid-air. Sheridan put her hands on top of her head as the phone rang again.

Rob quickly answered it, keeping his voice low as the room buzzed with the news of Daniel Parks' death.

Anna turned to Sheridan. 'We need to find out which prison Jennifer's in. When she finds out that Daniel's dead, she'll do the same thing.'

Sheridan slumped back in her seat, slowly shaking her head. 'Jennifer's already dead.'

'How do you know *that*?'

'Because they will have planned it that they died together. Trust me.'

Rob finished the call and after slowly placing the receiver down, he looked at Sheridan.

'Well?' she asked, prompting everyone to focus their attention on him.

'Jennifer Parks was found dead in her cell this morning.'

Sheridan looked at the floor. 'Don't tell me, she hanged herself, too?'

'Yeah.'

Hill walked back in. 'My eclair better still be there,' she barked before noticing the expression on everyone's faces.

'Fucking hell, has someone died?' She looked around the room. 'Well?'

CHAPTER 107

As she drove through the Kingsway Tunnel, Sheridan gripped the steering wheel and ignored the tears that stung her eyes. The Parks case was over, in every sense of the word. They were all dead, all gone. She had all the answers, the truth about what really happened.

After Jennifer and Daniel were charged and sentenced, the chief constable had congratulated her and the team for their commitment and diligence. Sheridan had smiled as he shook her hand and informed her of the impending commendation, which under normal circumstances would have filled her with pride and a huge sense of achievement. In her years as a senior investigating officer, she had secured numerous convictions, locked away murderers, rapists, violent and dangerous criminals, and each one had left her with the knowledge that the streets might just be a little safer. But the Parks case was different. It was the only one that had left her feeling doubtful that justice had truly been served. Watching Jennifer and Daniel being led to the cells had made her feel uncomfortable. Throughout the whole investigation, Jennifer had managed to convince her that she was broken, a daughter mourning her parents, a sister aching to find her brother's body, a victim in every sense of the word. And all the while, she was playing the cleverest of games. And she had almost won. She had almost pulled it off and, strangely, Sheridan admired her for it.

There were times after she'd interviewed Jennifer that she had wanted to lock her up and toss the key away. And there were other times when all she had wanted to do was open her and Daniel's cell doors and let them go. Let them disappear together and try to build a life from the ashes of their past.

As she opened the front door, Maud ran down the hallway to greet her and Sheridan scooped her up, burying her face in her warm fur. She could hear Sam on the phone, laughing, as she walked into the kitchen still holding Maud. Sam smiled and kissed her on the lips.

'I'll call you back.' Sam put the phone down. 'What's wrong?' she asked.

'How do you always know when something's wrong?' Sheridan kissed the top of Maud's head before gently depositing her back on the floor.

'Because you've been crying.' Sam frowned and took her hands.

'I've just had a really shitty day.'

'Tell me everything.' Sam reached into the fridge and pulled out a bottle of wine.

'Jennifer and Daniel Parks both committed suicide last night.'

Sam spun around. 'No fucking way.'

'I'm just mad at myself, Sam. I should have seen it coming.'

'You couldn't have done anything to stop it, and from what you've told me, this was the only way it *could* have ended. They wouldn't have survived without each other and so they chose to be together in the only way they knew how.' Sam shrugged her shoulders and poured Sheridan a glass of wine.

'You're bloody lovely. Do you know that?'

'I know. It's a natural gift.'

CHAPTER 108

Hill closed her front door and walked across the road to her neighbour's house. Using her key, she let herself in and called out as she pushed the living room door open. 'It's only me, Gloria.'

'Hello, Hill.' Gloria looked up, prompting Barney to jump down from her lap. He stretched and wagged his way over to Hill as she bent down, scritched his head and lifted the carrier bag away from his nose.

'Happy birthday. I got your favourite cake. Shall I put the kettle on?'

Gloria turned the television off and, reaching for her walking frame, she pulled herself up from the armchair and followed Hill into the kitchen.

'Where's my card?' she asked, setting out two plates while Hill undid the box and slid out an enormous fruit cake.

'Here.' Hill took the card out of the carrier bag and handed it to her, opening the drawer and taking out a knife. She proceeded to cut a small piece of the cake off for herself and a large piece for Gloria.

Gloria dropped two teabags into the pot and took her card out of its envelope, reading the words out loud.

'To G, from Hill.' She shook her head. 'You have such a magical way with words, you couldn't even be bothered to write my whole name.' She turned the card over. 'And you've left the price on the back.' Gloria flicked the card at Hill and it fluttered to the floor, prompting Barney to sniff it and tap it with his paw.

'You're welcome, you miserable old bat.' Hill shrugged her shoulders, pulling the fridge door open to retrieve the milk.

'And you couldn't even be bothered to put candles on my cake.' Gloria tutted, breaking off a piece and shoving it into her mouth.

'You're eighty-two, you'd probably drop dead trying to blow them out.'

When the tea was made, they stood face to face and clinked cups.

'Happy birthday,' Hill said, smiling, and Gloria smiled back, revealing the sultanas that were stuck to her false teeth.

They sat in the living room chatting, while Barney tore the card up into little pieces and deftly flicked them off his tongue and on to the kitchen floor. An hour later, Hill got up to leave.

'How's the bet going at work on what your real name is?' Gloria asked, picking cake crumbs from her jumper and popping them into her mouth.

'It's up to a hundred and twenty quid.'

'And they still don't know that you know about the bet?'

'Nope.' Hill winked, leaned down and kissed Gloria on the cheek.

'Anyone guessed it right yet?'

'Nope.' Hill took her keys out of her pocket and made her way to the front door.

'Thanks for popping over,' Gloria called out.

'You're welcome,' Hill called back.

'Cheapskate,' Gloria shouted as Hill opened the door, smiling broadly.

CHAPTER 109

Saturday 18 October

Stacey Coates had been waiting for twenty minutes, having arrived too early. The instruction was clear. Be there at 10 a.m. and be done by 10.30. Checking her watch again, she got out of the car, looking around nervously before making her way through the cemetery gates. A light drizzle had been falling all morning and the grass beneath her feet was glistening wet. Pulling her hood over her head, she walked purposefully along the row of headstones, glancing at each one as she turned right towards the grave.

Ronald and Rita Parks' grave.

Opening the carrier bag, she took out the trowel and as she knelt down on the wet grass next to the headstone, she began to dig up the plant, pulling it out by the roots and laying it to one side. It didn't take long before she found it, buried another six inches down, wrapped in plastic. The package. Her eyes widened as she pulled it from the ground and wiped the dirt away. And then she smiled.

Setting the plant back in place, she stood up, ignoring the fact that her jeans were soaked through at the knees. Stacey Coates didn't care. She dropped the package into the carrier bag and tucked it inside her jacket before quickly making her way back to her car and driving off.

Half an hour later, David Palmer reversed into a space almost directly opposite the cemetery gates. He took out his mobile and checked the time, 10.59. It was time.

Gripping the small canvas bag tightly, he got out of the car and made his way across the road and through the gates.

As he reached Ronald and Rita Parks' grave, he quickly looked around before kneeling at the foot of the grave. Pulling the trowel out of his bag, he dug the plant up and tossed it to one side. Then he began to dig until his trowel hit the cold hard plastic. He reached inside the hole, pulled out the package and dropped it straight into his canvas bag. Then he shoved the plant back in the hole before making his way back to his car.

Stacey Coates and David Palmer had never met and didn't know each other. But they had one thing in common.

Stacey's husband was in prison. And so was David's sister.

Daniel and Jennifer's cell-mates.

Inside each package was twenty thousand pounds. Payment to do one thing on the night that Jennifer and Daniel hanged themselves.

To keep their eyes shut and not sound the alarm until the morning.

CHAPTER 110

Sam carried the tray upstairs, managing not to trip over Maud, who raced past her and dived on to the bed, waking Sheridan.

'Sorry about her. She's just had a big poo in her litter tray and has been racing around the house in celebration.' Sam set the tray on the bedside table and leaned over to kiss Sheridan, who laughed as she reached for her coffee.

The phone rang and Sheridan answered it, while Maud sniffed the toast and stuck her paw in the butter. Sheridan chatted away to her mum before agreeing to a game of crazy golf. After arranging where they'd meet up later that day, Sheridan ended the call and put her head back on the pillow, cradling her coffee.

'A letter came for you.' Sam handed Sheridan an envelope and lay across the bottom of the bed, feeding Maud a piece of crust.

Sheridan recognised the writing and, putting her coffee down, she opened it.

> *Dear Sheridan,*
> *I never got the chance to tell you how truly sorry I am*
> *for everything we put you through with the investiga-*
> *tion and I wanted to explain a couple of things.*
> *I want you to know that it was never about*
> *the money. It was about making things right. Some*

people might say we were evil, but were we? Or were we made evil by circumstance?

My parents taught me one thing. How to be the perfect liar. I lied to you throughout the whole investigation and for that, I am so sorry.

The truth is, I never imagined that I could feel such hatred for another human being, and I never thought I could become the person I did. The person you got to know.

I told you that the night I went to Crosby and stood in front of the Iron Man statue, I wanted to know how my mother had felt in her last moments. I remember saying to you how frightened she must have been. I hope she was frightened, I'm sure she was, and I hope her last thoughts were of what they all did to us.

I'm not scared of death. I welcome it. I can rest now, knowing they will never harm anyone again.

Daniel and I are safe now. All the children are safe from them.

You see, Daniel and I were broken, in every way a person can be broken. If our final plan has worked, then we're both gone now. But the truth is, we were already dead. We felt like we had died a long time ago. Now we're together again, as we were always meant to be.

We planned everything so carefully, even this. This was always the plan if we got caught. You probably saw me and Daniel smiling at each other just before the judge sentenced us. We were smiling because we knew we didn't have to endure being without each other any longer. I signed to you before they took us back to the cells, I hope you know that it meant 'sorry'. I really am sorry for all the lies I told. You were so good to me and never once looked at me like I was some sort of monster.

Maybe you would have done, if I had told you the final part of the story.

When I was fourteen, I fell pregnant and hid it from everyone, except Daniel. He was there when I gave birth in the cottage one morning, but the baby was stillborn. I remember holding him tightly before Daniel wrapped him carefully in a white towel. I asked Daniel to take care of him and he told me he'd buried him, but I never wanted to know where. It was the only thing that Daniel ever kept from me. He did it for me. The last time I spoke to him, I asked him where he had buried my baby and he said he was by the big fallen tree behind the cottage. I'm sorry that I never told you.

Maybe I am a monster after all. If there is a God, then I expect He will judge me for what I have done.

I've sent you an envelope, you should get it in a day or so, it's the only thing I ask of you.

Now you know everything. You know how and why it all happened. But it's over, it's done. We did what we needed to do. I can rest peacefully and take with me the last words Daniel said to me as we were taken back to the cells at the court – he whispered, 'I love you, Jen. This ends now.'

Look after yourself, Sheridan.

I hope one day they find the person who took your brother from you.

Jennifer.

When Sheridan had finished reading, Sam put a hand on her arm. 'You okay?'

'Yeah.' Sheridan handed her the letter and put her head back on the pillow.

Once Sam had finished, she pulled herself up to rest her head on Sheridan's chest.

'So, you'll have to try and find the baby's body now?'

'I know where it is. I was there. I've sat on the fallen tree she's talking about.' Sheridan blew out her cheeks.

Sam lifted her head. 'Do you think she's a monster?'

'No.'

'What do you think is in the envelope she's sent you?'

'I don't know, but if it arrives and I'm not here, don't open it.'

'Why not?'

'Because it could be *anything*.'

CHAPTER 111

Anna parked the car outside and Sheridan craned her neck to look up at the flat. They sat there for a moment and Anna rested her head back.

'Are you going to Jennifer and Daniel's funeral next week?' Anna asked.

'I really don't know. I'm so torn because one minute I just see them as calculated murderers and the next, I just see them as victims. What do *you* think I should do?'

'When we interviewed Jennifer, she asked you what you would have done in her position, and you said you'd have reported it to the police. So, I think that's your answer. You believe that what they did was wrong, because *you* wouldn't have done it. So, in short, if that's what you believe, then you shouldn't go.'

As they got out of the car and made their way up to the front door, Sheridan gripped the envelope tighter in her hand. She rang the bell and looked up at the sky, watching the sun peeking out from behind the clouds.

The door opened and Sheridan cleared her throat, again noticing the resemblance he bore to Daniel and Jennifer.

'Jason?'

'Yes. I'm Jason.' He stood back to let them in, and they followed him through the narrow hallway into the living room. The place was immaculately clean, if a little sparse.

'Please come through to the kitchen. Can I get you a tea or coffee?' He turned as Caroline walked in. 'You've met my mum.' He smiled.

Caroline touched his face as she passed him, putting her hand out, which Sheridan and Anna both shook.

'It's nice to see you both again.'

They sat at the kitchen table and Sheridan watched as Jason stood waiting for the kettle to boil. His dark hair was draped across his forehead. Just like Daniel's. It was apparent that Jason was a little slow, his speech was slightly impaired, and he walked with a faint limp. He reminded Sheridan of someone who had suffered and was recovering from a stroke.

'So, you wanted to talk to us about something?' Caroline asked as she sat down.

Sheridan placed the envelope on the table. The same envelope that had dropped through her letterbox a week before.

'It's a letter to both of you, from Jennifer.' Sheridan watched Jason's face as he walked over and stood behind his mother, placing his hands gently on her shoulders, before pulling a chair up and sitting next to her. Caroline took a deep breath and they began reading.

> *Dear Jason and Tanya,*
> *I can only imagine what you have both been through and I pray that you both now feel safe. He's gone and I want you to find some peace with that. I expect if we'd had the chance to meet and talk, our stories would not be dissimilar.*

Our father always denied that he had done any-
thing wrong, he always said that you abandoned him
and took Jason with you. He even denied that Jason
was his son. But then, he denied a lot of things in
his life.

You did something our mother never even tried
to do, you protected your child. You made sure that
he was safe, and I imagine you made sacrifices to
ensure he was kept out of harm's way. That's what a
mother should do. Protect her children.

May the rest of your lives be peaceful. May you
find happiness, because if nothing else, you deserve
that.

God bless
Jennifer Parks

They read the letter twice. When they'd finished, Jason placed his hand on top of Caroline's, scooping a hand through his hair with the other.

Caroline talked openly about how she wished she had known Jennifer and Daniel, how things could have been so different for them. Her love for Jason echoed in her words, how she would have laid down her life for him, rather than let any harm come to her beautiful boy. She knew that getting away from Ronald Parks was dangerous but her decision to run was the only choice she had. She apologised for lying to Sheridan and Anna about not knowing where Jason was, and Sheridan assured her that they understood.

Jason apologised for not handing himself in to the police when he found out that they were looking for him. He explained how he'd panicked when he realised that the letters he had sent to Ronald might incriminate him and make him a suspect for the murders. Sheridan asked him why he had been living in Liverpool rather than with Caroline in Cornwall. He said that he wanted a better life for them and working in Liverpool gave him the opportunity to earn a higher wage. He regularly sent money to Caroline, which she saved for their future. He hated being away from her, but knew if he worked hard and kept the money coming in, that would give them a fighting chance. A chance to start again.

He spoke about all the places they had lived when he was a little boy. The bedsit in Manchester where he and his mum had huddled together on a single mattress on the floor. How she had shivered against the wind that whistled through the broken windows, while she wrapped herself round him. Protecting him. The time they had slept on the seats at a railway station. How she had gone hungry but always made sure he was fed. He sensed she had been through much more than he could ever imagine. He was too young back then to know and she was too selfless to expose him to the truth. He recalled the endless nights they had lain awake, when his mum would tell him stories until he fell asleep. Stories about how one day they would settle down and live quietly and happily in a little house by the sea.

Jason smiled at the memory and, looking up from his coffee cup, he turned to his mum.

'You always seemed so happy when you talked about that house, and I remember how you would describe every room in detail. I used to dream about it, and I always woke up happy. Our little house in Cornwall by the sea.'

Sheridan smiled and stood up. 'Well. It was nice to finally meet you, Jason. We'd better be off now.' She shook his hand.

And just before she and Anna left, she slid another envelope across the table.

On the drive back to Hale Street, they chatted about Jason and Caroline.

'They deserve a better life, don't they?' Anna said, looking out of the window.

'Absolutely.' Sheridan nodded.

'Do you think they'll be okay?'

'Absolutely.' Sheridan smiled.

EPILOGUE

Sheridan and Anna delivered two envelopes that day. The first contained Jennifer's letter to Caroline and Jason. The second contained a copy of Jennifer's last will and testament. As the house and land were deemed to be the proceeds of her crime, the only thing Jennifer legally owned was the bookshop, which she had already sold. She left the money from the sale to Jason and Caroline.

Caroline and Jason now live quietly in Cornwall together. In their house by the sea.

The police discovered the remains of the stillborn child. DNA samples were taken, and it was confirmed that the child's mother was Jennifer Parks. The father was Ronald Parks.

Jennifer and Daniel were buried together. Only a handful of mourners attended the funeral, including Caroline and Jason, who read out the one-line eulogy that Jennifer had written:

Judge us not for what we have done but only for the reasons why.

There to hear her words, sitting quietly at the back of the church, was Sheridan Holler.

Anna believes that Steve is living and working in Glasgow. The truth is, he continues to watch her house.

Stephen Tubby was visited by the cold-case team. He admitted to being the man in the photograph but told police that at the time of Matthew's murder, he was away, working in Wales. He remains in the house on Gladstone Road with his daughter and six-year-old grandson.

The investigation into Matthew Holler's murder continues. Stephen Tubby is still a person of interest until his alibi can be confirmed.

Sam finally agreed to take cookery classes. She was the worst student the tutor had ever had. She is now enrolled in a first-aid course.

The last time Hill checked, the ongoing bet to guess her real name was up to £190. To date, no one has guessed right.

ACKNOWLEDGEMENTS

And now to the acknowledgments. There's quite a lot to get through because I don't do this on my own, although of course, I probably take all the credit.

So, firstly, you the readers. Thank you for buying my book, I will never take your support for granted and I will always try to entertain you with my stories and characters. I'm glad to have you on the journey.

Thank you to all the wonderful reviewers out there, who have taken the time to leave reviews. Trust me, I read every single one.

Okay, as always, to Susie. I hope you know that I couldn't do any of this without you. Your faith in me, your enthusiasm and patience is unerring and I promise I'll take you dancing when things quieten down. Teeny confession here, you ask me if I'm comfortable working at the kitchen table. Well, yes I am, because when you're not looking I grab a handful of Maltesers out of the freezer. There's a secret stash in the top drawer behind the ice. Did I mention I'll take you dancing soon? I love you. Can we get a dog? And some cats? I was joking about the penguin, by the way.

Moving swiftly on . . . Now to my gatekeepers, Breda Byrne, Michael Doherty, Lorraine Burns, Katharine Robinson and Detective Sergeant Jane Edwards (retired). Now look you lot, I think I said enough wonderful things about you all in the acknowledgements for my debut novel, *Long Time Dead*, so don't expect this every time. I was emotional back then and you caught me off guard. You all know how amazing you are. And just to confirm, as always, remember that you do what you do because you love me and I will not be paying you for your time. I love you all too. And you can't put a price on that.

Supt Sonia Humphreys, as always you are just there, at the end of the phone, whenever I need a weird question answered. I've known you for, what is it? Twenty-three years? Holy shit mate, how come you haven't aged and I'm frantically plucking hairs out of my chin on a daily basis?

Paul Sturman, my firearms expert. Cheers again for all your wonderful advice. I know I still owe you that beer. Don't shoot me. See what I did there? No, you shut up.

Danny Jamson, HM Coastguard. Danny, when I first contacted you about some of the scenes, you were totally amazing and I promised I'd mention you here. Thank you so much for taking the time to explain the technical stuff to me. We really must meet up one day, maybe at Crosby to admire the Iron Men statues.

Joanne Farrelly, senior probation officer. Jo, it was always such a pleasure working with you back in the day and I am so grateful for your help and advice. I promise we'll have a proper catch-up when I'm next in your neck of the woods.

Broo Doherty, my wonderful agent. The ride just gets better doesn't it? I just can't say enough good things about you. Shall I just leave it there? I can see you rolling your eyes at me. Okay, you're bloody amazing, there I said it. You are not allowed to dump me.

Helen Edwards, Helen, the quiet assassin, working behind the scenes and doing that thing you do. Thank you my lovely. Did you know you look just like that woman who does the foreign deals for DHH?

Lizzie Curle, for trusting me to appear at Capital Crime, you are very brave. But I still want to see that video of me dancing with your mum.

Everyone at DHH Literary Agency, what a team, what a family. Proud to be a part of it.

Victoria Haslam, my brilliant editor. Vic, I know that with you, I am in the safest of hands. Smiling and laughing all the way through this crazy journey.

Sammia Hamer, thank you for everything. You are a total star.

Russel McLean, my dev editor. The picky one. Thank you for all your hard work once again. You are picky, though.

The proofreaders and copy editors, I hope I don't give you too many headaches. Your attention to detail is sublime, thank you for all you do.

Riot Communications team, Jessica Jackson, Emily Souders, Sofia Saghir and Ruby Fitzgerald. I am honoured and privileged (spoilt) to have such a wonderful team behind me. Thank you.

Belle, Newman will live forever now, within these pages.

Twitter gang, you know who you are, my amazing band of followers (friends). Thank you for putting up with me and supporting me all the way. Maybe soon I'll actually get to meet some of you. I'll bring vegetables.

One last note, I turn to a lot of experts and advisors to make my novels as procedurally accurate as possible. But as always, I may have decided to tweak things a little, because it is fiction at the end of the day. So, any mistakes are mine.

And finally (okay, so the last note wasn't the last note):

Two beautiful parents, Nelly and Micky Doherty. I never got to meet you, but I'm told that Susie has so many of your wonderful ways. Strength, courage, humour and devotion to family. The very best of people, the kindest and most loving. May you forever walk together, through your fields of gold. I want you to know that I will always look after your girl. Okay, I might have taken my eye off the ball that time when she flew down a snow-covered mountain at a hundred miles an hour on a child's plastic sledge. But in my defence, I can't account for her being a little bit bonkers.

And to my mum, Marion. I know I told you when I was a kid that I wanted to be a palaeontologist and you were fine with that. But I'm sorry about the time when I was about eight years old and I dug up them chicken bones and brought them home, I honestly thought they were from a baby dinosaur. Well, I didn't become a palaeontologist, but I did become an author and I know you'd be so proud of me. I miss you every day, but you already know that. I know you're taking care of everyone up there. I'm doing my best to do the same down here.

ABOUT THE AUTHOR

Photo © 2023 John McCulloch @ Studio 900 Photography

T. M. Payne was born in Lee-on-Solent, Hampshire and now lives on the Wirral with her wonderful partner.

Having worked in the criminal justice system for eighteen years, the last fourteen of which as a police case investigator within the Domestic Violence Unit, she has now taken a break to concentrate on her passion for writing crime novels.

T. M. Payne is crazy about animals and if you walk past her with your dog, she will probably ask if she can pat it on the head. Or take it home with her. Or both.

She loves laughing, Christmas, playing golf (badly), walking along New Brighton beach (not walking her dog because she hasn't got one), snow, sunshine, sunsets, family and friends.

She dislikes beetroot.

Follow the Author on Amazon

If you enjoyed this book, follow T. M. Payne on Amazon to be notified when the author releases a new book!

To do this, please follow these instructions:

Desktop:

1) Search for the author's name on Amazon or in the Amazon App.

2) Click on the author's name to arrive on their Amazon page.

3) Click the 'Follow' button.

Mobile and Tablet:

1) Search for the author's name on Amazon or in the Amazon App.

2) Click on one of the author's books.

3) Click on the author's name to arrive on their Amazon page.

4) Click the ,'Follow' button.

Kindle eReader and Kindle App:

If you enjoyed this book on a Kindle eReader or in the Kindle App, you will find the author 'Follow' button after the last page.